DEMONS, DATABASES, AND DANGER

THE OTHERWORLDLY ADMIN BOOK 3

JANELLE SEEGMILLER

Demons, Databases, and Danger

Cover Design by Rachel Whitehurst

ISBN 979-8-9914035-9-7 (paperback)

ISBN 979-8-9938874-0-1 (ebook)

First Edition: 2025

For those who end meetings on time.
The rest of you, get it together.

1

Ilka hissed loudly at the front door. It startled me, and I turned in time to see her with back arched and hair standing on end. The light coming through the living room windows suddenly dimmed, like a cloud blocked out the sun. A pressure change in the air made my ears feel like they needed to pop; I opened and closed my jaw, trying to force a yawn to clear them.

Ilka hissed again toward the door.

She wasn't the type of cat to react to things so strongly. In an act of stupidity or bravery, I made my way to the front door. It would have been smarter to check the doorbell camera stream to see if anything was out there. But I felt a pull to just open the door.

I swung the door open wide. A tall woman dressed in a three-piece suit as if she was going to a business meeting stood there with a half smile on her face. A panic radiated up from my gut.

"Are you Linda Moss?" the woman asked. It was like

two people were speaking. The primary voice was soft and polite. She sounded a bit like Helen, my boss, when she was talking to a client. But there was another voice that slipped around the polite words. That voice crackled like logs splitting in a fire.

"Yes," I answered in almost a whisper. "Can I help you?"

The woman smiled back at me. "I think you can."

There was no way I would invite her into the house. Luckily there were two chairs on the front porch. I motioned toward them and asked her if she wanted to sit down. A warning meow sounded from Ilka as I closed the front door.

"Your cat doesn't like me much," the woman said as she looked toward the front window over our shoulders. I looked back and saw that Ilka had perched on the table in front of the window and was glaring unblinkingly at the woman.

"She doesn't like very many people," I responded on autopilot.

"That's fair, cats can be very discerning," she said and then turned back toward me. "I'll make this brief."

I nodded and tried to swallow the lump that had formed in my throat. Strangely, I was both drawn to and repelled by her. The part that wanted to hear why she had shown up at my front door won out.

"Something was taken from me, and I need the agency's help to recover it," she said plainly, never breaking eye contact with me.

My mind raced. Why didn't she contact Helen directly? Why was she sitting on my front porch asking for help? I was just the executive admin, and I had only worked there for five months. How did this woman know I worked for the agency, and how did she know where I lived?

"What was taken from you?" I asked. My curiosity always won out over practical questions.

"A painting," she answered. "A very important painting."

I finally asked the question that any sane person would ask: "Why are you here asking me for help?"

"You were the easiest one to approach," she replied cryptically.

I squinted and thought through what she could mean. I was never good at controlling my facial expressions when I was thinking.

"Please relay my request to Helen in the morning," she continued. "Let her know that Doria requests the agency's assistance in recovering a stolen item."

Doria unfolded herself from the chair. I stood to match her and followed behind as she made her way to the steps. I hadn't agreed to tell Helen, but I knew that I would.

"She'll know how to reach me," Doria said before she headed down the stairs. I watched from the front steps as she continued on the sidewalk and out of sight.

When I went back inside, Ilka met me at the door. Uncharacteristically, she wound her way through my legs, rubbing up against them. Seemingly satisfied that I was back in one piece, she gave me a final glare and then disappeared up the stairs.

Back on the couch, I replayed what had just happened. On the whole, it wasn't much. A woman—I assumed some kind of otherworldly person—had come to ask for help. The only strange part was that they had come to my home.

The panic that I had felt was probably because it was unexpected and unusual. Nothing Doria had said was threatening. Doria herself was a bit odd, but I couldn't place my finger on anything specific that caused me concern.

Doria had said to let Helen know in the morning. A missing painting didn't seem to warrant an after-hours phone call to my boss. Still feeling a bit off, I decided to text Annie to get her thoughts on it. She was my best friend at work and in general. She would give me a good second opinion on whether or not I should be freaking out. I wasn't sure if I could trust my own opinion on this.

Me: Sorry to bug you, but I just had someone show up at my house to ask for help from the agency

I watched my phone for a couple of minutes until the little dots showed up and let me know that Annie was typing. The dots came and went for about a minute. Annie was clearly trying to figure out how to respond. Finally, text appeared.

Annie: what?

Me: a woman showed up and asked me to tell Helen about the request tomorrow

Annie: do you know this person?

Me: no. that's strange, right?

Annie: yeah, that is strange

Annie: are you okay?

Me: yeah, I think so. She wasn't threatening or anything. It was just weird

Me: what do you think I should do

Annie: if you feel okay right now, I guess just tell Helen in the morning?

Me: okay

Annie: do you want me to come over and stay the night?

Me: no, I think I'll be okay, but thank you

Annie: okay. Lock your doors and text me if you change your mind

Me: will do, thank you!

THE LAST GOLDEN sunlight of the day filtered through the window. Days were getting longer as we moved out of the dark of winter. We were in the middle of what would likely become a fake spring. Days had been warmer, and the streets were filled with people seeking sunlight while they could. Anyone familiar with Seattle knew we'd still have weeks of gray and rain before summer finally broke out, so it was best to enjoy the pockets of warm weather and sunshine while they lasted.

Ilka had already devoured her dinner and then slunk off to find a ray of sunshine to lay in. That turned out to be right in front of the doorway between the kitchen and living room, as if she wanted to keep watch over both spaces. She stretched out her big cat body and refused to move, even when I almost tripped over her. All I got in response was an ear twitch and a glare.

Even though it was Sunday night and a strange woman

had shown up at my door, I felt more at ease than I would have a few years before. Ever since starting work at the OPT Agency, the normal Sunday scaries had stopped. I no longer had the pit in my stomach that grew over the course of the day that was full of stress, worry, and dread for the week ahead.

I looked forward to going into the office, which was actually a huge mansion. I looked forward to seeing my teammates and talking about our weekend. I looked forward to our work, even when it was a bit tedious. And I really looked forward to the meals that Mrs. Clark, the in-house chef and caretaker, prepared for us.

That was the case at least three of the four weeks each month. This week, I was at home and would get to go into the office. I tried hard not to think about the week after, when I'd need to go to the Council offices in San Francisco.

Four months prior, I had started an apprenticeship with Director Owens. She was in charge of the North American region and the only other known oracle on the continent. Director Owens, or Cora as she insisted I call her, was also a founding member of the OPT Agency. I didn't know the whole story, but Cora and Helen had a falling out years before when the third founding member had died. Cora left the agency and joined the Council.

Helen didn't like her or trust her. Neither did I. We had a growing theory that Director Owens was using the Council's resources to keep the otherworldly communities separate and fighting by abducting and murdering people who threatened her control, then framing rival groups. The theory felt solid, but there was no evidence. When

Director Owens insisted I apprentice with her, Helen negotiated for me to do it part-time so I could keep working at the agency. This would also allow me access to Council records and to talk to the people who work there to hopefully find evidence of her crimes. What we'd do once we found the evidence, I had no idea.

Once a month for the last four months, I packed a bag and took the agency's private jet to San Francisco. I stayed in a luxury penthouse that the agency owned in the city. A friend of Mrs. Clark's stocked it with food and dinners for me. I walked to the Council's offices, located in a high-rise building, and tried not to be suspicious as I looked for the secrets that would help us stop Director Owens. Three trips and I had learned nothing helpful.

I put that thought in a neat little box in my head so I'd stop thinking about it. I settled into my cozy couch to read and distract myself for the rest of the evening. I was in the last few chapters of a fun romance novel that contained just the right amount of spice. Obviously, the two main characters would end with a happily ever after, but I still looked forward to seeing how things would wrap up.

THE BUS WAS a few minutes late the next morning. That added to my simmering bad mood. The previous night's unexpected visitor had my nerves standing on end. I woke up several times during the night and checked all the security cameras that Steve had installed shortly after I started working at the OPT Agency.

Steve handled security for the agency, and apparently that included personal security for all of us as well. I had thought it was just another odd perk of working there, but I was beyond grateful that I could make sure no one was trying to get into my house without leaving my bed.

When I finally made my way into the giant house that served as our office, I was greeted by the smell of coffee and cinnamon rolls, my favorite breakfast pastry that Mrs. Clark made for us. Like Steve's security, Mrs. Clark's food was a perk of working at the OPT Agency—and the best one, if you asked me. She took care of the house and fed all of us while we were working. Mrs. Clark's food was better than any restaurant or home-cooked meal I had ever had. No offense to my mom, but when she was alive and decided to cook, it was good but not great. Mrs. Clark was an introvert and kept to herself most of the time. In my first weeks of working, I had taken that as her not being involved with the cases. I could not have been more wrong; she had been critical in helping the team solve cases several times. She seemed to know about everything and connected dots others didn't. Also, I was pretty sure she was a witch, but asking seemed rude.

When I walked into the kitchen, I found Annie and Angela talking at the kitchen table, halfway through a cinnamon roll each.

"Hey," Annie called out as she saw me walk in. "Come join us."

I checked the clock on the kitchen wall and saw that we still had almost thirty minutes until the morning meeting at nine. It would be nice to sit and chat as we almost always did in the morning, but I needed to talk with Helen.

"Sorry," I said as I added a cinnamon roll to a plate, "I've got to try to catch Helen before the morning meeting."

"Oh right," Annie said almost apologetically. "Yeah, you should talk with her."

"What's going on?" Angela asked. She wasn't rude about it, just genuinely curious.

"Annie can fill you in, and you'll probably hear about it at the morning meeting too," I answered, then grabbed the plate and mug of coffee I had poured, balancing them carefully to head upstairs.

Up the stairs from the first floor, where the kitchen and rooms we used for clients were, was like changing worlds. The second floor was a modern office space that was superbly decorated. No sad gray walls and cubicles were to be found. The main room held a conference table surrounded by chairs. The walls between the doors to the offices had cabinets and expertly lit artwork. A couple of whiteboards on wheels were scattered around but mostly stayed pushed out of the way.

A few of the office doors were open. All those offices were occupied by my coworkers. I had learned early on that each office was a representation of its occupant. Beyond the conference table and the two walls of doors was my office.

As Helen's executive admin, my office was strategically placed outside hers. Double doors opened to my space from the main room, and then another set directly across opened up to her office. Luckily, those doors were open, which signaled that Helen was in there and that she wasn't busy.

I quickly dropped off the plate, mug, and bag at my desk. I took a quick sip of coffee to fortify myself and then made my way into Helen's office.

"Helen," I called out as I poked my head through the door.

She looked up from a paper she was marking up with a red pen. "Good morning, Linda," she responded cheerfully. "Did you need something?"

"Yes." She gestured for me to have a seat, and I settled into my normal one, on the right of the two wingback chairs in front of her large walnut desk. "I'm not really sure where to start," I said quickly, the words tumbling over each other. I wasn't sure why I was nervous. I hadn't done anything wrong. But I was already feeling short of breath.

"Just start at the beginning," Helen prompted gently.

"So, last night after dinner, someone knocked on my door," I started off at the beginning as she suggested. "I answered it. It was a tall woman that I didn't recognize." My words were still coming fast. I paused and took a deep breath.

Helen's face looked calm, but her eyes were concerned.

"She knew my name. I didn't invite her in, but we sat on the porch." I wasn't sure why, but it felt important to be clear that I didn't invite this woman into my home.

Helen nodded, encouraging me to continue.

"She said that she needed help from the agency. A painting was taken from her. She asked me to relay that message to you and have you get in touch with her," I continued.

Helen's calm face started to slip, but not into concern. It was more anger.

"Her name was Doria," I said finally, but Helen's face clearly showed that she already knew her name.

Helen was nodding slightly; it looked like she was turning over what I'd shared in her head and deciding how to respond. I tried hard to catch my breath without making it obvious.

"Did she say anything else?" Helen asked softly. I knew that tone: she was holding back emotion.

"No," I answered quickly. "It was a very quick conversation."

"Okay," Helen said. She steepled her fingers and leaned back in her chair.

We both let the silence hang for a minute. I'd learned to give Helen space to think and wait through the silence. It was extremely uncomfortable initially, and I always felt like I was in trouble, even when I hadn't done anything remotely wrong. From experience, I'd learned that it was just Helen processing a lot of information and being careful about how she responded.

"The security system Steve set up for you is still working, right?" Helen asked.

I almost laughed out loud. I had spent most of the night sending him thanks through the universe for doing that. "Yes, it is," I answered quickly.

"Good," she said quietly, mostly to herself. "Good."

We went back to the silence of thinking.

"Alright," Helen finally said as she leaned forward on her desk. "Sounds like we have a new client."

"Oh," I said, slightly surprised. "Sounds good."

I shouldn't have been surprised that Helen would take on the case. In my five months working there, we'd helped with a variety of cases. Some were simple ones, like vetting people for werewolf pack recruitment or cataloging an estate for a vampire family. But we'd also had more serious cases, like a missing vampire and a murdered witch. A missing painting probably fell somewhere in the middle.

"Do you want me to start a case file?" I asked, wanting to be helpful and knowing that my statement would be the first document to add.

"Yes, after the morning meeting," Helen said. "We'll fill in the rest of the team with what we know so far."

"Alright," I said and started to get up. A cinnamon roll was waiting for me, and hopefully my coffee was still warm.

"Oh, Linda, one more thing," Helen said. "I don't want you to be concerned, but you should know, Doria is a demon."

2

The smell of coffee, cinnamon, and bread filled the meeting space alongside the easy chatter of people who got along. It was nice to sit and listen to the little conversation snippets, although I couldn't join in. My mind was occupied with Doria, the fact that she was a demon, and the new case that Helen would be announcing to the team. I tried to keep a smile plastered on my face. It was not the time to fall apart.

Annie had refilled my coffee for me. The steam rose above it, but I didn't drink it quickly like normal. She made a concerned face my way. She gestured at the untouched food, noting my surprising restraint on both the coffee and the plate of cinnamon rolls sitting in the middle of the table. I returned her concern with a grimace and a shrug.

Fortunately, before we could engage in a battle of unspoken facial conversations, Helen sat at the table and everyone settled in to start the meeting.

Helen gave us a warm smile. "I hope everyone had a

good weekend. We have a new case today. But let's begin with an update on Malinda's case. Hank?" Helen said, turning her gaze over to Hank.

I perked up at that and so did everyone else. We'd spent the last four months working on pretty mundane cases. Alongside that was the ongoing push of solving my mom's murder, which was firmly in the cold-case category.

Almost three years before, my mom, Malinda, was murdered. Yes, she named me after herself. Men did it; why couldn't she? What I originally thought had been a heart attack was actually poison. Only after joining the OPT Agency did I learn that from Helen. Helen and the team had been investigating it from the start. In that same meeting, I also learned that my mom was an oracle and that I was one too. It was a lot for one meeting.

It took me over a month of working at the OPT Agency before I was ready to start digging into my mom's case. Jax, the agency's contracted psychologist, had suggested that I form a team instead of trying to tackle it on my own. I was so glad I listened to them. The team had started out small, but eventually it included everyone at the agency.

However, much like before I joined the agency, we were stalled. They had spent two years before I joined OPT working on the case, only to hit wall after wall. A few leads related to Enid's murder case and an organization called Moonstone Haven had us feeling confident. But a few weeks into chasing down those leads, we had ended up right back at a dead end. Everyone had reassured me that this was normal and that we'd just need to continue looking and keep our eyes open.

"As you all know," Hank started in his even voice, "we've been keeping tabs on the house associated with Moonstone Haven. Activity has always been low, and it didn't seem to have an occupant. But we haven't seen activity for over a month. I went and checked it out, and it does appear to be fully abandoned now. They've moved out."

The Moonstone Haven house was owned by the local coven. They had not been forthcoming with information about it, even going so far as to deny that they knew anything. Helen was eventually able to get the coven leaders to admit that they owned the house and paid the taxes on it, but they claimed that it was a charitable donation and they weren't privy to any information about how it was used or by whom.

Over five months, we'd cataloged a few people going in and out of the house during the several stakeouts we had time for. They never stayed in the house. It looked like they were slowly moving out.

"Did they leave anything at the house?" Cam asked and brought my wandering attention back to the conversation.

"Some odds and ends and bigger furniture," Hank replied. "Nothing that seemed important."

"And we have no idea why they left?" I asked softly. I had intended to think that, but like usual, my mouth got ahead of my head and I said it out loud instead.

"No," Hank answered plainly.

I nodded in thanks for his answer but shrank down in my chair, a bit embarrassed by the question. Obviously if he had known why they left, he would have told us. As one of the only connections to my mom's case, Moonstone

Haven being abandoned made me sad. I had secretly hoped someone would move in, that we'd talk to them, and they'd be able to give us a fresh lead. It wasn't going to be that easy.

"Thank you, Hank," Helen said, clearly wanting to move us on to the next topic. "Any other questions about Hank's update?"

Everyone shook their heads. I did as well. I wanted to talk about it more, but we weren't going to get anywhere on it in the morning meeting.

"Okay. Let's move on to our next topic," Helen said and then looked my way. "Linda had a visitor last night who requested our assistance."

Helen was a stickler for transparency in most things, so I wasn't surprised she'd let the group know where the new client had come from.

Steve, sitting on the other side of the table, looked the most startled at Helen's statement. He looked my way and I could see the concern behind his eyes even though he didn't say anything. Most likely, we'd be having a conversation later about beefing up security around my home.

I was lost in thoughts about how that conversation may go when I heard Helen calling my name. Looking her way, I realized she may have said my name a few times.

"Linda, would you mind sharing what happened?" Helen said once she got my attention.

"Yes. Of course," I said and sat up straight in my chair. I told everyone about the encounter I had the night before, speeding through it without pausing, despite the various reactions on my colleagues' faces. It was better to get through the retelling in one go; the group did have a tendency to tangent on questions when given the opportunity.

"And so, I told Helen this morning as Doria requested," I finished up the story with a little bit of a shrug.

"Thank you, Linda," Helen said with a nod and a smile in my direction. Then she turned to the rest of the group. "For those of you not familiar with the name, Doria is a demon."

Based on the gasps and reactions, about half of the table did not know Doria was a demon. I was glad to see I wasn't the only one in the dark. The other half of the table looked concerned and skeptical.

"Jordan, can you give us a quick overview of demons so that everyone has the same context?" Helen asked politely. Not only was Jordan a doctor, researcher, and all-around badass, but she was also a walking encyclopedia for the supernatural and otherworldly.

"Of course," Jordan responded with a smile. "Demons are one of the oldest species of supernaturals, and there are some theories that other otherworldly species evolved from or were even created by demons."

Jordan was great at teacher mode and everyone was transfixed with her explanation.

"The origins of demons themselves are complicated and not confirmed," she continued. "Many human religions describe them as fallen angels who were kicked out of heaven. But the supernatural scientific community has yet to prove the existence of angels, so that origin for demons is unlikely. Rather, we know that demons are beings who are able to traverse dimensions. The general consensus is that they originated in another dimension but have chosen to reside in ours."

I thought about Doria's voice when she talked. She had sounded like two voices but like one was an echo from somewhere else. Maybe that somewhere else was another dimension.

"Demon is more of a category than a species," she continued. "There have been about a hundred cataloged individual demons since records on them have been kept. Each individual demon has unique qualities and abilities. Their powers are highly eclectic, with no two demons being exactly the same. Records from the Middle Ages make claims of a demon who could blight crops, while another is said to be in two places at once. Each individual only seems to have one or two specific abilities.

"They are classified as immortal," Jordan shared with some hesitation. "But some of the scientific community, myself included, think that this is not accurate." She paused and looked thoughtful.

I couldn't help myself again and blurted out, "What do you mean?"

She smiled at me, and I was glad I asked.

"Well, there is no record of them dying or being killed in this dimension," Jordan answered. "But there are records of them disappearing. I think they may live a long time but then decide at some point to return fully to the dimension they originated from."

Heads around the table nodded. Jordan was brilliant, and if that's what she theorized, who were we to argue?

"That all seems pretty harmless," Annie said when Jordan paused. "Why do they have such a bad reputation?"

"A few reasons," Helen answered. "First, there is one specific demon whose ability is possession of humans. Despite the Council's efforts over the last couple of centuries, that individual continues every decade or so to cause some mischief and stir things up with humans.

"Secondly, in general, they do not respond to enforcement of discretion or guidelines set by any authorities, and they are unpredictable," she said with a sigh and a glance toward me. "Most often, they don't cause any trouble. They live their lives and stay out of the spotlight. But every now and then, something happens, and when it does, there is very little anyone can do except contain the exposure and clean up the aftermath."

"Also," Jordan added, lowering her voice slightly like it was a secret, "the hundred-ish that we have a record of is very likely not the total number of demons in our world. Those are just the ones that have either willingly made contact or have caused enough trouble that we know about them."

"So, is Doria one that we already knew about?" Cam asked.

"Yes," Helen answered. "Doria is known. She willingly made herself known a long time ago to the agency. Doria lives most of the year in the Seattle area."

Helen looked toward Steve, and he added, "We've been keeping tabs on Doria since she made contact. While there have been no incidents with her during that time, demons have been known to have sudden behavior changes."

"Do we know what Doria's ability is?" I asked.

"No," Helen answered with a hint of frustration.

"And we are sure she's a demon?" I asked, confused and unsure if we should just take Doria's word on that. She could be another type of otherworldly person.

"Yes," Helen, Steve, and Jordan answered firmly in unison.

My eyes went wide at their strong reaction to a simple question. Something was being left unsaid. I just nodded in understanding, not wanting to press the issue.

"Do we know anything more about this painting that was stolen from her?" Annie asked. I caught her eye and gave her a grateful smile for moving the conversation on.

"No, not yet," Helen said. "I'll contact Doria after this meeting to get more information. For now, Linda will be starting a case file and adding her notes on the initial contact."

"I'll send the link out to everyone later this morning," I confirmed.

"Jordan," Helen said in her *let's get down to business* voice, "will you please add a summary on demons and links to any additional pertinent information for the group?"

"Yes," Jordan responded, typing some notes on her laptop.

"Steve," Helen said, turning to him, "can you pull the last year of surveillance logs on Doria? Add those and a summary to the file as well."

"Of course," Steve answered.

"Once I get more information, I'll let you all know,"

Helen said, then moved on to other topics and updates that weren't nearly as interesting.

After the meeting ended, everyone dispersed as usual to start on their tasks. I gathered up my laptop and coffee mug to head back to my desk. Annie caught my attention before I left.

"We are still on for a workout after lunch, right?" she asked.

"Yes," I answered. "Unless Helen comes back with something urgent on Doria's case."

We had started working out together once a week on Mondays in the office gym. Exercising did get done, but it was also a nice time for us to chat and catch up on the weekend activities. Cam joined us when she could.

"Should we ask Cam if she wants to come?" I asked.

"Yes," Annie answered. "I know Sarah was out here for the weekend, and I want an update from Cam."

"Things do seem to be getting serious between those two."

"Right," Annie agreed with a half smile. We were both happy for Cam, but we also knew that their relationship was not an easy one.

DESPITE HAVING plans to work out after lunch, I still indulged in seconds of the vegetable stir-fry that Mrs. Clark made for lunch that day. And also a cookie that should have waited for after.

The hidden elevator in my office wall took me down to

the third-floor basement. It had taken me over a month of working in the office to learn about the three floors of the basement that were built under the mansion. It was wild to think about everything that might have been down there. I hadn't made it to every room yet.

The third and lowest floor of the basement, that I knew of, held the gym and lap pool. When Jordan gave me a tour of the space, she told me that I would never want to go to another normal gym. She was right. Our gym was more like a spa. It had all the equipment you'd expect, but the aesthetic was calming, and it always smelled like a mix of lavender and citrus.

My workout clothes were clean and waiting in my locker. Another perk of the office was that Mrs. Clark would wash our workout clothes for us if we asked. I took her up on the offer, as it meant I wouldn't need to keep a stinky bag full of clothes that I'd need to remember to take home, wash, and bring back. Not having the right clothes couldn't be an excuse not to exercise.

When I got there, Annie was already in the gym stretching, so I hustled and got ready to join her. I changed quickly and stowed my work clothes in the cubby with my name.

"Hey," I said as I walked out.

"Hi. Are you ready to lift heavy things today?" Annie replied cheerily. Jordan had put us both on strength training programs, and we acted as each other's spotters and cheerleaders.

"Yes," I replied with some hesitation. We were

supposed to move up in weight, so I knew I'd be feeling sore later that afternoon.

We settled in on the mats to stretch. Halfway through our stretching routine, the door opened, and Cam walked in. Annie and I both met her with smiles.

Cam smiled back. "Room for one more?"

"Always," I answered.

"I'll go change and be right back," Cam said as she walked over to the changing room doors. A few minutes later, she was back sitting next to us, stretching.

"So, what do you both think about the Moonstone Haven house being abandoned?" Annie asked.

"I'm not sure," I replied as I tried to get my fingers to touch my toes. "It seems strange that they'd just move out. Maybe they'll be back."

"Do you think they found out that we were watching the house?" Annie asked. She had her body fully draped over her legs, the top of her head almost touching her toes.

"That could be the case," I admitted. "But I thought we were so careful."

Cam nodded in agreement. "I can't imagine that they would have caught on to us. Hank took all the precautions we normally take around witches. If they did catch on, he's not going to be happy about it."

"What does unhappy Hank even look like?" I asked with a hint of sarcasm. Both of them laughed. Hank was known to always be neutral. He rarely got excited or upset. I'd learned to appreciate that about him even though I couldn't really relate.

Annie straightened out and rested back on her

hands, waiting for Cam and me to finish stretching. She looked thoughtful for a minute. She was plotting something.

"Do you want to go check out the house?" She finally asked in a half whisper.

"Yes. I do. Very much," I answered quickly. "We'd need to go soon. I'm in San Francisco next week."

"Oh, that's right," Annie said. "How is that going?"

Annie and Cam didn't know the real reason I was going to the Council's offices once a month. Helen and I had decided to only share the apprenticeship part of things, not the plan to search for evidence of Director Owens's schemes.

"It's going alright, I guess," I answered with a shrug. "I'm not really learning anything new. We talk a lot about visions, but I don't think she has any more answers on how it works than I do. And the work I'm doing is mostly organizing documents and writing up summaries."

"Well, let us know if you learn anything interesting," Cam said. For a minute I wondered if she knew the real reason I was going out there. I looked at her for a clue but couldn't tell.

Annie caught my strange look and changed the subject: "So should we go to Moonstone Haven house this weekend?"

I nodded.

Cam squinted and considered it more cautiously. "Yes, but we need to be careful. We don't want to disturb anything if the witches are planning on coming back."

"Perfect," I said.

"Speaking of being careful," Annie said and looked at Cam, "how was your weekend with Sarah?"

Cam made a playfully annoyed face that quickly became a smile. "It was great, but short. She had to go back last night because of some pack business that came up."

Annie and I both knew better than to ask what the business was. Sarah was a member of the Northeast werewolf pack in the Boston area. They were often clients of ours and had been at the center of a missing vampire case six months before. Technically Helen had a rule about not dating clients.

Cam had dated Sarah in secret for several weeks before it came to light. Helen was not happy about it, and it had been an uncomfortable week for all of us. Helen and Cam had come to an agreement about Sarah. I didn't know all the details, but I did know that Cam and the rest of us could not ask Sarah about pack business.

Cam was looking wistfully into space, probably wishing she could spend more time with Sarah. Annie and I exchanged a knowing glance. Cam was in love, even if she wasn't calling it that yet.

"Do you have any future visits planned?" I asked.

"Yes," Cam responded. "I'm going out there in a couple of weeks to stay for a full week."

"That will be great."

"It will be. We haven't had a long stretch of time together in a few months."

I was the last to be done stretching and stood up to join the other two. "Time to lift heavy things. Who gets to pick the music today?"

3

Tuesday was my favorite: breakfast burritos. Mrs. Clark made everything fresh, including the tortillas and salsa. The smell of the spicy sausage and eggs greeted me at the door. I was glad that I had decided to come in a bit earlier. That meant I could sit in the kitchen and enjoy a leisurely breakfast. I was not the only one who had that idea.

Jordan and Steve were sitting at one end of the kitchen table, talking quietly between bites. They both looked up and said hi when I walked in but then went back to their conversation. It didn't look too serious, so I decided to join them.

"Morning," I said with a smile as I put my plate down and pulled out the chair to settle in.

"Good morning," Jordan replied cheerfully. Steve did not look as cheerful.

I sat awkwardly and started to eat, not knowing how to

start up a conversation. Maybe if I just ate my food, they would start talking again.

Steve smiled awkwardly at me and asked, "Any new visitors last night for you?"

"Nope," I answered. "Just Ilka and me alone at the house."

"Good," Steve said and then seemed to hesitate. "You didn't invite her in, right?"

I knew he was talking about Doria. "No, I didn't invite her in."

"Good," he said mostly to himself. Jordan gave him a subtle shake of her head. I wasn't sure he saw it.

Steve gathered up his plate. Before he left, he leaned toward me slightly and warned, "Be careful who you invite into your home."

I nodded, unsure of how to respond to a statement like that. Steve left and I looked at Jordan for any help deciphering what had just happened.

"He's just worried about you," she said. "He worries about everyone."

AFTER FINISHING my breakfast burrito and with my second cup of coffee in hand, I made my way upstairs to my office to get ready for the morning meeting. I had just enough time to check emails and schedules for myself and Helen before needing to be at the conference table.

An email in Helen's inbox made my heart skip a beat. I'd come to recognize the email address. It was from the

Council. The email had already been opened and marked as read, so Helen had already seen it. Looking at the clock, I realized that I didn't have time to read it; their emails tended to be long and took a while to get to the point. I'd take a look after the meeting.

Annie and Steve were already at the table looking at their laptops and drinking their coffees. I did a double take when I also saw Mrs. Clark at the table. Usually Mrs. Clark didn't join morning meetings, even though I'd learned that she kept up to date on all of our cases, and she'd often join in on critical or more urgent cases. That day she sat at the end of the table, mug of tea in hand, eyes scanning the group chatting casually around the table.

Mrs. Clark's joining raised red flags. It was not that I didn't want her there or that she shouldn't be there. Rather, if she had joined, it probably meant that something big was happening.

As usual, the morning meeting began right on time at nine o'clock. Everyone was ready to start when Helen cleared her throat to get things going.

"We have two major topics for this morning," Helen said calmly.

The vibe around the table had started to shift. I couldn't put my finger on it quite yet. It was either the fact that Mrs. Clark was there or that Steve was sitting with his arms folded and a very grumpy face.

"First, I was able to get in touch with Doria," Helen shared. "She was not very forthcoming over the phone, and I have decided to have her come to the office for an interview."

Most of the people around the table looked shocked or upset by that statement. The two relative newbies—myself and Angela—both looked confused by the reaction. It was not uncommon to have clients come to the office. In fact unless they weren't local, we almost always had them come to the office for interviews and meetings.

Helen clearly understood the reactions and was expecting them. She didn't flinch, but when muttering and side conversations started up, she wrangled things back into focus. "I understand the concern," she said calmly but firmly. "We will need to adjust the wards on the office to allow Doria to come in."

The reactions started to make sense, but it also brought up more questions for me. As usual, I blurted out the first thing that came to mind. "What wards?" I asked with the simplicity of someone who was clearly still learning about this otherworld.

At the question, Helen's eyes moved to mine. I chose not to be embarrassed. If almost everyone knew about it, then I should know too.

"Steve, would you like to explain?" Helen asked him gently.

He unfolded his arms and put both hands palms down on the table in front of him. "This office and the grounds are protected with magical wards that were put in place at the creation of the agency," Steve began to monologue. "They are steadfastly maintained and have never been altered."

The pieces were starting to click into place on why

everyone reacted strongly to Helen's decision to change the wards.

"In addition to other protections, the wards allow admittance to invited guests," he continued. "However, because of demons' unpredictable nature and the fact that they have never knowingly worked with or sought help from the agency, the wards are designed to never permit them entrance."

"Can we even change that?" Jordan asked.

"Yes," Helen said despite Steve's contrary glare.

"We don't know for sure," Steve retorted. "And we don't know what else might also change if we do."

"Why does she need to come to the office?" Angela asked sincerely, changing the topic slightly. It was a question that was on the tip of my tongue as well. Looking around the table, it was clear other people also were wondering.

"As Steve mentioned, we've never had a demon seek to work with us or ask for our help." Helen's calm tone helped to counter Steve's grumpiness. "Helping Doria gives us an opportunity to forge an alliance with a powerful individual and possibly even demons in general. Having her come to the office is a sign of good faith and that we are taking her case seriously."

Steve harrumphed a little at that, but I could see he was softening and considering what Helen was saying.

"We know that things are changing." Helen didn't need to say the obvious out loud. It had been a constant pulse of worry for all of us for five months. Everyone was aware of the working theory that Director Owens was manipulating and possibly murdering members of the supernatural and otherworld community. "If we discover that what we fear is true, we will need allies," Helen said softly, every word a solemn pronouncement.

I turned to look at Steve and could see him start to slowly nod in agreement.

"You're right," Steve conceded. "I understand that. But I am still nervous about a demon asking us for help. It doesn't make sense to me why she would now and for something that seems relatively trivial."

"I agree," Helen admitted. "I'm worried about that too. And that's something we'll need to figure out. Steve and Mrs. Clark, I'll need both of you to talk after this meeting."

At the mention of her name, I looked down the table at Mrs. Clark. With Steve's grumpiness pulling my attention, I had almost forgotten she was there. Her normally cheerful but quiet demeanor was completely replaced with an emotion I couldn't quite put my finger on. It was like fear, sadness, anger, frustration, and worry took turns dancing across her face. Whatever it really was, she was clearly not happy with Helen's decision. Despite that, she nodded in understanding and didn't offer a word of disagreement.

"Alright," Helen said in the way she did when she wanted to change topics. "We'll update everyone on the plan with the wards later today. Now we need to talk about another visitor."

Everyone looked confused. I thought back to the email from the Council in her inbox that morning and I just knew what she'd say next.

"The Council has requested a review for next Monday," Helen said quickly and evenly.

We had lucked out and the Council had canceled the first quarterly review they had scheduled. As part of some agreements to approve Angela's adoption into the Southeast vampire family, the family had required that Angela serve part of her two-year pre-adoption probation with the OPT Agency. Director Owens, with the Council's authority for the region, signed off on all adoptions. It was usually a rubber stamp, just a formality. But in this case, she had said no.

Negotiations to get her approval had included allowing Council representatives to do quarterly reviews of the agency while Angela was working there. Although we all knew it was going to happen at some point, no one was happy about it, and everyone's faces reflected that.

"I know this isn't something any of us are looking forward to," Helen said, putting words to everyone's reactions. "But we can handle this. Steve, I'm going to need you working on the wards. So, Linda, I'm going to have you take point on preparations for the Council visit."

I almost choked on my coffee. That was a big, important job. Steve had been the point person on the original review that had been canceled. I'd just assumed he would be the point person on all the reviews.

"But I won't be here," I blurted out. "Next Monday I'm supposed to be at the Council offices."

Helen tilted her head in thought. "That's right. We'll ask for you to be here on Monday and go on Tuesday instead."

"Okay," I agreed. That sounded simple enough, and I wouldn't mind one less day at the Council offices.

"Steve can hand off any details that were in place for last time," Helen said, glancing his way to confirm with him. He nodded and smiled my way. "You should be able to use the playbook he created."

"Okay," I said again, as confidently as I could muster. "I can do that."

"Also," Helen continued, looking around the table, "everyone will be involved, so please be responsive to any of Linda's requests."

They all gave some positive indication to the instruction, and I tried not to show any concerns with the assignment on my face. I doubted that I was successful. If I was lucky, the Council representative would be someone I was already friendly with from the San Francisco office.

"If Linda is taking point on the Council visit, do you want her in the meeting about the wards too?" Steve asked Helen. "Just so she's in the loop in case there is anything pertinent to the visit."

"That's a great idea," Helen agreed. "Linda, will you please join us in my office after this meeting?"

"Of course," I replied. I was excited for the assignment if it meant I got to learn more about the magical wards. I still had so many questions. A few dots had begun to connect, and I wondered if they had put wards on my house.

~

Steve had pulled up an extra chair to Helen's desk. Mrs. Clark and I sat in the wingback chairs, me in my normal chair on the right. The three of us gave Helen a moment to get settled behind her desk. She shuffled papers and items around and then leaned forward.

"I know there are concerns with what I'm proposing with the wards," she said gently. "And I don't want to discount those. Is there anything I'm not thinking about that I should be?"

I loved the way Helen worked with her team. She was firm and decisive but also open to feedback and compromise. Multiple times, I watched her take in new information and pivot based on that. When she didn't change her mind or decide on something despite objections, she always made it clear why. I had a feeling that would be the case again.

"I understand why you want Doria to come to the office," Steve started. "I am mostly concerned about why she asked for our help."

"That is one of my concerns, too," Mrs. Clark said.

I nodded in agreement. Even though I had just learned about demons, if those two had concerns, then I did too.

"I understand. I'm concerned about that as well," Helen acknowledged and wrote something in a notebook in front of her.

"I'm also concerned about doing anything to the wards," Steve said. "We've never changed them before, and I don't know what will happen if we do change them now."

"Mrs. Clark, any thoughts?" Helen asked instead of responding directly to Steve.

"I think they can be changed safely," she responded softly. "We'll need some time to review things, but I think the change we want is fairly localized. Did we want to open it to any invited demon or just Doria?"

"How hard would it be to do just Doria versus any invited demon?" Helen asked.

"Any invited demon would likely be easier and also easier to reverse if we changed our minds," she answered confidently.

Several months before, I concluded that Mrs. Clark was a witch. I didn't know how widely that was known among the team, and I didn't know if Mrs. Clark knew that I knew. I was embarrassed to admit that it took me until that moment to realize that Mrs. Clark was likely the one who was at least maintaining the wards, if not the one who put them up in the first place.

"Let's do that then," Helen said decisively. "And, I agree that we should try to do it in a way that we can reverse if needed. Linda, Steve, any other thoughts or questions?"

"Not really," Steve answered first. "I'll work with Mrs. Clark to review the wards. How soon do you want this done?"

"As soon as possible," Helen replied. "I don't want Doria to rethink her request. But don't rush it if you are unsure about the change."

"Will do," Steve said and looked toward Mrs. Clark.

"I think we can have it changed before lunch," she said.

"Alright," Helen said. "Keep me posted. Linda, any questions?"

The three of them looked my way, and I remembered

why I was invited. I quickly thought through how it could be related to the upcoming Council's visit.

"Does the Council know about the wards?" I asked. "Will they notice a change in them and ask questions we don't want to be asked?"

"That's a good question," Steve said with an encouraging smile. "Director Owens would know. They were up while she was working here. As far as we know, she wouldn't notice a change unless she was actively surveilling them with a witch from her team. If she did ask about it, she'd have to admit to a level of surveillance that is not allowed and that she probably doesn't want us to know about. So I don't think they will ask, even if they do notice something."

"Okay, that makes sense," I said as confidently as I could. "I don't think I have any more questions right now."

"Great," Helen said and clapped her hands together once. "Sounds like we have a plan then. Mrs. Clark and Steve, let me know when you have a firm timeline and plan with the wards."

"Will do," they both said.

"Linda, I'll let you know when I'm free this afternoon to answer any questions about the Council visit," Steve said, looking in my direction.

"Sounds good," I responded. That gave me some time to look over the documents again to refresh my memory so that I would have some questions to ask. Maybe I could find a moment to ask him if there were wards on my house.

IT WASN'T EVEN an hour after I had sat back at my desk to review the documents put together for the Council visit that I got a ping on the messaging app. Steve was alerting everyone that the wards would be adjusted in thirty minutes. We weren't likely to notice anything, but if we did, we were instructed to contact Steve immediately.

The message was straightforward and benign. I trusted that Mrs. Clark and Steve knew what they were doing. But seeing the words on the screen made a nervous ball of dread start to build in my stomach. I tried to go back to reviewing the document, but my attention kept returning to the message.

After twenty minutes of that and only ten minutes until the wards would change, I decided that there was no way I was getting more work done. I needed to get up and move. I needed to go find someone to talk to.

Steve and Mrs. Clark were busy. I didn't really want to talk with Hank. Jordan's office door was closed. Cam wasn't in her office. Angela's office door was also closed. Heading down the stairs, I could hear Annie humming to herself from the living room. I'd just pop in and see if she was busy.

"Hey. Knock, knock," I said to get her attention as I walked into her view.

"Hey, Linda," Annie replied cheerfully. "How are you doing?"

"Good," I answered with some hesitation. "Actually, this

thing with the wards is making me antsy for some reason. Can I come hang out with you for a bit?"

"Of course," she responded quickly.

Annie didn't have extra chairs by her desk for me to lounge in, so we both moved over to the couches set up as a waiting room for clients and visitors.

"I know what you mean," Annie said as we settled in. "I'm not sure I love that we are changing the wards for the first time ever. Did Mrs. Clark or Steve have any more information in the meeting you went to?"

"Not any specifics on how it all works," I replied. "But Mrs. Clark did say that she thinks it can be changed in a way to reverse it if needed."

"Oh, that's good," she said and then changed the subject. "Any other thoughts on checking out the Moonstone Haven house?"

"Yes," I said, happy for the distraction. "I still think we should go. I know we probably won't find anything, but I want to check it out."

"I agree," Annie said. "But I do think we should tell Helen. I don't think she'd tell us not to go."

"Yeah," I agreed, but with some hesitation. I wasn't as confident as Annie that Helen wouldn't try to stop us from going. And I was even less confident that I would agree not to go if asked not to.

"When do you want to go?" Annie asked.

"I have a feeling that this new case is going to take up a fair amount of time this week, and we have to get ready for the Council review," I replied, thinking through the timing of things out loud.

"Do you have anything this weekend?"

"No. Do you?"

"Nope. Maybe we should try to go on Saturday," Annie said, "if we don't have time to go during the week."

"That'd work," I said with an excited smile. It also meant that we wouldn't have to explain to the rest of the team why we were leaving the office during the day and would be unavailable. I didn't want to explain to everyone why I was so interested in visiting the house that was likely empty. I didn't know the answer to that.

We sat in silence for a minute, and then Annie's head jerked up to look at the clock on the mantel. I followed her gaze and saw that we were less than a minute away from eleven thirty, the designated time that the wards would be changed.

Annie and I locked eyes and we both held our breath.

The clock clicked to the half-hour mark. At that moment the lamps in the room blinked off and then back on. A ripple-like shadow circled around the perimeter of the room and then flashed out.

With wide eyes, I looked back at Annie. Her face mirrored mine.

"Did you see that?" she asked in a whisper.

"Yes," I replied, matching her whisper.

"Should we tell Steve?"

A ping from both of our phones made us jump. We reached for our respective phones and read the same message.

Steve: The wards have been changed. No adverse events noted.

"I guess it's okay," I said. "They probably saw it too."

"Yeah," Annie said in a normal volume again. "They probably did."

"We should still say something, right?"

"You're right," Annie agreed.

I sent a quick message back to Steve about what we had noticed downstairs. It took a few minutes but he wrote back.

Steve: noted

4

Lunch was delicious but uneventful. Everyone but Helen and Mrs. Clark had decided to eat in the kitchen around the table. It was easy chatter, but it felt like people wanted to avoid talking about what was going on. No one talked about the wards or the weird shadow that rippled through the rooms when they were changed. We also didn't talk about Doria's upcoming visit to the office or the Council's upcoming review.

I'd been around this group long enough to know that sometimes everyone just wanted to chat about inconsequential stuff. We often dealt with stressful and sometimes scary situations. Those moments when Hank could tell funny stories about his dog, Juniper, or when Jordan shared the new scientific articles she was excited about were worth preserving.

We all enjoyed Mrs. Clark's chicken alfredo, and then, as if on some invisible cue, everyone gathered up their plates to take to the sink to rinse off. On the way out, Steve grabbed my attention.

"Hey, we may not have time this afternoon to talk about the Council stuff," he said cryptically.

I made a confused face.

"I think this afternoon is going to be busy," he half explained. "But we can make some time to talk tomorrow."

"Okay. That's fine," I replied calmly. Inside, I wondered what he knew that I didn't. I wouldn't need to wait long to find out.

NOT TWENTY MINUTES after we had all scattered to our desks to continue working, a message popped up. Helen was asking for an ad hoc meeting in ten minutes. That would be ten minutes that I would not be getting any work done, so I decided to go refill my still mostly full water tumbler and then sit at the conference table and wait for the meeting.

I wasn't the only one who had that idea. Five minutes before the requested meeting time, more than half the table was full. Jordan and Hank were chatting about something that sounded confusing. Cam and Angela were talking toward the other end of the table. I couldn't hear what they were saying, but they looked calm. Annie came in and sat across from me in her normal seat.

"What do you think this is all about?" Annie asked in an exaggerated whisper as she leaned toward me over the table.

I shrugged. "Your guess is as good as mine."

"Well, at least most of us don't know," she said as she looked around the table. Steve, Helen, and Mrs. Clark, if she would be coming, were the only missing people and likely the three who had an idea of what we'd be talking about.

"Do you think it's about the wards?" I asked after noting who wasn't there.

"Maybe," Annie replied. "I guess we're about to find out."

She had turned to look at the stairs. I followed her gaze and saw that the three missing folks were making their way upstairs to the meeting. The pit that had been steadily growing in my stomach all day jumped in size when I saw the grim set of their faces.

"Thank you all for joining on such short notice," Helen said as she sat down. "We'll make this update quick, but I wanted to do it in person in case there are any questions. The protection wards were successfully changed." She glanced strangely toward Mrs. Clark. "As successful as we can tell at this point. Doria will be coming in for an interview at three this afternoon."

"Is there anything we need to do to prep for her visit?" Annie asked.

"Yes," Helen answered. "We'll use the back parlor for the visit. If you and Linda could check the room over and make sure it is ready, that would be great."

Annie and I exchanged a quick glance and a smile. The room wouldn't need anything done. Mrs. Clark kept all the office spaces immaculate. Likely with magic, but that wasn't confirmed.

"Also, Mrs. Clark, if you could prepare some refreshments please?" Helen asked.

"Of course," Mrs. Clark replied.

"Other than that, we'll have myself and Linda in the meeting," Helen said calmly.

My head snapped up at the mention of my name, and I must have looked confused. Helen noticed.

"I'll have you take notes during the meeting," she said softly, looking in my direction.

"Oh, right. Yes, of course." I stumbled over my words.

Doria and I had already met, and taking notes for Helen's meetings was technically part of my job description. It shouldn't have been weird that just Helen and I would be in the meeting. But Steve usually attended meetings if Helen was worried about safety. I guessed she wasn't worried about that with Doria.

THE BACK PARLOR was my favorite meeting room in the building. Several months before we had moved out the conference table and replaced it with a circle of four wing-back chairs surrounding a walnut coffee table. Soft lighting, dark green paint, and heavy drapes made it feel like the back room of an old library. Originally the room had been changed to accommodate the visit of Winthrop, a vampire. Since then it had been used almost exclusively for his visits and my therapy sessions with Jax, so it was strange to see someone other than Winthrop sitting in the chair opposite Helen.

Doria sat confidently with a teacup held delicately in her hand. She was as tall as I remembered from our meeting on my front porch, but in the office I also noticed that her dark hair had a purple sheen to it when the light hit it just right. Her eyes seemed to change color, and I wondered if it was related to her mood. Her features were bold and looked more symmetrical than was natural. She was wearing a striped dark gray three-piece suit. It was clearly tailored to her. The neck was open without a tie, and a pocket square was a pop of orange on the otherwise dark and white ensemble.

Helen, opposite Doria, matched her confidence. I just tried not to jiggle my leg too much.

"Thank you for having me here today," Doria said after Helen had completed what turned out to be unnecessary introductions. It was clear Doria already knew exactly who Helen was. Doria's voice still had the crackling echo that I had noticed when I first met her. It seemed less pronounced right then.

"Very happy to have you here and to be of service," Helen said in her client-facing, professionally polite voice. "If you don't mind, I'd like to start at the beginning. Can you tell us what happened?"

"Of course," Doria responded, matching Helen's polite tone. She set her teacup on the coffee table and recrossed her legs. "Last week on Thursday, I became aware that a valuable painting was missing. I was unable to determine who had taken it or how. And I have not been able to retrieve it. I would like the agency to help me get it back."

"Can you tell me more about the painting?" Helen asked.

"It's a portrait of myself," Doria said. "Well, a version of myself."

"Where was the painting located before it was taken?" Helen asked.

"In the attic of my residence," Doria said simply.

Not what I was expecting. Who kept a portrait in the attic? Did she not like it? If she didn't like it, why did she want it back so badly? Helen didn't ask any of those questions.

"Does anyone else have access to your residence?" Helen asked instead. I guessed that was a pertinent question.

"My housekeeper, but I've already spoken with her," Doria replied, still seemingly nonplussed by the whole situation.

"Would it be alright if we talked to her?" Helen asked.

"Sure."

"Have you had any recent guests at your residence?"

"No."

"Have you noticed anything unusual recently?"

"No."

"Is there anyone you suspect of taking the painting?"

"No."

"Have you had any incidents like this in the past?"

"No."

"Do you have any security measures at your residence?"

"Just me."

I was startled a bit. At that answer, her voice was like a log suddenly breaking up in a fire.

Helen paused for a moment. I looked up at the change in cadence. Helen was thinking. I should have used that time to catch up on the notes I was taking. Instead, I watched the subtle changes in Helen's face as she came to a decision of what to ask next.

"Why do you need our help?" she finally asked, her professional tone slipping slightly into obvious curiosity.

Doria picked up her teacup again and took a sip. Both women let the silence hang in the air for a minute. After a couple of sips, Doria set the teacup back down, crossed her legs in the other direction, and let out a sigh.

"Okay," Doria said, clearly preparing to start an explanation. "The painting is a self-portrait. But it is also what you all would call 'magic.'" She put air-quotes around the word *magic* and looked at both of us as if to see if we were following along. We were. So far. "The painting is tied to my physical self in this realm. It allows me to offload any damage to this physical body to the painting."

I held my tongue, but I had so many questions. Luckily, Helen had questions too.

"Can you help me understand more about what you mean by that?" she asked in her interviewer's tone. I probably would have just said, *What?*

"Any damage to this body, like a cut or even aging, is..." Doria paused to search for a word. "Let's say, absorbed by the painting. But there are some restrictions. I need to physically make contact with it to transfer the damage from this body to the painting. Clearly, with it gone, I can't do that. So, stuff like this"—she held up her left hand, which I saw had a bandage on it—"will not heal properly."

"Like ever?" I blurted out.

Doria turned toward me. "It will eventually heal. But slower than normal, even slower than humans would heal. Also, I'll start to age, and I do not want to do that," she said with a small chuckle.

My high school English teacher would have been ashamed about how long it took me to connect that to the famous story that had been assigned reading. Annie and Cam had told me in my first week at the agency that most stories about magic and otherworldly beings were based in some reality. This was just another example of that. I made a mental note to get a copy of that story to reread.

"Alright, that is helpful to know," Helen said calmly, getting attention back to her and the conversation. "Is there anything else we should know?"

"Yes," Doria said with some hesitation. "I don't know how long it will take for the effects of not having the painting to manifest." She paused and broke eye contact with Helen. Then for the first time she sounded scared. "And I don't know what will happen if somebody tampers with or destroys it."

Helen tilted her head with empathy and gave Doria space to collect herself. A few moments and a small cough were all it took for Doria to regain her confident, *nothing can touch me* posture.

"I'm trusting this agency because I've been told that you all are very discreet and very good at what you do," Doria said, the crackling undertones in her voice becoming more pronounced. "I need that painting found and returned as soon as possible."

HELEN WALKED Doria to the front door after the interview. I headed upstairs to type up the notes and add them to the case file. The conversation wasn't that long, so I was able to complete it and email it off to Helen for review before four o'clock. I double-checked the new case file to make sure it was ready for the team.

Several people had already started to add materials and fill in documents with information. Normally I would start reading through everything that had been posted, but I was feeling antsy and didn't want to get started on anything so late in the day. Outside my office doors I could see Annie and Angela sitting at the conference table with their laptops out and chatting. I decided to go see what they were up to.

"Hey," I said in greeting.

They both popped their heads up and looked a little guilty, like they'd been caught conspiring on something.

"Oh, hey, Linda," Annie said with some relief in her voice.

"What are you two up to?" I asked, very curious about what was going on.

"Boring stuff," Angela offered with a smile.

"Like what? Anything I can help with?" I said as I sat

down at the table. "I'm having trouble being motivated to do anything at the end of the day."

They both smiled and nodded in understanding.

"We were just going over the expenses on the office redecorating projects for this last year," Angela said. "I'm trying to see what we can deduct for taxes."

"Oh," I responded, trying not to make a face. "That sounds fun, I guess."

Angela laughed. "It's fun for me. Which is good because it's all I've been doing for the last few months."

"So did we spend too much?" I asked jokingly.

Annie and I had spruced up three of the suites upstairs after many of the furniture pieces had been repurposed into the back parlor room. The results were widely loved. Even by Hank. Annie was a genius when it came to interior design. The results were all thanks to her. I played the assistant role and loved every minute of it.

"For a normal company, I'd say yes," Angela said, half joking. "For this agency, you probably could have spent double and I wouldn't have blinked."

"Really?"

I knew the agency had a lot of money. We were all paid very well. The office had quiet luxury in every room. And the agency had a private jet on standby. But unlike some other companies, we never talked about the financial state of the business. In every other job I had worked at before, monthly company meetings were filled with financial updates and always a push to see the numbers go up and to the right.

"Yes," Angela said and then leaned in toward the both

of us and lowered her voice. "If all of our retainers stopped paying and we didn't have any cases, the agency would be fine for years."

"Well, that's good to know," I said, still jokingly. "But it would get boring without cases."

"Speaking of cases," Annie said, also leaning in and making our little talking circle tighter, "how did the interview with Doria go?"

"I thought you'd never ask," I answered softly. Everyone would find out as soon as they read the case notes, so I wouldn't be spilling any secrets I shouldn't. And I loved telling a story. "First, Doria may give Winthrop a run for his money on who is most intimidating in a closed room."

"Don't tell him that," Angela said with a laugh. "He'll just want to try harder."

Annie and I both laughed along with Angela. She would know better than all of us. Angela was engaged to the five-hundred-year-old vampire. First, she had to spend another year and a half working with us at the OPT Agency, and then she'd become a vampire, adopted into the Southeast vampire family. Then Angela and Winthrop would be mated, the vampire term for married.

"I won't say a word to him about it," I promised. "The interview was pretty standard, but we learned more about the painting."

"What?" Annie asked. "I've been curious about what is so special about a painting that a demon would need our help."

"Jordan may have some more insights, but here's what I know," I replied, and then recounted what I had learned.

"I can see why she wants it back so badly and so quickly," Annie said solemnly. "Jordan said that demons are considered immortal. I guess that's how it works, at least for Doria. That's interesting."

I had learned early on that no supernatural was fully immortal. Not even vampires. Many supernaturals and otherworldly beings lived very long lives, but everyone eventually died. And everyone could be killed.

5

"Let's start with an update on Doria's case," Helen said at the regularly scheduled meeting Wednesday morning.

The energy was low across the board. I knew why I was having an off day. Ilka had been sulky the night before and had spent much of the evening standing by the front door. It was unlike her and made me worried that we'd get another unexpected visitor. We didn't, but it had kept me on edge all night. That was my problem, but I had no idea what was going on with everyone else.

"Did everyone have a chance to read the interview notes from yesterday?" Helen asked, surveying the table.

Half-hearted nods from the group confirmed that everyone had read them.

"Any questions or thoughts from that?" she pressed the group to engage.

No one jumped right in, but Helen was an expert at sitting in silence until people started speaking. Usually it wasn't needed. Usually, the team was engaged and excited. And, when there was silence, I was the one to crack first. It had become a bit of an inside joke. That day, though, I wasn't going to be the one to speak first.

Instead I watched how everyone else reacted to the uncomfortable silence. It had been about thirty seconds. Across the table from me, Annie was focused on her open laptop as if she were reviewing the notes. Cam was tapping her pen and staring straight ahead. Jordan was glancing thoughtfully at Helen with a small smirk, like she knew what Helen was doing. Hank's eyes were darting around the table at each of us and trying to make eye contact. I narrowly missed getting locked in a staring contest with him. Angela was staring at Jordan with a confused or curious expression, hard to say which. Steve seemed to be staring down Cam or trying to get her attention.

And Helen. Well, Helen was looking at me. We were probably only at the one-minute mark, but to me it felt like ten. I couldn't take it anymore.

"I still don't get why she needs our help," I finally said. The relief of filling the silence was worth the smirks I caught from both Annie and Jordan.

"I'm still wondering about that, too," Steve said.

I silently thanked him for backing me up.

"I know you addressed this in the interview," Steve continued, "but it still feels suspicious."

Helen nodded once to indicate that she understood, but instead of addressing the statements, she glanced around the table to see if anyone else wanted to add anything.

"Are there any records of demons working with any agency?" Angela asked calmly, the ever-practical one. Exactly what you'd want in your accountant.

"No," Helen responded just as calmly. "Not that we are aware of. But I also think that we can be smart about this." Her tone picked up strength and resolve. "This may be an opportunity for the agency to learn more about demons and build lasting relationships that could help us in the future."

"Doria could still be unpredictable," Jordan offered.

"You're right. I propose that we continue with the case and split into two groups." I could hear the excitement behind Helen's voice as she laid out the plan. "Group one will work the case like we normally would with any client. Group two will be working on theories for why a demon is asking for our help. This will allow us to serve the client and cover our backs," she concluded with a small smile. "Thoughts?"

"I like that plan," Cam offered first.

Everyone but Steve indicated their agreement. Helen tilted her head and looked at him. I held my breath. He had seemed the most suspicious of Doria, and since he was head of security and one of Helen's more senior people, I didn't know if she would continue the case without his support.

"Seems like a good approach," Steve finally agreed.

"Alright," Helen said with a clap of her hands. It was her signal that it was time to lay out the plan. "Jordan and Steve, I'd like you each to lead a group. Is there one either of you feel strongly about leading?"

"I'd like to be the leader of group two, the one working on why she is asking for our help," Steve answered first. There were no surprises there, and I thought we'd all feel better with him leading that group.

"Great," Helen said. "Jordan, would you be okay being lead for group one?"

"Yes," Jordan answered.

"For the rest of the team, let's talk about which group would be best," she instructed and turned to me. "Linda, you are already taking point on the Council visit, which we still need to talk about. So I'd recommend you not be assigned to a specific group until after that's finished."

"I'm fine with that," I responded. I'd still get to read all the reports and participate in discussions, so it wasn't really a big deal for me not to be in a group so I could focus on the Council visit.

"I'd like to be in group one," Cam said. "I have a feeling we'll need some forensic analysis of the scene that I can help with."

"Good point," Helen said. "Hank, thoughts?"

"Group two, please."

Helen and Steve both nodded in agreement to his request.

"Annie?" Helen prompted.

"I think I could help out best with group two," she said. "I'm guessing we'll have a fair amount of research to dig through."

Steve responded, "I think you're right, and you are the best at that."

"Angela?" Helen asked, turning to her at the end of the table.

"Group one," Angela said. "With it being a theft of an item, even a magical one, there may be a monetary motive. I can help with the forensic accounting side of things."

"That's a very good point," Helen said and gave her an approving smile. "So we've got Jordan, Cam, and Angela in group one. You three will be working the case as normal. Of course, you'll keep the whole team updated and include anyone you think could be helpful."

"Understood," Jordan confirmed.

"Steve, Hank, and Annie, you three have a more ambiguous job," Helen said. "Go wide and don't discount anything at this point."

"Of course," Steve confirmed.

"Both teams, I'd like a plan outline by the end of the day," Helen instructed. "Oh, I almost forgot: Doria said that we are welcome to visit their residence at any point to investigate the scene and collect evidence. Jordan, just let me know when you'd like to go and who you need."

"Will do," Jordan said.

"Great. Let's move on to the Council's visit," Helen said and then turned to me. "Linda, any updates there?"

I straightened up and cleared my throat. "Yes. Steve shared the prep document he had already done for the last time. I've read through that and we'll be meeting later today to go over any open questions. It looks like we'll just need to check on a few records to ensure they are up to date and then I'll write up a few summary documents of our activities the last two quarters. I'll send those out for review to everyone."

"Do you know when the summary documents may be ready for review?" Jordan asked politely.

"Not for sure, but I'll try to get them out by the end of Thursday," I offered, holding back a grimace. That would only give the team a day to review them, or we'd be working over the weekend.

"That would be great," Helen replied with a smile and then turned to the rest of the group. "I know it's a tight turnaround, so be sure to hold some space on Friday for those reviews."

Everyone indicated that they understood, and no one complained. We were all used to fast turnaround times when it was needed. This work was like hills and valleys. You enjoyed the slow times in the valleys when they were there because you knew that soon you'd be on a steady run uphill again.

Jordan had given me that lecture in my third month there when she saw that I was always picking up new tasks. I had felt the need to always be busy, constantly at 110 percent capacity. That mentality had been drilled into me in my other corporate jobs. It had never felt sustainable even in the midst of doing it, but it didn't feel like there was another option. I had to be at capacity always or risk being let go. It was the looming threat always there in the background. But being over capacity hadn't saved me from being let go in the end.

After Jordan's lecture, I reminded myself on a regular basis: Hills and valleys. Don't run when you don't need to.

Build up the energy for when the sprint is needed. Then sprint hard, get it done, and rest after.

Steve caught my attention as we all got up to leave the meeting. "What does the rest of your morning look like?"

"I don't have anything else scheduled right now; I just need a block of time to start the summary reports." I answered, looking at the calendar on my phone. Ideally I could get in two hours that morning and knock out a first draft of the reports that day.

"I've got some time right now. Does that work for you?" Steve asked as he similarly checked his calendar.

"Yes," I replied. That would be perfect. We could get through the questions, and then I could be heads down on the reports until lunchtime.

"Great, do you have what you need? Do you want to head to my office?" Steve asked.

"Yes, that works," I said and grabbed my laptop and coffee.

Steve's office had become one of my favorites, even though I didn't spend a lot of time in there. He was one of the parental figures in the office, and his space reflected that. The vibe was like a cool den where your mom or dad would settle in after dinner to read or work on things away from the noise of the kids. At least that's what television taught me. Growing up an only child with a single parent, I spent evenings with my mom lounging on the couch. Usually both of us read or we would watch TV together.

I made my way to the chairs in front of his desk Instead, Steve motioned to the lounge chairs set up on the other side of the room around a coffee table. He grabbed his laptop from his desk, and then we both sat down oppo-site each other.

"Where do you want to start?" Steve asked, kicking things off for us.

"Honestly, it all seems pretty straightforward, so I want to make sure I'm understanding it right," I said as I pulled open my laptop to the document I had been reviewing of the game plan Steve had already put together.

"That's good," he said with a chuckle. "We worked hard to make it as simple and straightforward as possible."

"Well, you all did a good job," I replied. "From what I understand, we need to provide the Council with an over-view of the cases that we worked on over the last quarter. Or, in this case, the last two quarters because they missed a visit."

I looked up to see if I was on the right track. Steve was nodding along.

"I looked at the write-up you had for the quarter that they didn't come," I said, pulling up that document. "I'll just use that same format and add in the new cases."

"Perfect," he offered as encouragement.

"I did see there are a couple of things you left out." That was where I had concerns. "How did you decide what to leave out or what to include?"

"Great question," Steve said. "I didn't decide, Helen did. I provided her with a complete report, and then she made comments on what she wanted removed."

"Okay." That made sense, but I was a bit troubled by it.

"Take a look at row four," Steve instructed. I did and could see his cursor in the spreadsheet as well. "That case is the full report. We didn't take anything out of it. That would be the best example to use to write up the other ones."

The case in question had been a simple review of a werewolf pack's properties and investments for insurance claims. For this agency, as tame and mundane as a case can get.

"Okay, that's helpful," I replied.

"After you get the cases entered, send it over to Helen and she'll let you know what to remove," he continued. "She's pretty quick with it, so I wouldn't stress about it too much. But you will want her to do that before you write up the summary."

"Do you want me to update the playbook with that step?" I asked offhandedly. It seemed like an important step in the process that we'd be doing every quarter.

"No," Steve said and his tone shifted. "I know it seems sneaky, but the Council will be looking at the procedure that we wrote up and then the documents that we provide. As long as we follow the procedure, we pass the review. Or at least that is how it is supposed to work. If we include in the procedure that we review and redact sensitive information, then they will ask questions about that. And we don't want them to."

Steve looked at me as if waiting to see how I'd react. I still had my questions about the Council and especially Director Owens. The theory that she had killed my mom still percolated in the back of my head. I hadn't let that go. But we hadn't been able to uncover any corroborating evidence.

What I did know was that I trusted Helen and Steve.

"That makes sense. I'm fine with that," I replied firmly.

"The only other thing they may check is specific cases," Steve said, changing the topic slightly. "Again though, they should only be checking that we have a procedure for how we handle cases and that we followed that procedure for the case."

I made a face. That would be a lot more work than I could get done in less than a week.

"But that won't happen in this review," he reassured me as if he had read my thoughts. "Helen got them to agree to a three-month notice for specific case reviews. So they may give notice for specific case reviews this time, but those won't happen until next quarter."

"That's good," I said with relief. That was clearly the bigger and more nerve-wracking part of the visits. I remembered reading that in the playbook, but it was good to have Steve explain it. "Anything else I should know?"

"Nope. You won't need to be in the meetings when they are here. We'll probably want you in the building in case we do have questions or need support, but you shouldn't have to talk with them."

"I'm good with that." I had been pretty sure that was how it would work, but when I was asked to lead the prep efforts, I worried that I needed to be involved in the actual meetings. "Do we know who from the Council will be coming?" I asked, still wondering if it would be someone I knew, like the head of the records department.

"No," Steve answered. "I'm hoping that we can get that

established and have the same person every time. But so far they won't commit to anyone specific."

"That seems weird," I said what I thought out loud.

Steve laughed a little bit. "It is weird, but the Council is weird. Do you have any other questions?"

"No," I answered confidently.

"Great. Remember I'm here to help if needed or if you have any questions," he offered with a smile and stood up.

"Thank you," I said and closed my laptop.

Steve walked me to the door of his office, and we said polite goodbyes. I checked my phone as I walked away. I had a good chunk of time to work on it before lunch; if I was quick, I could probably finish it.

THERE WERE ONLY seven cases in the last quarter, and none of them were complicated. It was easy to fill in the document, and I was done well before the two-hour block I had set aside. Doria's case file didn't have anything new, so I didn't need to worry about that. Instead I decided to pull up my notes from my apprenticeship and work on my secret project, finding evidence against Director Cora Owens.

Every night when I was back in the safety of the apartment in San Francisco, I meticulously wrote down notes about my day. I included what I did, who I interacted with, and any conversations I had. A secure file on my laptop hard drive held all my notes, and I was the only one who had access to them.

Helen and I talked about the notes when I came back to debrief, but we hadn't uncovered anything useful yet. She was okay with that and reassured me it would take time. I was getting frustrated by the lack of progress.

I knew I couldn't expect Cora to just come out and tell me about her plotting and scheming. It was also unlikely that any of the staff at the Council offices really knew about her plans. If they did, they were likely part of it and not going to tell me anything useful.

The staff members I had worked with so far had all been friendly. They seemed to be good people just trying to do a job and doing what they were told. The only fault I could find in any of them was that they were too quick to follow directions and never asked questions. It was a very top-down control system and very micromanaged.

I shadowed and helped one of the record clerks, Willow, a witch who was checking coven memberships. We were supposed to catalog specific magical gifts. There was a spreadsheet with checkboxes for different gifts and abilities. We read the report supplied by the covens, entered a name, and checked the boxes. Some gifts weren't listed as options. When I asked Willow if we should add those, I was told no and that coming up with the categories wasn't part of our job.

I was shocked at her lack of curiosity and that her boss wouldn't want them to bring that to their attention. It seemed like a big gap in the process. But the beaten-down look Willow gave me when I asked stopped me from pressing further. This was not a group of people who were encouraged or rewarded for speaking up about anything.

6

A nnie, Angela, and I were a few bites into our lunch of Mrs. Clark's artfully created cobb salads when Jordan walked into the kitchen. She wasn't her usual breezy self. A few quick glances around the room, and she settled her gaze back on the three of us. Our forks hung in midair and our eyes were wide, waiting to see what was going on with her.

"Well, at least two of you are here," Jordan said as if she was already mid-conversation.

"What?" Annie asked gently.

"I need Angela and Linda, but I'm also looking for Cam," she replied.

"What can we help you with?" Angela asked just as gently as Annie had.

I had decided to go back to my salad. Whatever was coming, I wanted to get as much lunch into me before it did.

"The four of us are going to Doria's house as soon as

possible," Jordan said. She was still clearly distracted. "Did you not get my message?"

Angela and I exchanged worried looks. Jordan didn't sound angry, but she was a little out of sorts. I pulled up the messaging app on my phone. There wasn't a message from Jordan or anyone about going to Doria's house.

"No, sorry," I apologized.

"I didn't get a message either," Angela added.

Jordan pulled her phone from her back pocket, clicked around a bit, and then let out a sigh. The frustration in her voice got heavier. "I didn't hit send," she said and deflated a bit.

"Have you had lunch yet?" Annie asked calmly.

Jordan shook her head and looked longingly at the salad bowls on the kitchen island that were waiting to be picked up.

"Why don't you sit down and eat something?" Annie said as she got up to help get Jordan some lunch. "You can tell Linda and Angela what you need. And I'll help you track down Cam while you eat."

"Okay." Jordan sighed again. "That would be good. Thank you."

I continued to quickly eat my salad so that I'd have time for dessert. Jordan and Annie rejoined the table with a bowl of salad and juice from the fridge. Jordan lowered her eyes and concentrated on eating a few bites, allowing the three of us to exchange worried glances. Jordan, much like Helen, was usually a rock for the team. I didn't think I'd ever seen her so frazzled.

"So, what's going on?" I asked Jordan between her bites.

"I was looking at the weather for the past week," she said and then took another small bite before continuing, "Surprisingly, it hasn't rained since before Doria found the painting gone."

We all nodded, but if the other two were like me, we hadn't made the connection yet.

"It's supposed to rain tonight," Jordan said and took another small bite. "If we can get to the house before it rains, we might be able to find evidence outside."

Another bite. Another round of nodding. That time we all got it.

"That makes sense," I replied. "So we need to go soon."

"Yes," Jordan said, slightly less agitated. "But I need Cam to help make sure we have all the right equipment, and I can't find her."

Annie and I exchanged worried glances at that. It wasn't like Cam to be unavailable, but she had been more distracted recently and was spending more time in her basement lab.

"I've messaged her," Annie said. "We'll give her a couple of minutes to respond, and if she doesn't reply, we'll split up and check the office spaces again."

"Is there anything we can help prepare?" Angela asked.

"I guess we can start pulling the evidence-collection kits and checking them over," Jordan said. "Cam always handles that, but she has a checklist for each kit, so we should be able to get started without her."

"Well, let's finish eating, and then Linda and I can get started on that while you and Annie find Cam," Angela cheerfully replied.

I had already finished my salad. Instead of sitting around and watching the others eat, I got up and dished out four plates of the white chocolate raspberry cheese-cake that was in the fridge for dessert. If it was already in front of them, they'd be less likely to suggest we skip it. We could eat fast.

AFTER WE ALL devoured the cheesecake slices, Angela and I went down to the first floor of the basement. Jordan and Annie had set off to look for Cam, who still hadn't returned either of their messages.

The racks of bins in that part of the basement held the equipment used most often. Angela and I had both helped to inventory equipment a few months before. I was told this was an activity we could look forward to every six months. I didn't look forward to it. It was dusty and sweaty work. I was getting stronger, but I still didn't like to sweat.

Each bin had a QR code that we'd scan with an app on our phones—an app and system that Cam had created for the agency. In that same app, we could type in what we were looking for, and it would display an augmented-reality view of the racks to highlight the bin we needed.

"Jordan said that there would be a list for the evidence kits, right?" I asked Angela, hoping she remembered better than I did.

"Yes," Angela confirmed. "But she didn't say where."

"Maybe it's in the bin," I said and typed the evidence kit into the app's search bar. The app returned two options: to find the bin or to see its contents. I clicked on See Contents, and a list of items replaced the screen. "Oh, it's in the app. Impressive."

I shouldn't have been surprised. All the inventory checking had been through the app too. Thinking about it, I would have been shocked if it had been a piece of paper in the box. That wasn't how Cam did things.

"Found it," Angela said. She had been clicking through the app on her phone as well. Angela held up the phone and then pointed out two boxes one row up and to the left. "It's those two."

We each pulled out a bin and set them on the ground so that we could open them. My bin was a collection of smaller boxes and bags, each with its own label. I was able to quickly remove the four items that we'd need and set them aside. Angela had also removed a few items from her bin. We were about to open them up to check the contents when footsteps in the room caught our attention.

"Oh good, you found them," Cam said as she walked toward us. "Sorry I'm late."

"No worries," I lied. There were worries. This was not normal Cam.

Cam already had her phone out and was confirming that we had pulled the right items. "Let me just check these real fast and then we can load up the van," Cam said as she stared at her phone.

"Okay," Angela answered for us. "Is there anything else we can help with?"

"No, that's alright," Cam replied and dug through the

bags. "Jordan should be down in a few minutes. She just needed to update Helen."

"Is Helen coming with us?" I asked, curious if she'd come along. I was hoping that she would. Not that we couldn't handle it, but it always felt safer when Helen was around.

"Probably," Cam replied, zipping up the bags now, "if she doesn't already have something scheduled."

"Sounds good," I replied with a smile. I knew her schedule and that she didn't have anything that afternoon.

We loaded all the equipment into two duffel bags. Cam went to pull the van from the detached garages to the basement garage door so that we could load up more easily. Jordan and Helen came down just as she was pulling in. We all gathered in the loading bay, waiting for Jordan's instructions.

"We'll split up into two groups when we get there to do a quick sweep," Jordan said. Her normal confidence and easygoing vibe had returned. "Cam and Angela, I'd like the two of you to take the outside." She looked at each of them.

"Got it," Cam replied, and Angela nodded in understanding.

"Helen, Linda, and I will start inside," Jordan continued. "We'll regroup after our first sweep and decide if we want to do another round. Any questions?"

I had questions—this was my first evidence-collection mission—but I knew I could ask them during the task. Mostly I'd just be doing as instructed anyway.

"Alright. Let's load up," Jordan said excitedly.

Angela, Cam, and I ended up in the back of the van.

Jordan and Helen sat in the front chatting, but it wasn't loud enough for us to hear. Cam stayed glued to her phone. Instead of being upset with Cam for not responding right away when we needed her, I decided to strike up a conversation with Angela.

"How are things going with Winthrop and the adoption process?" I asked with real interest. She'd shared regular updates with us and didn't mind answering questions. It was really interesting to hear about the process from an adoptee's point of view.

"It's going well," she replied. "I'm about a month away from completing the first course. And then I'll need to head down to Louisiana to meet the rest of the family."

"Do you think the course has been fairly accurate?" I asked gently. It turned out that most groups, including vampires, werewolves, and witches, had their own education courses that their adoptees or young people took to learn about the supernatural and otherworldly communities. I had asked if I could take one or all of them. So far the answer had been no. Luckily, I had all the agency files and documents that held the information I wanted, so I didn't push the issue.

"Mostly," she said with a squint of her eyes. "It for sure has a slant toward the vampires' experience. And the history is probably missing some points of view."

"I guess that's to be expected," I offered. "It's the same for human history and education in different parts of the world."

"That's true," she replied, seeming to become more at ease with that comparison. "And I'm lucky that I get more exposure to different ideas at the agency. It's giving me a more well-rounded view that I'm hoping will be helpful once I join the family."

There had been a question that had been eating away at me, but it never felt polite to bring it up. But Angela and I were good friends and she had just said something that made it an easy pivot to ask.

"Do you know yet if you'll still work with the agency after you join the family?" Even saying that as nonchalantly as I could, it was still laced with some anxiety. It would be hard to have her go. We were the two newest members at the agency, and I felt connected to her with our shared newbies experience.

Angela smiled sadly. "I'd like to stay with the agency. Winthrop is supportive, but we're not sure how the family will react."

"Oh," I uttered, not sure what to say.

"We're going to wait to ask when the adoption gets closer," she said a bit more cheerfully. "I think the chances of them letting me stay will be higher if I'm more established here and have passed most or maybe all of the adoption milestones."

"That makes a lot of sense," I replied, trying to match her cheerfulness. "For what it's worth, I'd like you to keep working here."

"Thank you. That means a lot."

Cam looked up from her phone. "I want you to keep working here too."

"Thank you," Angela said.

I smiled back at Cam, glad that she had chimed in.

"What are you working on?" I asked Cam. Whatever it was must have been important or exciting if she was missing messages from us.

Cam looked anxious for a moment, but quickly hid it. "It's a new device that we need. Nothing too crazy."

I squinted at her in confusion. Cam usually talked at length about any gadgets or inventions she was working on, no matter how mundane they were.

"Can you tell us about it?" I pressed.

"Not much to tell yet," Cam deflected. "I haven't figured it out, but Helen wants it soon."

That just added to the mystery. I was trying to think of another question to ask that would get her to reveal what the new device was when Jordan turned down a residential block and parked the van in a driveway.

"We're here," Jordan said loudly from the driver's seat.

Helen turned around to face the three of us in the back seat. "Jordan and I will go make sure Doria is home, and we'll let her know what we are doing. You three get the van unloaded and wait for us here."

We all nodded in understanding.

Jordan and Helen walked up the steps of the two-story mansion we had parked in front of. The circular driveway was empty except for our van, but Doria had said she'd be home. Cam, Angela, and I stayed back, waiting for them like we'd been told. It didn't take long for Jordan and Helen to return.

"Doria gave us the go-ahead to look around," Jordan said and then pointed to the south corner of the house. "Cam and Angela, she said the painting was usually at that end of the attic. I'd say start on that side, but try to circle the whole property if you can before it rains."

We all looked up at the sky. It was overcast, but that was pretty normal for that time of year. A few darker clouds were to the west. Those were the ones we'd need to worry about, and it looked like they were moving in fast.

"Will do," Cam answered and hefted up one of the dark duffel bags.

Jordan grabbed the other bag from the open van door. "We'll head inside and start from the top down. When you two finish, come inside and we'll see what else we need to do."

Cam motioned to Angela, and they walked off toward the south side of the house.

Jordan hefted the bag up onto her shoulder and then looked from Helen to me. "Let's go see what we can find."

7

The inside of the house matched the outside. It was a huge Tudor-style home filled with intricate woodwork, built-in shelves, and glass-front cabinets filled to capacity. Directly across from the front door was a giant fireplace with a green tile surround flanked by two benches filled with pillows. It looked like the perfect spot to cozy up with tea and a book on a rainy afternoon.

Doria wasn't around, so I didn't feel bad about staring and trying to peek around every corner. Annie would have loved the house and probably would have gotten some ideas for the office.

"Linda, we're heading upstairs," Jordan called out, snapping me out of my gawking.

"Sorry," I said sheepishly. "I'm coming."

"First, put these on," she said and handed Helen and me a pair of black latex gloves and some blue shoe covers.

I struggled to put them on, but Jordan and Helen both snapped theirs on with practiced ease.

The ornate wood stairs took us up to a landing overlooking the foyer. I followed Jordan and Helen down the hall to a closed door. They must have been given directions because they walked right up to it and opened it, revealing a set of narrower stairs that led to the attic space where Doria had said the painting had been stored.

"Helen, can you take the photos?" Jordan asked after we had made it up the stairs and stood in the expanse of one large room. Four dormer windows filled the space with soft gray light. No one had made a move to turn on any lights yet.

"Yep, I can do that," Helen answered and knelt down to dig through the duffel bag that Jordan had brought up.

"Linda, you and I are going to collect fingerprints and any other evidence we can find," Jordan said, turning my way. "I'll have you do the labeling and note what we find. Just be careful where you step, try not to touch anything, and let me know if you see anything interesting."

"Okay," I said, a bit concerned that I was out of my depth.

Jordan handed me a clipboard, a pen, and a sheet of stickers. She had taken out a smaller black case that opened like a tackle box.

"We'll start with fingerprints around the door and light switch," she said. She pulled an aerosol-type can and something that looked like a fancy flashlight from the case. Aiming at the doorknob, she sprayed the area. A fine white mist floated over the surface, but it didn't look like anything had happened. Jordan sprayed once more and then looked closely at the section of the door. I guessed she was satisfied because she set the spray can down and clicked on the flashlight.

The special flashlight shined over the area that was sprayed. I gasped as neon-green sets of fingerprints lit up.

"Pretty cool, right?" Jordan pressed down another button on the special flashlight that made a series of audible clicks. "It's something that Cam came up with. It's way more effective than dusting for prints. The light has a built-in camera so you can just shine it on the print and get a picture of it." She moved the light around and clicked the button a few more times as she explained, "The images of the prints will get uploaded, and then we can look for matches."

"That's so cool," I said and then offered, "Do you need me to clean up the dust stuff?"

"No," Jordan said with a smile. "It will evaporate in about half an hour, no need to clean it up. And it doesn't disrupt the prints, so if you ever get to a scene before the official investigators, you can still get prints without interfering. As long as you have thirty minutes to let it clear out."

"That's amazing," I said. I was constantly impressed with what the team came up with.

"I'm going to give you a series of numbers that go with these images. Can you write that down and the location where we found them?" Jordan asked.

"Of course," I said, readying my clipboard. Jordan read off a five-digit code and dictated what I should write. We repeated the whole process with the light switch just to the left of the door.

"Writing down the location part is the only thing we have to do by hand. We are trying to automate it," Jordan explained more as we worked. "We haven't been able to get the coordinates precise enough, but it's getting close."

"Sure," I offered in support, but I didn't really know what she was talking about.

"Jordan, I think I found something," Helen called out from across the room.

We made our way over to Helen with our tools. She was standing under one of the dormer windows that was slightly open. I was turned around in the house, so I wasn't sure if it was the south window that Jordan had pointed out before we had gone into the house.

"Doria said that she didn't touch anything after she found the painting missing," Helen reminded us. "This window is the only one open up here. And look." She leaned in closer to the window frame and pointed out a deep gouge in the wood. "The frame is scratched and the locking mechanism is bent."

"Good find," Jordan said. "Did you already get pictures?"

"Yes," Helen replied, straightening up.

"Great. We'll see if we can find any prints," Jordan said. "Have you found where the painting was stored?"

"I think it was over by that wall," Helen answered, pointing to the wall perpendicular and about ten feet away. "If you've got it covered here, I'll go take a look and get some pictures."

"That would be great, we've got it here."

Jordan turned to me with the spray can held out. "Do you want to try this one?"

"Oh." I hesitated. "I don't know. I don't want to mess it up."

"You can't really mess it up," Jordan said with a smile. "Just point it to the area where the scratch is, spray once for about three seconds, wait five seconds, and then spray it again."

"Okay, I guess I can try," I said and took the spray can she offered. It was surprisingly lightweight and felt cold to the touch. "Do I need to shake it?"

"No. That's not necessary," Jordan answered with a small chuckle.

I followed her instructions, counting the seconds in my head to get the timing right. After I finished with the spray, Jordan looked it over.

"It looks great," she said. We swapped the can for the flashlight. "Now just shine the light around the area. Turn it on with the big button on the top. When you see some prints light up, click the other button. It will keep taking pictures as you hold it down."

I nodded my understanding and shined the flashlight at the area I had just sprayed. I started to panic. There weren't any fingerprints, so had I done it wrong?

"I'm not seeing anything," Jordan said calmly. "Let's spray the lock and see if we get any there."

"Okay," I said and started the process over.

Jordan wasn't looking; rather, she was making some notes on the clipboard.

"I don't see any here either," I said as I shined the light around.

"They probably used a tool to get it open," she said, still calm. "Let's just double-check the whole frame, and then we can join up with Helen. Are you okay to keep going?"

"Yes." I was confident by that point that I knew what I was doing.

It was fun. I sprayed around the full edge of the window's large frame. Switching over to the flashlight, I started in the lower right corner and methodically made my way up and around, looking for any sign of fingerprints like we'd seen on the door. I was starting to feel deflated about the lack of fingerprints when I got to the left edge and the neon-green prints lit up. A clear set of four fingerprints.

"Oh," Jordan let out. "It looks like this is where they gripped the frame. Get some pictures, and then let's see if we can get any on the outside of the window frame."

I clicked the button and held it to capture several sets. When that was done, Jordan nodded and then opened the window all the way.

"Spray around there," she said, pointing to the outside where it would align with the inside set.

I leaned out the window to get to the right angle. "Got it," I said excitedly. A single large print that looked like a thumb stood out neon green on the frame.

"Awesome," Jordan said. "Let me make a few notes."

Helen walked over, probably because we had been making so much noise. "What did you find?" she asked.

To answer, I shined the light on the four prints that

were inside the frame, then leaned out the window but left room for her to lean out too.

"There's one out here, too," I said, pointing to the outer frame. We exchanged places so she could lean out to take a look.

"That's certainly something," she said, mostly talking to herself.

"What are you thinking?" Jordan asked before I could blurt out the same.

"The print orientation," she said. "This would only make sense if they were grabbing the frame to climb into the attic, not to just look out."

We all looked at it again. And then we all looked out the window again. It was a long way down. Technically, the attic was the third floor of the house. No normal ladder would be big enough to get up there.

"That is strange," Jordan agreed and then shook her head as if to clear out a thought. "Did you find anything near where the painting was?"

"No. I did take some pictures. But the two of you should come take a look," Helen said and gestured for us to follow her. "More eyes are helpful."

I could see the shadow of a square on the wall where something had hung for a long time. The bare wood around it in the uninsulated attic had aged from the sun, creating a perfect outline. I was about to say that, just looking for the right witty words to use, when my eyesight tunneled, and I snapped into a vision.

I was in the same attic. It was disorienting. For a moment, I didn't know if it was a vision or if I'd just had a momentary blackout. But the life-size portrait of Doria hanging on the wall in front of me, which had just been bare, confirmed that I was having a vision of the past—or, if the painting had been returned, maybe the future.

Visions still came when they wanted to. I had learned to let go of trying to control when and how they happened. I just needed to breathe and let the vision show me what it needed to. I looked around for any clues that could help me figure out if it was past or future. Then a small sound off to my side caught my attention. It was footsteps. Multiple pairs. And it sounded like they were coming up the stairs.

I panicked and searched for a place to hide. Then I laughed at myself. They probably wouldn't see me, and if they did, so what?

The attic door creaked open and two people walked in. At least I thought it was two people. One of the two was a dark shape, roughly person-sized, if a bit too tall. The light around it seemed to be sucked in like a black hole in space. The shape was followed by another woman I didn't recognize.

They were speaking to each other, but I couldn't quite make out the words. I noticed the crackling undertones coming from the black void that were constant in Doria's voice when she spoke. The other woman had a melodic voice. It was like a choir harmonizing with every word she spoke. It was breathtaking and drew me in.

I was wrapped up in listening to them, trying hard to glean any words of their conversation. Abruptly, they stopped talking. The woman I didn't know raised her hand in a gesture to be silent. She looked confused and then concerned. I had no idea where the maybe-Doria void was looking.

The woman turned back to the door and then began to make a slow turn around the room as if searching for something. It felt like she was searching for me. I closed my eyes in an instinctual effort to not be seen. If I couldn't see them, maybe they couldn't see me.

Peeking open my eyes, I made eye contact with the woman. She reached out toward the black void and then faded into it herself. I let out a swear, startled at the sudden change, then felt the pull in my stomach that snapped me back to the present reality.

Jordan and Helen looked at me with concern and curiosity. I blinked a few times and then decided to sit on the floor cross-legged and compose myself. I wasn't surprised that I'd had a vision. Over six months, my therapist, Jax, and I had figured out what often triggered them and how to deal with them effectively.

The visions were often triggered when I was feeling engaged and motivated in something that I internally felt was helpful. This made it sound like I had control over them. I didn't. The feelings couldn't be faked and it wasn't a sure way to trigger a vision. They came when they wanted, and there was no forcing them despite how hard I tried.

As for dealing with them, I struggled for months with worry about how they would be interpreted and used by the team. They were not clear answers and often left me more confused. At first, I had thought of them as a view into reality at a different time. I would recount them to the rest of the team and I would be sick with worry that I had gotten something wrong. Or missed something that could be critical to a case. Or that I focused on something that would lead us down the wrong path.

With a lot of practice, I did the best I could and reminded myself that the team had solved cases before I was there. They'd continue to solve them without a vision if needed. Also, the team wasn't going to run off on a whim; we'd get evidence first. Knowing that, the visions had become easier for me.

Normally a short and relatively simple vision wouldn't have landed me sitting cross-legged on the dusty floor of an attic with my boss and a senior colleague standing over me. But this vision had something new. I was getting sick of new things in visions.

"Do you need some juice?" Jordan asked in her doctor's voice. She was already reaching into the duffel bag and pulling out a Pacific Cooler flavored Capri Sun, the best kind. I nodded and took the juice with the straw already in place, courtesy of Jordan. After a few sips, I was ready to talk.

"It was fairly simple, and I'm afraid not very helpful," I said. I had gotten over a lot of hang-ups with my visions, but I still had a habit of caveating what I would tell. Everyone put up with it. "It was this room. The painting was hanging on the wall. But I couldn't tell if this was in the past or the future." I took a couple more sips of the juice pouch. "Two people walked in. A woman I didn't recognize and someone I think was Doria. They were talking, but I couldn't make out what they were saying." I slurped the rest of the juice, flattening the pouch with a loud sucking noise. "The woman I didn't recognize had a voice that sounded familiar-ish, but I couldn't place it."

Helen and Jordan both made their thinking faces.

"What do you mean you think it was Doria?" Helen asked, picking up on that point quickly.

"Well, I recognized her voice," I said and pictured what I had seen in my head. "But where she was in the room was just a black void. It was like pictures of black holes, where the light is being sucked in and it's just nothing."

"Interesting," Jordan whispered, mostly to herself.

"But it was her voice?" Helen pressed.

"I think so," I replied but then hesitated. "Well, the voice was like hers. It had that crackling undertone. But I guess it's hard to say for sure."

"Okay," Helen said. "Anything else?"

"The other woman turned into a black void too. She was reaching toward Doria when it happened. That's about it," I replied and then promised, "I'll write it out as soon as we get back to the office."

That had become the standard procedure. I found that writing it out like a screenplay helped to get all the details out. Even the details that I didn't think were important could be later on. I also tended to add some of my own narration over the write-up. I was a very sarcastic narrator. No one had complained about it yet. Jax said it was a coping mechanism but wasn't hurting anyone so I should keep doing it if it helped.

"Alright," Helen agreed with only a small side-eye and

then turned to Jordan. "Anything more you want to check out up here?"

"No," Jordan answered, looking around the space. "Well, let's do one more sweep, and then we'll see if we can get prints on the other door up to the stairs and the entrance doors on the main floor."

"Sounds good," Helen agreed, and I nodded.

"Linda, do you want to get started on the fingerprints while we do a sweep up here?" Jordan asked.

"Yes, I can do that," I said, excited to be given a job I knew how to do. I picked up the case with the tools and headed to the door.

Down the stairs, I had just started spraying around the door handle when Cam and Angela walked up.

"Find any good prints?" Cam asked, setting down their duffel bag.

"Not sure down here yet," I answered as I gave the door another spray. "But we found some sets upstairs. Jordan and Helen are doing a last sweep up there." I pointed up the stairs with my head.

"Cool. We'll wait here so we don't interrupt them," Cam answered.

I concentrated on the task I'd been given. As expected, several prints showed up neon green under the light. I clicked the button to take several pictures at different angles. Then I repeated the procedure on the other side of the door. Cam and Angela stood patiently off to the side as I finished and then stowed the tools in the case.

"I need to do the other entrance doors too," I said, ready to continue on.

"Oh, we already got those," Cam answered. "And any windows that would be accessible."

"Awesome," I answered, relieved. It was getting late, and although I had just had a juice pouch, I could really use a snack.

As if on cue, Jordan and Helen headed down the stairs, duffel bag in hand.

"All done outside?" Jordan asked.

"Yep. And we got all the entrances for prints. Doors and windows," Cam answered.

"Excellent."

"Does this house have a basement?" Jordan asked, turning toward Helen.

"I think just a cellar," Helen answered. "But we should check it out. I bet it's just behind these stairs."

We all followed Helen as she walked through the hall toward the back of the stairs. As expected, there was a small, unassuming door. Unassuming if you didn't count the huge metal bar and padlock that secured it closed.

"Well, I think we'll need Doria if we want to look down there," Jordan said once she saw the lock.

Doria hadn't been around for any of our time in the house. I assumed she was tucked away in some office or back room, waiting for the five of us to leave her home. That's what I'd probably do.

"I'll go see if I can find her," Helen answered and walked away toward the back of the house.

"Do we really want to go into a basement that's padlocked shut?" I blurted out in a half whisper once Helen had left our sight.

Everyone smiled. Some smiles were more nervous than others.

"Are you scared of basements?" Angela teased.

"Yes," I said, only half joking. "We all should be."

"Well, you can stay upstairs if you'd like," Jordan offered gently with a small laugh.

"You can all stay upstairs," Helen said, rounding the corner and responding to the overheard conversation. We all jumped slightly and looked at her, confused. "Doria said that she'd allow me to take a look in the basement, but only me."

I would not have been as calm as Helen sounded. That sounded like something someone would say to get you alone and have you never come back. I wasn't the only one concerned.

"Are you sure?" Jordan pressed in a whisper.

"Yes, it will be fine," Helen said, still as calm as could be. "If I find anything pertinent to the case, I can share that with you all. But I've been asked not to share anything else I see down there." And then I swear she stared directly at me. "So don't ask."

"I won't," I answered automatically. I probably would.

Doria rounded the same corner that Helen had come from. She had a large key ring in her hand that held several keys. "Ready?" Doria asked Helen.

"Yes. The team will wait by the front door," she said, more as an instruction for the four of us.

We nodded and walked slowly toward the foyer. We stood in a half circle so that we could be close to one another and all see the direction of the basement stairs.

Helen gave a little half wave before she followed Doria through the door.

"I'm giving her five minutes," Jordan said under her breath. We all kept our eyes focused on the direction they had gone.

It was less than three minutes before we heard happy chatter coming up the stairs. We heard Doria pull the bar back through the rungs and secure the padlock. Helen and Doria appeared in the hall. They chatted a bit more in quiet voices and then shook hands. Helen walked toward us and Doria disappeared into the back rooms of the house.

"Alright, I think we can head out," Helen said cheerfully as she passed us and went out the front door. We all looked at her with wide-eyed curiosity. But no questions were asked as we followed her out to the van.

8

The ride back to the office was mostly quiet. We were all exhausted from the rush to get out there and the high-anxiety basement situation that was still a mystery.

As we pulled into our basement garage bay, rain started to fall. We all helped to unload the van, but then Helen said we could put away everything the next day. She suggested that we record any pertinent notes from the evidence collection and then head home early. The next day would be a heavy day of going through evidence and she wanted us well rested.

I took her up on the suggestion and started on the task with a cup of tea handed to me by Mrs. Clark. It took me only twenty minutes to type up the basic notes of the vision I saw. I could add more details to it the next morning once I looked at it with fresh eyes. Jordan had already outlined the evidence collection of the attic, so I was able to add some notes to that document instead of starting my own. All done in under an hour and on the early three o'clock bus home. Ilka was not overly pleased that I was home early and wouldn't give her an early dinner that her not-so-polite meowing was clearly requesting.

THE NEXT MORNING started off well. I had a great night's sleep. The morning bus ride and walk to the office were peaceful. The rain from the night before had continued but settled into light, misty rain that barely seemed to fall. I was early so I walked slowly, letting the drops collect on my green raincoat and face.

At the office I shed my coat and boots at the door and stowed them in a coat closet for wet things. I had taken to keeping a pair of sneakers in that closet for rainy days. It was a bit chilly in the office, but I had a cardigan upstairs on the back of my chair that I could grab.

First things first: coffee, bacon, and whatever sugary pastry I could also smell baking in the kitchen. Checking the time on my phone, I realized I was still early enough to sit down and enjoy some breakfast before getting to the morning meeting.

Mrs. Clark was at the stove humming a tune that I recognized. There were a few tunes that she hummed over and over. I'd only ever heard them from her and I couldn't place them, but they carried a comforting stillness that I associated with warm bread, good coffee, and soft lighting.

I made a small noise so that I wouldn't startle her. She glanced over her shoulder and smiled.

"Good timing. The bacon just came out and the eggs will be ready in just a moment," she said and turned back to the stove. It was a good morning.

Grabbing a plate, I loaded up a couple of slices of the crispiest bacon I could find on the platter and grabbed a cinnamon-sugar scone. Setting the plate at a spot at the kitchen table, I then filled up a mug with coffee and added a splash of half-and-half. Turning to head back to the table, I saw Jordan and Annie walk in, both smiling and chatting softly.

"Good morning," I called out cheerfully as I sat down.

"Good morning," they said in unison and with a similar level of cheerfulness.

They similarly loaded up their plates, grabbed coffee, and then joined me at the kitchen table. A few moments later, Mrs. Clark walked over with a pan in hand. Expertly seasoned scrambled eggs were transferred from her pan to our plates. We all said our thank-yous and then dug into the delicious breakfast.

"How did you all sleep?" I asked after half my plate had been emptied.

"Good," Annie was the first to answer as Jordan was chewing a large bite of scone. The sugar coated her lips and I smiled at the joyful picture.

"Also good," Jordan finally said and licked the sugar off her lips. "Actually, surprisingly good."

"Me too," Annie said. "Maybe it's because we worked so hard and then went home early."

"Well, whatever it was, I'd be happy for a repeat," I offered. I then took another big forkful of eggs, with a little piece of bacon balanced on top for a perfect bite. I looked up after my bite and saw Mrs. Clark watching the three of us with a smile on her face. I smiled back.

Talk continued over little things. Other team members filtered in and grabbed breakfast to go or sat with us for a minute. Soon it was quarter to and we all needed to get our things together for the morning meeting.

THE HAPPY, small chatter continued as we all settled into our semi-assigned seats for the meeting. Topics shifted to the reports that had come out of the evidence collection. Theories were beginning to develop and more questions to ask.

"Let's get started," Helen said right at nine o'clock. "We need to talk about Doria's case and the Council's visit on Monday."

I sat up straight at the mention of that. With the visit to Doria's house, the Council's visit had slipped to the back of my mind. I secretly hoped that they would cancel again. But either way, I was ready.

"Let's start with the Council's visit," Helen said, turning to me. "I think Doria's case update will take longer."

"Sure," I replied. "We've cataloged the cases, and they are with you for review."

I paused briefly at that to see if Helen would respond. She just nodded, so I continued.

"I'm still on track to have the summary reports and the cases spreadsheet out to everyone for review later this afternoon," I said and looked around the table. "I'll send out a message as soon as it's ready."

"Great," Helen said. "I've also just confirmed that you, Linda, will be here on Monday for the review. You can go to San Francisco on Tuesday morning."

"Got it, I'll check in with the pilots to change the travel plans," I responded and made a note for myself so I wouldn't forget.

Helen continued, "Also, we don't have the list of Council representatives for Monday. They said that there were some changes in schedules and they'd get back to us as soon as they could."

A few grumbles around the table echoed mine. I really wanted to know who they would be sending to meet with us.

Helen didn't acknowledge the grumbles but asked, "Any questions?"

"Who needs to be available on Monday for those meetings?" Hank asked.

"Steve and I will meet with the Council representatives," Helen answered. "We would like the rest of you in the building and available, but we hope no one else will need to be in the actual meeting."

I couldn't tell by Hank's face if he was happy with that decision or not. The rest of the team looked happy to not have to sit in a conference room reviewing documents with members of the Council for hours. Hank was still a mystery to me sometimes.

"Any other questions?" Helen asked the group. A round of shaking heads and a few muttered *nopes* indicated there weren't any. "Alright, let's move on to Doria's case." Helen turned to Jordan and gestured for her to start.

Jordan looked around the table as she shared. "We were able to get out to Doria's house yesterday and collect prints and photos. The images should be in the case folder, but I haven't fully annotated them yet. I'll send out a message as soon as that is done later this morning. Instead of sharing our running theory right now, we decided that we'd like unbiased fresh eyes on some phys-ical evidence collected," Jordan said somewhat cryp-tically.

I had helped with the collection but hadn't been part of that conversation. I wondered what they could be talking about.

"So, there will be some blank spots in the annotation," she continued. "We'll regroup on the case after lunch. I'll need the core team there, but anyone else who would like to come is welcome. Just let me know, and I will send you the calendar invite."

I did some quick mental math to see if I could get my report done that morning so that I'd have time to go to that meeting. I also had my weekly therapy session with Jax, and they frowned on me skipping appointments. If Helen got the spreadsheet back to me soon, I may have just enough time.

"Thank you," Helen replied to Jordan's summary. "Any questions or thoughts?"

Another round of shaking heads. *Good, this may be a*

quick morning meeting, I thought to myself, proud I didn't blurt it out loud.

"Steve, is there any update on the other project related to Doria's case?" Helen asked, looking at him.

The *other project* had become the work to theorize why a demon, for the first time ever, had decided to seek an agency's help. We had started to call it the conspiracy project, but Steve didn't like that, so we were stuck with the boring-sounding *other project*.

"Yes," Steve said and cleared his throat softly. "We've outlined three theories that we will be exploring in more detail. They cover the two extremes and the middle ground."

They had submitted a document outlining all of that in the folder for the project, but with everything going on, I hadn't gotten to it yet. Based on the faces around the table, I wasn't the only one.

Steve seemed to catch this, so he went into more detail: "On the benign end, Doria sincerely wants our help for this specific case. On the concerning end, this is a setup so that Doria or demons in general can infiltrate the agency. Somewhere in the middle is that Doria is bored and set up the theft for something to do. We have some other theories, but we plan on working through those three first."

Glancing up, I caught Annie's eye and made a questioning face. She half smiled and nodded slightly. I'd get more information from her later.

"Sounds good," Helen replied. "Any questions on that project?"

There weren't any questions. At least not any that people wanted to ask right then.

"Alright," she said in her *wrapping things up* voice. "Remember to review the reports for the Council when Linda sends those out, and let Jordan know if you want to attend the afternoon meeting on Doria's case."

Everyone disbanded pretty quickly. It was going to be a busy day for all of us. I was gathering up my things when Helen caught my attention.

"Linda, I need to just check one more thing and then I'll have the case document back to you," she said quickly as we walked toward our offices. "You did a great job, I just have a few things to edit."

"That's great," I replied. "I'll look it over as soon as you send it and then get started on the summary report."

I did just that. There were very few things that Helen wanted redacted, so I wasn't too surprised. The cases last quarter were all fairly straightforward—more legal stuff than investigation work. The summary report was an easy template to update. It included things like the number of cases, average length of cases, categories by type, and other boring things that bureaucrats cared about. It was very data and numbers heavy.

Checking the clock on my laptop, I saw that I probably had just enough time to wrap it up and send it out before my session with Jax, ahead of schedule.

~

JAX and I settled into our regular chairs in the back parlor with steaming mugs of peppermint tea in hand. The heavy drapes were open and let in soft light. They gave me a moment to settle in and take a few deep breaths before we dived into what we'd be talking about that day.

I'd come to love our Thursday morning sessions. Just a month before, we'd dialed it back from the twice a week that had been required as part of my return-to-office compromise after my incident with a newly adopted vampire and a wannabe werewolf. Like most of the team members, I'd probably continue to take advantage of the onsite sessions no matter what was going on.

"Any specific topics you want to cover today?" Jax asked patiently, pushing their blue hexagon glasses frames back up to the bridge of their nose.

"Just the usual, I guess," I said with a sigh. The usual in this case was my mom's murder and how to cope with the gift of visions that I'd inherited from her.

"Why the sigh?" Jax pressed gently.

I tried hard not to roll my eyes. I should have known that they would pick up on that.

"It doesn't feel like I'm making any progress with either," I replied, trying not to sound ungrateful.

"What would progress look like to you?"

"I don't know."

"Think about it for a minute. There's no right or wrong answer."

I closed my eyes and cupped the mug between both of my hands, letting it warm them up. Using the strategies that Jax had taught me, I took a few deep breaths to steady my thoughts. The smell of the peppermint tea was pleasant and it opened up my sinuses a bit. I relaxed and let myself think about the question.

"I guess for my mom's case, progress would be solving it and knowing what really happened to her," I said softly. That seemed obvious.

"Okay," they responded and then let the silence hang in the air.

I knew that Jax would let us sit in silence for as long as it took. There was no winning that battle of wits with them. So after about three seconds I said, "And then there's the visions. Progress would be actually being able to control them and have them be useful."

"Do you feel like you're learning anything new from your time with Director Owens?" Jax asked nonchalantly. They were aware of the apprenticeship but not the secret mission Helen and I had attached to it. Jax encouraged me to get the most out of my time there.

"Not really." I knew I sounded like a petulant teenager, but if you couldn't be that way in therapy, where could you?

Jax sat in silence with a blank face, giving me space to think of a better answer. I took another sip of tea and tried to think of something more constructive to say.

"Director Owens tells me about how she experiences visions, and I've been keeping notes and reviewing them," I answered. "But there isn't anything jumping out at me that seems helpful. And I've tried her way. It doesn't work for me."

"Let's talk through it again," Jax suggested.

"She says she is able to focus on a specific person," I started out, thinking how best to summarize it. "It's someone she knows. Or at least, it seems like it is always someone she knows by the way she talks about them."

I paused and considered the examples she had shared. They were all fairly neutral visions involving people who worked at the Council's office.

"She said she used to use noise-canceling headphones and an eye mask to block out things going on around her so she could concentrate on the person she wanted to learn about. Now she doesn't have to." I hadn't seen her actually do this—she'd never offered and I hadn't asked. "All the examples she shares are of things that are currently happening for that person."

Jax leaned forward, a rare look of surprise in their eyes. "Are you sure about that?"

"Yes." I hesitated and rethought through the examples Cora had shared. "Yes, I think so. They all seemed to be things the person was currently doing, like getting lunch or working on a report. It's like Cora has a window to what the person she is thinking about is doing."

"And you've tried to recreate that experience?" Jax asked, settling back into their normal demeanor and tone.

"Yes, but it's never worked for me. I don't think that is how my visions work."

"Well, we do know that oracles' gifts are rarely the same," Jax reassured me. "I'm not surprised that it wouldn't work for you. But I'm proud of you for trying."

I smiled back at them. Their words were kind, but they didn't do much to assuage my worry about my gift.

Jax cleared their throat. "Have you had any luck getting access to the records of other oracles?"

"No," I said, back to the petulant-teenager tone. "Cora said that she wants me to have them but that she has to get permission from the Council Forum and that they don't meet again to review requests like that until the fall."

There was a pause in the conversation. Jax looked at their watch and then back at me. "We still have some time. Is there anything else you want to discuss today?"

I thought for a moment. "There is one thing with the last vision I had. I'm pretty sure our client, Doria, was in the vision, but there was just a black hole where she was."

"Have you had anything similar happen before?"

"No, just this time."

"Tell me more about what that experience was like."

I replayed the vision in my head and tried to pay attention to my emotions while I recounted the scene for Jax, then wrapped up with answers to the questions I knew they would ask: 'I had pretty neutral feelings. It didn't make me worried or scared. I think I was just surprised because it hadn't happened before."

"Why do you think that happened?" Jax asked. It felt like they had an idea but didn't want to bias my thoughts.

"Well, Doria is a demon, and Jordan told us that demons aren't from this dimension," I rambled, thinking out loud. "Maybe I can't see Doria because she isn't from this dimension. Or it could be an ability of hers, but Jordan and Helen didn't know about that, so I'm not sure." I trailed off, unsure where I was heading on that train of thought.

Jax smiled and waited to see if I wanted to continue. I didn't.

"I'd recommend you talk with the team more about the black-hole phenomenon in your vision," Jax offered. "Maybe try to devise an experiment to see if you can learn more."

I perked up at that and then deflated. An experiment would be fun, but I was still unable to control when I had visions, so I didn't see how that would be possible. Not wanting to be negative, I told Jax that I'd try.

9

W e gathered around the upstairs conference table after lunch. Although anyone could come, it was just five of us: myself, Jordan, Cam, Angela, and Annie. It was a busy day, so I didn't begrudge the others for not joining. But I had hustled that morning on the report so I could be there, and I was glad I did.

Jordan rolled over a whiteboard and listed out items that she wanted to cover, including fingerprint matches, trace evidence, and my vision. "We were able to identify three sets of prints. After excluding Doria and her house-keeper, the third is unknown. We found the unknown print on the window frame," Jordan started us off.

She pulled out two glossy printed images. One was clearly from a doorframe, and the other from the window frame in the attic. The neon-green outline of fingerprints glowed eerily against the wood.

Tacking them onto the whiteboard with a magnet,

Jordan wrote with a black marker *Unknown Print One* under the doorframe. She wrote the same under the image of the window frame.

"We can confirm that these two sets of prints belong to the same person," Jordan said. "We looked for matches in the human world on AFIS with no luck. So we may need to ask the Council for access to their database."

"I thought we had access," Cam said and scrunched her face up with confusion.

"We did, and we still technically do, but they just put out a new process. We have to fill out a form stating why we are using the database," Jordan said as calmly as she could, but her face was a softer mirror of Cam's.

"Are we sure we want to do that?" Cam replied and then offered with a glimmer in her eye and a wiggle of her fingers, "I could probably find a workaround."

Jordan laughed first at Cam's ridiculous face, and then we all joined in, dispelling the tension that had started to build.

"Let's keep that in our back pocket," Jordan said after a moment. She said it jokingly, but I thought she was at least somewhat serious. "For now, I don't want to do anything that would alert Director Owens or the Council staff about this case. So we'll hold off on the forms and the workaround."

"Why?" Angela asked.

"It's odd that a demon is asking for our help," Jordan answered. "The Director may want to get involved or want details about it that we don't want to share."

Angela frowned. "That makes sense, I should have thought of that."

"No worries," Jordan responded quickly. "I think we're also being extra sensitive about anything related to the Council right now."

At Jordan's statement, Cam shot me a look like she knew something. This was the second time Cam had seemed suspicious. I needed to corner her and ask her what was going on.

"I could ask someone about getting access to the records at the office next week in person," I offered. "That way it wouldn't be in writing, and maybe we could get it fast-tracked."

"That may be a good idea. Let's come back to that if we need to. Either way," Jordan continued and gestured toward the whiteboard, "we know we have an unknown individual who could have accessed the attic. Let's talk about trace. Inside, we collected some swabs from the gouge on the window frame, but that'll take some time to work out in the lab. Cam and Angela, do you want to talk about what you found?"

"Yes," Cam said, perking up. "There weren't any obvious footprints in the yard. But around the area under the window it did look like the ground was disturbed. We think someone tried to sweep away any footprints or other impressions that they could have left."

Jordan pulled another image out of her folder and hung it on the whiteboard.

"This is what it looked like right below the window that

was open in the attic," Cam said as we all looked at the image. "You can also see that the plants look disturbed, and there are several bent or broken branches on the hydrangea."

Jordan pulled out the next image from her folder and hung it next to the one of the ground and hydrangea bush.

"This was found snagged on the bush," Cam said. "We bagged it."

Jordan passed a small clear plastic bag over to me to look at and pass around the table. It looked like a collection of small feathers and some cloth.

"As you can see," Cam continued, "these aren't feathers that just came off of a bird naturally. They are attached to some cloth. We think the cloth snagged on the bush and ripped this from whoever was standing there."

"I think we'll be able to get DNA from the feathers," Jordan added. "At least one of the three has its base fairly intact. But I'll need until tomorrow for the results. It will have to sit overnight. In the meantime, I want to review the cultural practices of otherworldly creatures that often have feathers. This grouping of feathers is intentional, and maybe it is something that is commonly done. Although I can't think of anything like that off the top of my head."

"I can help with that," I offered. My report was done and out for review, so I had the time. I had been scouring the internal documents that the agency had curated on all the supernatural and otherworldly species since my first day there. That type of research was fun.

"I can work with Linda on that too," Angela offered.

"That would be great. Thank you both," Jordan said.

"Let's move on to Linda's vision and then we'll circle back on assignments and tasks. Linda."

I sat up straighter and put my hands in my lap so that no one would see them shaking. Dissecting my visions with the group was still a bit nerve-wracking. It didn't feel like it should be counted as evidence, but if it helped, I would keep doing it.

"Well, I wrote up the vision so everyone can read the details," I said, hoping this would get me out of recounting the whole thing. "So I'll just hit the highlights."

Jordan nodded, so I continued with that plan.

"It was in Doria's attic. The painting was there, but there wasn't a clear sign if this was past or future," I said, thinking again about what I saw, heard, and smelled in that attic, trying to grasp anything new. Nothing new came to me. "Two individuals entered the attic. One was a woman I didn't recognize. And the other was a person. I could hear their voice, and it sounded like Doria, but they were just a black blob." I paused, signaling to everyone that I was done and ready for questions.

"How confident are you that the black blob was Doria?" Annie asked politely.

"About eighty percent," I answered confidently. I'd been thinking about that a lot. "The tone and crackling echo her voice makes was prominent. But I haven't met any other demons, so I'm not sure if that crackling echo is common in demons or unique to her."

Everyone looked thoughtful. "I'm not sure either," Jordan admitted after a moment of thinking. "But that's a good question." She wrote it on the board.

"Any distinguishing features about the other woman?" Angela asked after a moment.

"She was probably a bit shorter than me. Blonde hair. Blue eyes. Fair-featured. She was wearing a loose-fitting dress." I rattled off as I pictured the woman in my head. Nothing about that was very distinguishing. Everyone stayed quiet and let me think.

"Her voice was interesting," I said mostly to myself.

Something tickled the back of my brain. There was something there I should know. Then it hit me.

"Oh!" My exclamation startled the group. "Her voice was melodic, like multiple people harmonizing. I've heard a voice like that before." I turned and looked at Annie. "It was like the voice of the siren who dropped off a package at the office my first week here."

Jordan exchanged a questioning glance with Annie. We hadn't told anyone about that encounter. It wasn't that we'd done anything wrong, but that first week had been a lot and it just got lost in the shuffle of everything else.

"The other woman in the attic was a siren?" Jordan asked, still a bit shocked.

"Well, I don't know that for sure," I responded. "But the voice had the same sound. Kind of like a choir was backing her up. And I was drawn to it."

"That plus the feathers does point us to sirens," Cam offered with a slight shrug.

"And a siren would be able to get in and out of the high attic window," Annie offered.

"Sirens do fit. But this seems out of character for them," Jordan mused out loud. "I have a hard time seeing what their motive would be that would be strong enough to mess with a demon."

"That could be said for almost everyone," Annie grimly replied.

"True," Jordan agreed.

"Are there a lot of sirens in the area?" I asked, looking around the room for an answer.

"Some, not a lot," Jordan answered. "But we should talk with Helen. She may have some thoughts."

"What about the housekeeper?" I asked, thinking back to the meeting with Doria.

"I talked with her this morning," Jordan answered. "It was just a phone interview, but she seemed to corroborate Doria's story."

"Is there any chance she could have been involved?" I asked.

"We haven't ruled her out," Jordan said. "But it seems unlikely. She's been working with Doria for years without any issues. We'll talk to her again if needed and keep an eye out for anything that would point to her."

The meeting wrapped up shortly after that. Jordan wanted to get started on testing the feathers. Cam was going to talk with Helen about the siren theory. And Angela and I decided to spend the rest of the afternoon digging into the research task we had volunteered for.

"FINDING ANYTHING INTERESTING?" Angela asked from the seat across from me.

We had brought our laptops and notebooks to the conference table on the second floor so that we could coordinate the research efforts. Not knowing where to start, we decided to do some keyword searching and see if anything popped up.

"No," I answered with some frustration. "You?"

"Not really," Angela sighed. "There are a lot of supernatural beings with feathers, but from what I can gather, they are all a natural part of their anatomy. The feathers we found seemed to be artificially attached."

"That's what I've seen too," I said and paused to think. "Maybe the feathers aren't special and it was just someone with an eclectic fashion sense."

"Are we even sure it came from the intruder?"

"That's a good question. Maybe we should see if Doria has any outfits with feathers before we spend the next several days on research." I wasn't trying to get out of work, but better to work smarter than harder.

Angela suggested, "Let's send the group a note and see if Jordan or Helen will ask Doria."

"That's a good idea," I agreed.

Angela sent the message to the group chat, and Jordan answered almost immediately. She suggested that we text Doria and see if she responded. A quick game of rock, paper, scissors, and it was up to me to text her.

Me: Doria, this is Linda with the OPT Agency. I have a quick question if you are available.

I messaged her and set the phone down where I could see it. Not quite five minutes later it vibrated with a new message.

Doria: Hi Linda. Happy to help. What's your question?

Me: Do you own any clothing with feathers?

The three little dots appeared. It took a moment for her to respond.

Doria: No.

I showed Angela the text. "She says no."

"Ask her about blankets or pillows," Angela suggested.

Me: Any blankets or pillows with feathers?

We both watched the phone for a response. It came quickly.

Doria: A moment, please.

Angela and I both shrugged. I imagined Doria walking around her house looking at the contents of her bedding. A few moments later the phone vibrated with another text.

Doria: Katya says no.

"Katya?" Angela asked.

"Her housekeeper, if I'm remembering correctly."

"That would make sense."

"Anything else you can think of that we can ask about?" I asked Angela.

"No," she said. "We can probably text her again if we need to."

"You're right."

Me: Thank you. That is helpful.

Doria: Anytime.

"At least she didn't ask us why," I said with relief. "I'm unsure if we should tell her now."

"I'm sure Jordan or Helen are keeping her up to date."

We returned to our research and soon had a list of supernatural and otherworldly feather-related beings.

Sirens still seemed to be at the top of the list. They were the most common on the list in the Seattle area, and my vision showed that a siren was, or would be, in the attic with that painting at some point. The research was winding down when Cam came through and stopped by the table.

"How is the research going?" Cam said as she sat down at the table.

"Done," I said. "At least for now. I'm unsure how helpful it will be to keep going without some direction."

"We did text Doria," Angela offered.

"What for?" Cam asked.

"We wanted to see if she had any clothes or things with feathers that they could have come from," I explained.

"That was a good idea. What did she say?"

"She said she doesn't," Angela answered.

"I believe her," I added. "She doesn't seem the type to wear anything with feathers."

Cam laughed. "I've only seen her twice, but I agree with you."

"How did your talk with Helen go?" I asked.

"Good." She shrugged. "She was skeptical that it was a siren, but she said she would make some phone calls and get back to us if she has any ideas of who might be suspicious."

"That's good," Angela said.

Cam smiled back but seemed worried about something.

As Cam got up to leave, I asked, "Are you busy? Do you want to grab some tea and chat?"

Cam looked nervous for a minute. "Sorry, I can't. I need to go back down to the lab and finish up something."

"Okay," I said, trying not to sound disappointed. I wanted to know what was going on with her.

Cam left.

When she was out of earshot, Angela leaned toward me and whispered, "Is everything alright with Cam?"

"I don't know," I whispered back. "I hope so."

10

F riday's breakfast was wonderful, as usual. I may have overindulged in the bacon-and-brie egg bites, but Mrs. Clark had made enough to feed an army, so I didn't feel too bad. The morning meeting was also pretty typical. Everyone gave their updates quickly and there wasn't a lot to discuss.

The DNA results from the feathers would be ready later that afternoon. Depending on those results, we might have an ad hoc meeting to strategize on Doria's case. It looked like Friday would be pretty calm.

I had a few minutes before my one-on-one with Helen, so I decided to make a quick phone call. Even though Jordan suggested we wait to reach out to someone at the Council offices for the records we needed, it wouldn't hurt to see if we'd be able to expedite the request when we needed it.

The direct line rang three times before Willow picked up. "Hello, this is Willow with the records department."

"Hi, Willow, it's Linda," I said as pleasantly as I could. Willow had been really kind to me and we'd worked together several times during my time at the Council offices. There was no need for me to take my frustration with the director out on her.

"Linda, it's so nice to hear from you." Her voice changed from clipped professional to friendly. "What's up, did you need something?"

I smiled behind the phone, happy that she seemed in a good mood. "I have a quick question. We are working on a research project and we may need access to some nonredacted records from the Council offices. I'm trying to plan out a timeline for the project and want to see if there is an expedited option for record requests."

Willow paused momentarily. "Is this a research project for the OPT Agency or for your work with Director Owens?"

"For the OPT Agency," I answered, trying not to let my rising concern reach my voice.

"Well..." Willow dragged out her response. "I'm afraid that nonredacted records can't be shared with the OPT Agency."

"What?" I blurted out too quickly. I took a breath and controlled my tone. "I was under the impression that we could request them when they were needed for a case or for research."

"That was how it used to work," Willow said. "But some new policies just went into place. The notice will probably go out sometime next week. I probably shouldn't have told you just yet."

"I won't tell anyone that you told me early," I said. No reason to get Willow in trouble.

Willow sighed with relief. "Thank you, and I'm sorry, Linda. I hope this doesn't mess up your research project."

Willow was just the messenger. I knew better than to press her to understand why the new policy was implemented. She wouldn't know.

"That's alright, Willow," I said, forcing my voice to stay light. "We'll figure out a different approach for the project."

"Oh good." She sounded relieved. "I'll see you next week."

"Yep, see you next week. Thank you. Bye."

That was going to upset everyone at the agency. It didn't make sense why they would change a long-standing policy like that. Fortunately, I had a meeting with Helen soon. I would keep my promise and not tell her that Willow had shared the news prematurely, but I would tell her what I knew.

HELEN and I settled into our normal seats in her office for our one-on-one. Helen was behind her large desk, framed by the picture window. I was in the wingback chair on the right in front of her desk, my laptop resting half open on the floor.

"The reports for the Council visit all look good," Helen said, starting us off.

"Yes. I think everything is ready and it should be pretty straightforward for Monday," I replied. Everyone had already given feedback on the reports, and I only needed to make some small edits.

"I agree," Helen said, but then paused like she wasn't sure how to say what was on her mind. That was worrisome. "We still aren't sure who is coming from the Council. But we can handle whoever it is."

"Do you think Cora will come instead of sending a representative?" I asked. That thought had been kicking around my head all week.

Helen half smiled, like she was trying to hide her concern. "I wouldn't put it past her, and she probably would just show up without telling us."

"Speaking of Director Owens," I said, changing the topic, "I learned just before this meeting that the Council has a new policy that they aren't releasing nonredacted records anymore."

Helen looked upset but unsurprised. "I was wondering when things would start locking down."

I looked at her, confused.

She gave a sad smile and continued, "Information is power, and I think Cora is feeling more threatened by us. She has already gotten more involved with the agency, using the quarterly reviews and your apprenticeship to get information. The next step would be limiting our access to information."

"Do you think she knows what we are doing?" I started to panic. "What if she has been using her oracle gifts to spy on us?"

I kicked myself for not thinking about that sooner. Everything she had talked about in regard to her gift had been so mundane that I didn't think it was a threat. But it was actually the biggest threat. She knew Helen, and after spending weeks with her, she knew me enough to use her gift. And there were probably others at the agency she knew. She could know everything.

"It's okay," Helen said, calming me down. "Take a deep breath."

I had started to breathe heavily. After a few deep breaths, I was somewhat calmer. "How will it be okay?" I asked, really wanting her to tell me.

Helen leaned forward and held eye contact. "I apologize that we didn't explain this better. The wards on the office protect us from any uninvited magic."

"Oh," I muttered. I knew that. That was why they had to be changed to let Doria enter the office.

"Not just magical people but magic in general," Helen explained. "That includes someone using magic like Cora's oracle ability."

"So she can't spy on us here?"

"Yes," Helen answered. "And she also can't spy on you at home."

"Our homes have wards, too," I said more than asked. I had been suspecting that was the case all week.

"Yes, they do," Helen confirmed. "Not as strong as the office's, but enough to help in this case."

"That's good to know," I said and took a few more deep breaths. "But what will we do about not getting access to the Council records?"

"Nothing," she said calmly. "At least for now."

I gave her another confused look.

She explained, "We need to act normal. We'll wait for the notice to come through, and I'll push back on it like I normally would. I don't expect that to work. We'll keep investigating." Helen leaned back in her chair and tapped the desk with her pen. I gave her space to think. After a few moments, she straightened back up. "I think it's time to bring the full team into our investigation plan on Director Owens."

"I'd be good with that, but why now?"

"Things are escalating faster than I thought they would, and if you are going to have a chance at finding anything during your time at the Council offices, we need to move faster."

My face dropped. I already felt guilty that I had not found anything yet, but I tried to have reasonable expectations. This was my first time being a spy.

Helen could tell I was upset. "I wouldn't have expected you to find anything yet. You've only been there three times. And if Cora weren't making moves, we'd wait a bit longer to give you more time."

"That's fair," I said, mostly trying to convince myself. "How do you think the team can help?"

"I didn't want to make you nervous," Helen said. "But I've already got Cam working on something that would let you download data from computers without it being traceable. She's been working almost nonstop on it for the last few weeks."

That revelation cleared up a few things. That must have been why Cam had been so secretive and unavailable recently. I was also relieved that she was already working on something.

"Is it ready?" I asked, thinking about my upcoming trip.

"I think so," Helen said. "Let me see if she can come to talk with us right now." Helen turned and typed on her computer, messaging Cam. A few more clicks, and she turned back toward me. "She'll be right up. Was there anything else we needed to talk about today?"

"I don't think so," I answered. "If I think of anything after, I'll let you know."

"Great."

Cam knocked on the door and Helen called out to come in. Cam settled into the chair next to me and gave me a questioning look.

"Cam, thank you for joining us so quickly," Helen said. Then she got right down to it. "I've let Linda know about the device you have been working on to help her with the data extraction."

Cam sighed and smiled over at me. "That's great and perfect timing. I think it's ready."

"Good." Helen was pleased. "Can you tell us a bit more about how it will work?"

Cam reached into her pocket and pulled out a pen, placing it on the desk in front of me. It looked like a normal pen with a cap. "The device is this pen," she said with almost uncontrollable glee. "There were a couple of problems I needed to solve. First, it needed to be something that, if someone found it on you, they wouldn't ask what it was. You aren't allowed to bring in electronic devices, and a flash drive would be too obvious. It also needed to be able to pass through metal detectors without setting off alarms."

I nodded. Every time I came to or left the Council offices, I had to pass through metal detectors and have my bag searched.

Cam continued, "It also needed to be something that was easy to use. You'll probably be nervous when you use it, so I wanted to make sure it was as easy as possible so that you didn't need to worry about it."

"That's good," I replied encouragingly. "So how does it work?"

Cam picked up the pen and removed the cap. "Helen, do you have some paper I could use?"

Helen slid over a pad of sticky notes.

"The pen works like a normal pen." Cam demonstrated by scribbling on the paper. "But it won't last long. There isn't a ton of ink, so try not to use it as a real pen much, and make sure I get to refill it between your trips."

"Will do," I replied quickly.

"There are two ways it will work." She picked it up and held it before me. "If you want to get information from a computer, you put the pen's tip into a USB or other port. Any will work except for the power port. Then press down and hold the end of the pen. It will extend the tip of the pen to make the connection and download any data that's on the computer. You'll need to hold down the end. When you release it, it will stop."

Cam paused and looked at me. I nodded that I understood, so she went on, "The other option is to get information directly from servers. This one is a bit more complicated. You'll need to find the data cable that is going into the server. Use the end of the pocket clip to puncture through the plastic coating on the cable. The hole it leaves should be really small, and no one would notice it, but you'll want to find a spot to hide it afterward. Once you make the hole, you'll need to push the pen's tip through it while holding down the other end. Then use the top of the cap to close the connection. If the cap and the tip of the pen lose connection, it will stop."

I watched as Cam demonstrated the steps in the air. It seemed simple enough.

"But how does it actually work?" I said my thoughts out loud. I wasn't technical, but I'd seen enough spy movies and knew the basics of how computers worked.

Cam looked panicked and glanced at Helen. Helen gave a sharp nod.

Cam grinned. "We aren't a normal agency and this isn't a normal spy pen. We got some magical help to boost the ability of the metal in the pen tip to conform to any port space and work like a flash drive would. I can't explain exactly how it works or how they did it. But I do know that it works."

"And it will work for me?" I asked. I may have had visions, but mine wasn't the type of magic that could turn a pen into a flash drive.

"Yes, it will, and you'll be fine using it," Cam said confidently.

Helen looked less convinced. "Do you have some things that Linda can practice on before next week?"

"For sure," Cam said, still excited by the new gadget she

had made with some magical assistance. "The other thing you need to know: the pen doesn't transmit the data. We didn't want to risk the data traffic being sniffed within the building. So you'll have to download the data to your computer or back here at the office to see it. I have a special docking station you can plug into your laptop and then dock the pen to get the data off it. You'll want to do that every night to clear up the storage space on the pen for more data."

"You can send the data back to us from the apartment," Helen added.

"Right," Cam agreed. "The apartment has a secure and encrypted connection back to our offices."

I looked at the pen still in Cam's hand, and it started to feel more real; I gulped down the lump in my throat. "Anything else I should know?"

Cam gave me a comforting look. "This isn't the only pen we'll have. Now that I have it working, I'll make more. If you need to dump it because you think someone may suspect you, you can."

"Cam's right," Helen agreed. "Your safety is more important than that pen or getting data from the computers."

"Thank you," I said and fought back the forming tears.

"Speaking of safety," Cam said hesitantly, "does Steve know what Linda is doing?"

Helen looked guilty momentarily and then recovered to a neutral face. "Not yet, but he will today. We're going to update the whole team on this mission."

LUNCH WAS WEIRD. The food was good like always. Mrs. Clark had made fried chicken with mashed potatoes and roasted vegetables. Most of us were gathered around the table eating, but the vibe was off. Helen had asked everyone to meet at one o'clock. Cam and I kept giving each other looks—we knew what the topic would be but didn't know if we should say anything to anyone just yet.

About fifteen minutes before the meeting, Helen came down and asked Steve if he could come to talk with her. He came back looking unhappy and gave both Cam and me weird looks. I was sure Helen had broken the news to him about my mission at the Council offices.

Everyone gathered around the table a few minutes before one. There was some uneasy chatter, but mostly everyone was anxious to hear what was happening that warranted a Friday afternoon meeting.

Helen cleared her throat and called the group's attention to herself: "I need to update everyone on a sensitive project." She paused but didn't let any side chatter start. "As all of you know, Linda is completing an apprenticeship with Director Owens at the Council offices in San Francisco."

Folks around the table nodded and looked my way. This wasn't news to anyone. It had been hotly debated whether I should do the apprenticeship, but Helen had dealt with all that effectively.

"What we didn't share with everyone is that Linda is

undertaking a data-reconnaissance mission during her time there," Helen said quickly and then paused.

Almost everyone looked shocked. Cam gave me an encouraging grin. Steve looked like he was grumbling under his breath.

No one spoke up, so Helen took a deep breath and continued, "I think everyone knows what type of information she is looking for. We need to know if the theory about Director Owens abducting, killing, and framing otherworldly community members is true. For that, we need evidence." Helen paused again to give everyone time to think.

Jordan broke the silence: "Do you really think we'll find anything?"

Helen and I had discussed that question repeatedly, always coming to the same conclusion.

"There is no way that she could have conducted these murders and manipulations on her own," I said firmly. "The Council is a bureaucracy, and like any bureaucracy, there is probably a paper trail." Helen smiled and nodded her head for me to continue. "It's not likely that it will be obvious, but this team is good at finding patterns. I just need to get the data. And Cam is helping with that."

All eyes shifted to Cam. She flushed slightly at the sudden attention. I grimaced; I hadn't meant to throw her under the bus. She gave me an understanding smile.

"With some help, I've put together a device that will allow Linda to discreetly download data and transfer it to her laptop," Cam explained. "As Linda said, we'll have to dig through a lot, but if there is something there, we'll find it."

Hank asked, "Have you got any of the data yet?"

"No," I replied. "I'll be trying to access computers and maybe the server room next week to get the first data cache for us."

Everyone was starting to look more at ease. Everyone except Steve. I tried to catch his eye to reassure him, but he was looking down at his hands.

Helen also noticed this. "Steve, do you want to share your concerns?"

Steve grumbled a bit but then looked up. "I agree that this is probably the only way we'll get any evidence on Director Owens, but it is dangerous for Linda. I need more time to think through some precautions and safety measures."

Helen nodded and smiled softly at him. "That would be appreciated, thank you."

"Not to rush you," I said softly, "but do you think we can have those sorted by Tuesday? I'd like to make a move before things get more drastic."

That was the wrong word to use. Everyone perked up, and Annie was the first to respond, "What is getting drastic?"

I shot an apologetic look at Helen. I wasn't sure she was ready to share with the team what I had learned that morning.

Helen didn't look worried and replied to Annie, "We learned this morning that the Council, likely Cora specifically, is enacting a new policy that will mean we no longer have access to nonredacted reports and documents."

Jordan was pissed. "She can't do that!"

"I'm afraid she can," Helen said calmly. "The Council gives wide discretion to their directors on how they manage their regions. It's unlikely that it would go our way if we appealed to them."

"Can we get the records from another region?" Angela asked.

"They wouldn't have all the same records," Helen answered. "And they would likely just point us back to our regional office."

"So Cora is starting to lock down information," Jordan summarized.

"Exactly," Helen confirmed. "We all know that information is power, and so does Cora. She is getting worried. We don't know what she knows. And, more troublesome, we don't know how she'll react if she feels cornered."

11

Cam picked us up just after nine on Saturday morning. Annie was already in the car, so I climbed into the back of her small SUV. The plan was to look around, hopefully get inside the Moonstone Haven house, and then go get brunch.

We rolled up to the familiar-looking house and parked on the opposite side of the street. I was ready to jump out and get started, but Annie and Cam weren't moving to exit the car just yet. Instead, they both turned in their seats to look back at me.

"We're just here to look around," Cam said, speaking directly to me. "I brought some gloves and evidence bags in case we find anything. But I don't want you to get your hopes up."

Too late, my hopes were up. I'd been thinking about this house all week, and we were finally there to look around. For some reason, I was sure we'd find something to help us. It wasn't a vision, just a feeling.

"Sure, I understand," I responded as sincerely as possible. They both knew me well and probably didn't believe me.

"Let's circle around the house, and we can see if there is an easy way to enter," Cam continued. "We promised Helen we wouldn't break in, but if a door or window is open, then we can go in."

"Right," I agreed, anxious to get moving.

Cam and Annie exchanged a look that I'd seen before. They'd be keeping an eye on me.

"Okay, let's go," Cam finally said.

We got a backpack out of the trunk. Cam handed us both a pair of gloves. I tucked mine in my back pocket until I needed them. Then we crossed the street.

The street was a typical residential area. Small and well-maintained houses lined each side, interspersed with shade trees that would soon dust pollen onto the cars in the small driveways. It was early and still slightly chilly. There wasn't anyone else outside. I was sure neighbors were either sleeping in or doing weekend chores behind closed doors. As long as we stayed quiet and quick, no one would think anything of us being at the house.

The Moonstone Haven house fit inconspicuously in with the neighborhood. It was well maintained, and someone had clearly been around to keep the yard clean. I made a mental note of that. Even if the house was no longer occupied, someone was still caring for it.

The gate to the backyard opened with a simple latch. The three of us made our way through it and closed it quietly behind us. Large trees surrounded the yard, creating a barrier of privacy. Small garden beds sat empty as if waiting for the summer vegetable plantings. A quaint greenhouse made out of old windows sat to one side of the yard. Everything was lovely but empty.

A back door waited for us at the end of the path we were walking on. Annie got to it first. She had already put on her gloves and tried the door. It creaked open with only a turn of the doorknob and a slight push. We all exchanged startled glances. That was unexpected.

I rushed to get my gloves on as well and followed Annie and Cam into the house. Inside the door was a landing with steps going down to a basement and a few steps up to the first floor. We went up the steps into the kitchen.

Much like the outside of the house, the inside was clean but empty. The kitchen led into a small room that probably had held a dining table and then into a front living room. Off of the hall was a small room and a bathroom. All the spaces were clean of dust but empty of any belongings.

The three of us took the staircase at the front of the house that led upstairs. Three rooms and a bathroom filled the upstairs space. A few large rectangles under dustcloths were against the walls in two of the rooms. A quick peek revealed they were dressers. The drawers were empty. We silently circled through each of the rooms and then back to the top landing.

"Looks like Hank was right," Annie whispered. "This place is empty."

"I don't think we are going to find anything here," Cam said, giving me an apologetic look.

The house had been our strongest lead for my mom's case and connected her to the coven and to another witch who had been murdered just months before. I had held out hope that something or someone at the house would help lead us to what really happened.

"You are probably right," I admitted sadly. "Let's check out the basement and then get pancakes."

I hated basements.

Something felt strange, like there was someone just out of my field of view who was watching. I kept glancing quickly over my shoulder to try to catch whatever it was. Every time I looked, nothing was there. Maybe the house was haunted. I shook it off, followed Cam, and thought about breakfast. At least the pancakes would cheer me up a little bit if we didn't find anything.

Cam led the way down the stairs and through the house to the back stairs that led to the basement. We'd managed not to turn on any lights in the house, but the basement was dark. Cam switched on a light as we went down the stairs, illuminating the empty space.

The basement was one large room. Remnants of shelves and workbenches lined the walls but were empty of items. We split up and each walked silently around the perimeter of the room. Something felt off.

I made one circle around the room and then looked up at the ceiling. I started to walk around again, this time counting my steps as I went. There were about thirty steps along the back wall and another thirty along the side of the house. The room was roughly square, but I counted the other two sides anyway. They matched.

I stared out at the space from the last corner I ended up in. Cam and Annie were poking through the drawers and cabinets to see if anything was left behind. Something was definitely off.

"Wait," I blurted out, probably louder than was needed in the enclosed space.

Cam and Annie were startled and looked my way. "What?" they said in unison.

"Did you have a vision?" Annie asked. Solid guess on her part. I had tried to push for a vision, but like every other time I tried to force it, nothing came.

"No," I said at a more reasonable volume. "This room doesn't make sense."

"Seems pretty standard for a witch's house. This would be their workspace," Annie answered.

"Not that," I said. I almost had my finger on it, and then it hit me. "It's smaller than it should be."

Cam and Annie looked around. I rushed forward with an explanation.

"Basements in these houses are usually the same footprint as the first floor," I said and walked to the center of the room. "This space is smaller. There should be another ten feet of room toward the front of the house."

"You're right," Cam said. "The upstairs is a rectangle, this basement is basically square. But they could have added on more space on the front of the house after it was built."

"True," I hesitated. "But I have a feeling that's not the case."

"You think there is a secret room down here?" Annie asked.

"Yes."

"Well, let's find it," Annie responded.

We all walked to the wall that would be at the front of the house if the space lined up correctly. It was filled with empty shelves. At first glance, it looked like one solid set.

"Look at this," Cam said from off to the side. "The wood is cut here and here." She pointed out two cuts on the boards that, had you not looked closely, would have gotten lost in the joint of the next vertical post. "There's a flashlight in the bag." She got down on the ground to look under the lowest shelf. "Can you hand it to me?"

Annie dug through the bag and handed her the flashlight. Cam clicked it on and pointed it around the underside of the shelf.

"The cut goes all the way to the back," she called out from under the shelf. "And there's a hinge. I think I can lift it."

Cam pushed on it, but it didn't move.

"I can't tell if it's just heavy or if it's caught on something," Cam called out.

Annie and I moved closer and grabbed the end that should swing up. We both pulled as Cam pushed to move it, but it didn't budge.

"There must be a latch or something," I said.

Cam scooted over a bit to the side where it was being

held in place. "Found it." Something clicked. "Try now," Cam instructed.

The shelf moved slightly but still wouldn't give.

"Look for a small circle that you can fit a finger in on the shelf above this one," Cam called out. "I think they are connected and move together."

I leaned under the second shelf, which was about chest level. There wasn't enough light to see, so I ran my hand from the back of the shelf toward the front. About halfway, there was a protruding board with a small circle. Ignoring the thought of spiderwebs and bugs, I put my finger in the hole and pulled it toward me. A soft click sounded.

"Got it," I called out and wiped my finger on my pants to remove the imaginary bugs.

"Okay, pull up on the shelves again," Cam instructed.

Annie grabbed the bottom shelf, and I pulled the one above it. As a set, they both moved up with just enough clearance to fit below the next shelf. We pushed them all the way up, and they latched into place. Cam stood back up, and the three of us looked at the awkward little doorway that had been created. A doorway to nowhere.

"This has got to be the door, right?" I asked, perplexed.

"Yes," Annie replied. "If not, that's a weird way to have shelves."

Cam shined the light around the edges and then swept the floor with it. We all followed the light with our eyes. A slight scratch on the floor made it clear that something had moved along it.

"Looks like we just need to figure out how to open it," Annie said with delight.

"Maybe it's just a push open and close," I said, thinking of the cupboards in fancy hotel rooms that didn't have handles. You just pushed on one side of it to open them. I stepped forward and placed both my hands on the side that should swing open based on the scratch marks on the floor. A quick but firm push against it was all that was needed. The door opened with a soft whoosh, and a musty smell wafted from the room.

"Awesome," Cam said under her breath.

The door stood cracked open, but none of us moved to open it all the way and go inside.

"Rock, paper, scissors to see who goes first?" Annie offered.

We nodded and stood in a tight little circle.

"One, two, three, shoot," Annie called out as we all made the motions.

I threw rock. They both threw paper.

"Okay, I'll go first," I said.

Cam handed me the flashlight. "We're right behind you," she reassured me. I felt her hand settle on my back, and I knew Annie would have her hand on Cam's back, forming a chain so we knew we were all together.

I pulled the door open slowly and let the flashlight shine in first. The room was closed off. No windows and no overhead light that I could see as I swept the light around the space. I felt Cam nudge me forward a bit, and I took a step in.

It was colder than the rest of the basement and had that musty smell that rooms get when they aren't used a lot. It wasn't dirty or dusty, but unlike the rest of the house, this room had boxes in it. Half a dozen medium-sized boxes were piled on one side of the room. There were no labels that would indicate what could be inside.

"Oh, they left something," Annie said as she spotted the boxes. "Let's have a look."

We all went over to the boxes. I held the light over them as Cam and Annie started opening them up. The first few boxes had some old clothing, nothing that looked familiar. The next box had some bottles of an unknown substance. The next box was filled with brown paper, the kind used to cushion items during shipping.

Sandwiched between the paper stuffing was an old leather-bound book. Cam pulled the book out and set it on top of one of the boxes we'd already explored. Opening the book, we all leaned forward to see what it was. It was filled with lines of handwritten notes.

"It's like an old accounting ledger," Annie said as she flipped to the next page. "There's dates, numbers, and symbols." Annie pointed to a row and we tried to follow it through. "There's letters, too, but they don't make sense," she added. "It's probably a code or initials."

"Initials seems likely and the dates are in order," I pointed out. "Go to the end. What's the last date?"

Annie flipped the pages until the writing stopped. "It's October of last year."

I whispered the thought that popped into my head: "That's just before Enid was killed."

We all paused and looked at each other with wide eyes. That seemed like too much of a coincidence. Enid was murdered five months before by a young witch who was being manipulated. During the investigation of her murder, we found Moonstone Haven and this house. A vision had also connected my mom to Enid, Moonstone Haven, and the house. But other than the vision, we had no concrete evidence of that connection. Maybe this book held the clues I was looking for.

"Do you think they are coming back for this?" I asked.

"They cleared out everything else," Cam replied. "Maybe the people who cleaned out the house didn't know about this room."

"Let's look through the rest of the boxes and then decide what to do." Annie suggested.

I nodded. That would give us some time to think and not make a rushed decision.

Annie set the book back down in the box on top of the paper stuffing. We opened the remaining boxes. There were more clothes and some blankets, but nothing interesting. Without deciding on it out loud, everything except the book was boxed up and put back where it had been found.

"I think we should take the book," I said. "We can always bring it back when we are done with it."

"I agree," Cam said, and Annie nodded.

I picked up the book and wrapped some of the paper stuffing around it. It stayed tucked under my arm as we left the room, closed the hidden door, reset the shelves, and left out the unlocked back door.

Back in the car, my desire to go to brunch was gone. I was hungry, but more than that, I wanted to look through the book. "How would you two feel about going to the office and finding some breakfast there?" I asked from the back seat, trying to sound nonchalant.

"I was hoping you'd suggest that," Cam said. "I want to start working on cracking the code in that book."

"Me too," Annie agreed. "And I bet Mrs. Clark has some food in the kitchen we can eat."

The change of plans agreed on, Cam drove us back to the office. The book remained unopened in my lap through the drive. It didn't seem fair for me to get a look at it without the other two. I held the edges of it and tried not to grip it too hard.

THE OFFICE WAS QUIET. It wasn't abnormal for people to be around on the weekend, but it wasn't that common either. Mrs. Clark was likely in her cottage at the back of the property, and Helen may have been up in her suite on the third floor, but the main parts of the office were empty.

We gathered in the kitchen around the table. Annie started the coffee while Cam and I pulled some fruit and leftover quiche from the fridge. We moved silently around the kitchen, preparing the brunch we'd share, but we all kept making quick glances at the book in the middle of the table as if it would get up and walk away if we didn't check that it was still there.

"Let's talk through a plan," Annie said between bites of the quiche we had divided up.

"I think we should take images of each page," I offered.

"That way, if we need to return it, we'll still have the information."

"That's a good idea," Cam agreed. "We can also upload the images and see if we can get a program to help us with the code."

"We also need to update the team on the find," Annie added. "They may have some ideas or be able to help."

"Okay, I can send an email," I agreed.

"Well, I don't think we need to tell them this weekend," Annie said with a smile. "We can update everyone in the morning meeting. We'll just give Helen a heads-up so we don't blindside her."

"If we can get the images taken today, then we can let everyone have access to them on Monday," Cam added.

It took us almost an hour to take images of each page in the book. We got in a pretty good rhythm. The book ended with about a quarter of the pages empty. Cam insisted that we take photos of every page, including the blank ones, to have a full copy.

After the photos were done and we confirmed that they were safely uploaded onto Cam's laptop and backed up to the office server, we pulled more food from the fridge for brunch number two. Luckily, there were almost always leftovers to eat.

"Now that we have all the photos, how should we tackle this?" I asked between bites of reheated fried chicken.

"I can print us all a copy that we can mark up," Cam offered. "But I don't think we should take the book or any of the pages out of the office until we know more about what is in it."

"That's fair," I said, even though I was disappointed that I couldn't work on it all weekend. It was probably for the best. I had a pile of laundry to get through.

Annie looked at both of us and offered practical advice: "We're all tired, and it's been a lot today. I think we shouldn't start on this until Monday."

Cam and I looked at each other and then back at Annie. I sighed. "You're right. A couple more days won't hurt."

We finished up our late lunch and then washed the dishes. I took the book up to my office and locked it in the credenza behind my desk. Cam drove us both home, where laundry, bathroom cleanup, and other chores waited. As I entered my home, I thought—not for the first time—if it would be worth the money to get a house cleaner.

12

All the laundry got done that weekend, but I was restless. I knew the book and, hopefully, clues were waiting back at the office. I rushed through getting ready Monday morning and caught an earlier bus. Even though there were a few folks in the kitchen eating breakfast, I grabbed mine to go and headed up to my desk. I needed to make sure the book was still there.

I had emailed Helen about it before we left the office on Saturday. Her response was *Good work; we'll look at it on Monday.* Cam had already added a new folder to the case file and uploaded the images we took of every page. We'd be updating the full team in about thirty minutes at the morning meeting. My heart felt like it was skipping beats. It was going to be a big day.

The Council representatives were scheduled to arrive at one o'clock for the review. We still hadn't been able to confirm who exactly was coming, but I had several hours before I needed to worry about that. I had time to spare, and the book was calling to me.

I unlocked the cabinet I had left it in and hauled it out onto my desk. It was smaller than I remembered, having built it up in my mind over the weekend. The pages were still filled with strange logs with initials, dates, and symbols. I had worried that it could have a magic spell on it and maybe all the writing would disappear when it left the house. That didn't seem to be the case.

My phone pinged, letting me know that it was five minutes to the meeting. My coffee and breakfast had gotten cold. I had only managed to stare at a single page and made no sense of it. I had hoped for a vision to be triggered. No luck.

I left my cold breakfast at my desk and brought my laptop and the book to the conference table. Cam and Annie glanced at me knowingly when they saw the book, but no one else gave it a second look. There were lots of old books in the office.

Helen sat in her chair at the head of the conference table right at nine o'clock. "We've got a big day today and several updates. Jordan, let's start with you this morning."

I caught some concerned glances around the table. Usually Helen outlined the agenda for everyone. That morning she jumped straight in, like she didn't want to let anything out until it was necessary.

"S-sure." Jordan stumbled slightly. "The feathers we found outside Doria's house finished processing Friday. I was able to confirm that they are not from a siren. It is not conclusive, but it looks like the feathers are actually from a phoenix."

If I hadn't been watching Helen, I don't think I would have caught the flash of relief that washed over her face when Jordan said it wasn't a siren.

"Whoa," Hank let out an uncharacteristic exclamation. We all turned toward him and he went a little red. "Sorry, it's just that phoenixes are really rare. I didn't know there were any around here."

Jordan confirmed. "You're right. They are really rare and very private. I wasn't able to find any known phoenixes near here in our records. And with the new policy at the Council, I don't think we'll have any luck asking them."

"How do you want to proceed?" Helen prompted Jordan.

"Let's start with the easiest path," she answered with a shrug. "We should ask Doria if she knows a phoenix."

"Good idea," Helen agreed. "If Doria isn't forthcoming, let me know if I can help."

"Will do."

Helen turned to me. "Linda, can you give a rundown on the Council visit this afternoon?"

"Yes." I straightened up. I already had the notes pulled up on my laptop, but I didn't need them. I recapped what we all already knew and added, "Annie and I have printed out the summary document and the case list. There will be copies for all participants in the conference room for you."

I paused and looked at Helen to see if I could get a hint at anything else she wanted me to share. She smiled and added to the group, "Please remember that we'd like everyone available if there are questions. We'll message you if we have a question, but you shouldn't need to come meet with the representatives."

Most of us were relieved that we wouldn't be needed in that meeting.

Helen looked around at all of us. "Any questions about this afternoon?"

No one had any questions.

"Great," she continued. "Linda, Annie, Cam, you three had another update for the team."

The three of us had talked about who would update the group. Annie and Cam insisted that I do it, as I was the lead on the case. Annie also said that I was the best story-teller in the group. I picked up the book and held it to my chest as if it would give me strength.

"On Saturday, we went to the Moonstone Haven house to check it out," I said and then paused to see if anyone would react strongly. We'd had Helen's permission, so I wasn't worried about getting in trouble, but I didn't want to upset anyone. Surprisingly, everyone nodded like it was totally expected. "We were able to get into the house through an unlocked back door." I continued to explain how we walked through the empty house and then got to the basement. When I told the group about how we discovered a secret door, eyes lit up around the table. "We found the latches and then pushed the door open. There were several boxes and in one of them was this book." I held the book out in front of me. Everyone looked eager to get their hands on it.

Cam looked at me and I gestured for her to continue the update. "We took images of every page and have them uploaded to a folder in the case file. Everyone has access to those, and we'll also have the book available if anyone wants to see that in person."

Hank and Jordan had their laptops open and clicked through. Based on their looks of concentration, they must have found the file and approved of our work.

I picked up the thread of the update again: "We haven't looked at it much, but there are initials and dates. We think it is a log and that there is some kind of code. Any help on figuring it out would be appreciated."

Helen wrapped up from there. She left us all with a few reminders and encouraged everyone to look at the book that we found. The meeting ended a bit earlier than usual. We all had a lot going on that day.

HELEN AND STEVE both reluctantly had other things they needed to do, but the rest of us stayed at the conference table to look at the book together. We huddled around one corner and pushed the book to a spot where everyone could see if they leaned in a bit. I flipped slowly through a few pages to give everyone a chance to see what was written.

Jordan and Hank peeled off from the group and set up their laptops to pull up the images for a closer look. I was getting frustrated that I wasn't seeing any patterns or helpful information yet.

Angela leaned forward and pointed to one of the symbols on a row. "I think I've seen something like this before."

Every head at the table perked up.

"Where?" I asked, trying not to sound too excited.

"I'm not sure exactly," she hesitated. "But this looks like some symbols I've seen on paperwork in Winthrop's study."

"Do you know what those symbols are?" I pressed.

"No, but I can ask." Angela grabbed a paper from the side cabinet and copied down several of the symbols that were in the book. "Do you think it's okay if I show him these?"

Angela had asked me, but I looked toward Jordan for an answer. She was quick to respond, "I think that's okay. Just don't show him the book, and if you can, don't tell him where they came from."

We all spent another ten minutes silently looking at the book and the images. Jordan broke the silence first and suggested that we plot the log against a timeline of known events in the otherworldly community. Hank and Cam were going to start researching the names that were listed. Angela would see if she could get any info on the symbols. Annie and I were going to continue to look for patterns in all of it.

A path forward decided on, people gathered up their things and headed to their offices to get started on that and other work that needed to be done that day. I had decided to keep the book in my office. No one disagreed with me.

WE WERE ready for the Council representatives. It had been decided that Helen and Steve would greet them instead of Annie. Helen wanted to keep contact between the Council people and the rest of us to a minimum. But Helen didn't say that we couldn't snoop from the window overlooking the front walkway.

Annie, Cam, and I perched at the window five minutes before one o'clock to see if we could spot the representatives. I had some guesses as to whom they would send, but the knot in my gut kept pulling me to one name.

Right at one o'clock, a big, dark SUV pulled up to the curb. A tall blonde woman stepped out of the passenger door, held open by the driver. She wore a tailored dark suit and large dark sunglasses. Her head tilted up, and even though she was wearing sunglasses, I knew that her piercing green eyes were looking at the three of us standing at the window.

Director Cora Owens had come personally for our review.

An involuntary shiver went through my body as the three of us stood frozen in place. I had gotten used to seeing Cora in the Council offices, but having her there, in a place I felt so safe, didn't feel right.

"Well," Cam whispered, breaking the silence. "We should have guessed she'd come."

Annie scoffed, "She could have at least let us know ahead of time."

"She wanted us to be surprised," I whispered back.

"It's fine," Annie said and reached out to touch my arm. "We're ready for anything."

We moved from the window to a spot at the stairs where we could hear what was happening in the foyer below but not be seen by anyone. Jordan walked by and saw the three of us huddled there.

"What are you all up to?" Jordan whispered.

I reached out and grabbed her arm so I could move her closer to us where she wouldn't be seen. "Cora showed up," I whispered back.

Jordan's scoff matched Annie's. "I knew it."

Annie leaned in closer and whispered, "We just want to hear what they are talking about. We'll get back to work when they go into the conference room."

So far we had only heard awkward welcomes and unnecessary introductions. Cora had brought someone with her. He had the stature and rugged attractiveness that was common among werewolves. I felt like I recognized him but couldn't remember the man's name. Cora had glossed over his name so fast that we didn't catch it. Footsteps proceeded through the living room and to the large conference room behind it. The doors closed and Jordan gave us the *time to get back to work* look.

"Who did she say was with her?" Annie asked quietly.

"I didn't catch the name," I answered. "But he's a werewolf, so either from security or operations." Those were the only teams that had werewolves on staff.

"Not records?" Cam questioned.

I could only shrug. Cam was right to ask. I would have thought one of the witches on the records team would come. They were there to review our records after all.

We all turned to head back to our offices. Jordan reminded us as we dispersed, "Helen or Steve will send out a message if there is anything important."

AN HOUR PASSED without any messages or updates. I was determined to stay at my desk and work on understanding the book we had found in the Moonstone Haven house. The notepad I was using was just filled with nonsense doodles and question marks. I tried to channel the emotions that I usually associated with a vision. No luck. I shouldn't have tried, it never worked, but it's easy to fall back into old habits when stressed.

A ping from my open laptop startled me and got my hopes up that we had news. We did; it just wasn't about the terrible director who was in the closed-door meeting with Helen and Steve.

Jordan had news from Doria. She wanted to add an update to the debrief meeting that we'd have as soon as Director Owens and her people left. I needed a distraction and was sure that Jordan would tell me what was going on. She probably needed a distraction as well.

Her door was open, so I knocked lightly on the frame and poked my head into her office. "Hey, what did you hear from Doria?"

Jordan smiled and closed her laptop. "Come on in. I need a break."

I sat down in the chair in front of her desk and waited
for Jordan to share her news.

Jordan leaned forward and smiled. "Well, the good
news is we won't need to ask the Council for a record that
they won't give us."

"Is there bad news?" I asked.

"Not really bad," she responded. "I'm a bit annoyed that
Doria didn't tell us earlier, but most otherworldly folks are
nervous about sharing too much. I should have guessed
that a demon would be the same."

I gave Jordan space to share her thoughts in the
rambling way that she did when she needed to let out
some frustration. Unlike Annie or even Cam, Jordan didn't
come right out and say she needed to vent about a problem. Instead, she would pepper a conversation with her
feelings, and if we stopped her or pressed her to get to the
end faster, she would switch to only the facts. I liked to
hear the feelings side of things.

"It's not really her fault, I guess we only just now asked
her directly about it," Jordan continued to wind her way to
the news. "Anyway, Doria does know a phoenix in the area.
The two of them have had some run-ins over the last
several decades. I get the feeling that they have an uncon-
ventional relationship. I can't really tell if Doria hates
them, loves them, or something in between. I'm still having
a hard time reading Doria."

Jordan paused in thought, so I prompted her to think
out loud: "Did Doria say what the run-ins were?"

"Oh," Jordan said. "She wouldn't say exactly, but she
made it sound like they were pretty petty."

"Does the phoenix still live in the area?"

"Yes, but she wouldn't say where."

"That's not as helpful."

"True. I'll have Helen call Doria and see if she can get the address."

"Helen does have a way of getting people to do what she wants, huh?" I said, which probably should have stayed an unspoken thought.

Jordan laughed. "She does. Which is good for us." A ping on both of our phones got our attention. Jordan was faster checking hers. "Steve says they are wrapping up and should be done in ten minutes. Helen wants to meet as soon as Cora leaves."

The message on my phone was the same. Nerves started to build. Either the quickness of the meeting was a testament to how well I put together the report, or I did so poorly that they had to cancel, and they would be coming back once it was corrected.

I hid my concern and stood up. "I'll go grab my laptop and get back to the conference table."

"I'll see you there. I just need to finish up this note on Doria's case," Jordan said and turned her attention back to her laptop.

I WAS NOT the only one who had decided to wait for the debrief at the conference table. By the time I got my laptop from my desk and walked back to the main room, Annie, Angela, and Hank were all sitting, quietly working on their laptops. I sat in my normal seat and opened my laptop to do the same. No one was typing. I laughed a little bit. We were all trying to look busy, but really we were all listening for any noise coming from downstairs.

A couple of minutes later, Jordan walked out of her office and saw us all sitting there, ears pointed toward the stairs to listen. She laughed at us softly but sat in her seat and joined us in the effort.

Not long after, the sound of a door opening floated up the stairs. We all leaned closer toward the stairs. Footsteps walked from the back room, through the living room, and into the foyer. We could finally hear what they were saying.

"Thank you again for being such an accommodating host," a fake sweet voice that I knew was Cora said.

"I'm glad that the review was successful," Helen said. "And we'll get you the requested data, Director Owens."

"Oh, Helen," Director Owens said. "I really wish you would call me Cora."

"My apologies, Cora," Helen said in her overly polite professional tone.

The folks around the conference table all exchanged glances. We knew what that tone meant: Helen was being nice but she wasn't happy about it.

"I'm so sad I didn't get to say hello to Linda or the rest of the team," Cora said.

"Well, the team is quite busy, and we didn't know that you would be coming personally for this review," Helen said, emphasizing the last part. We all made approving faces upstairs. Her voice turned professional as she continued. "Next time, if you let me know beforehand, I can try to clear the team's schedules to meet with you."

"That would be lovely," Cora said. "Maybe we can all go out for dinner and drinks after."

"Maybe."

We heard footsteps again, and the front door opened.

"Well, until next time," Cora said.

"Yes, next time," Helen responded. I imagined that they shook hands. Then, a few moments later, the front door closed. We could hear Steve's sigh all the way upstairs.

13

"It sounds like she suspects we are up to something," Jordan pressed after Helen's summary of the review meeting.

"It would be safe to assume that," Helen conceded. "We'll need to be careful about how we move forward with the investigation."

According to Helen, the review with Director Owens— or rather, *Cora*, as Helen and a few of us called her—and her assistant for the day had gone well. They had a few questions about the cases and wanted to see details about the pack's insurance claims we had assisted on.

The strange part of the meeting was when Cora asked about activities unrelated to cases. Specifically she had asked about any research projects or inventions that the team was involved in. I grimaced at that and wondered if Willow had mentioned anything about our phone call on Friday.

Helen had sidestepped that by telling her that we only

had research related to cases. This was technically true if you had a wide definition of a case. Cam and Jordan, our two primary researchers and inventors, were not happy to hear that those questions were being asked.

We were just about done with the debriefing when the doorbell sounded from downstairs. Helen, Steve, and Annie all checked their phones to see who was at the door.

"Angela," Helen said, turning to her. "Were you expecting Winthrop today?"

Angela looked surprised. "No." She paused and looked around. "But I sent him a few symbols from the Moonstone Haven book and asked him if they looked familiar." No one was upset, but Angela was quick to explain, "I didn't tell him what it was from. But he seemed really interested in what was going on. He may be coming to ask about that."

Helen smiled softly. "That's alright. Annie, could you go answer the door and see what he needs?"

Annie nodded and headed down the stairs. Like earlier, we all inclined our heads toward the stairway to see if we could hear what was being said. Unfortunately, Annie and Winthrop spoke softly at the front door, so I only heard mumbles that I couldn't make out.

A few moments later there were some sounds of footsteps and a door closing. Annie came back up the stairs.

"I asked him to wait in the living room," Annie told the group. "Like Angela thought, he wants to talk about the symbols from the book."

Helen leaned back in her chair and had on her thinking face.

The silence was making my mind race, and I blurted out, "It sounds like he could help us."

"You're probably right," Helen said with a smile. "Annie, would you invite him up here? Hank, could you grab another chair for the table?"

Both moved to do what had been asked. The rest of us sat ready to hear what the five-hundred-year-old vampire had to say about the mysterious symbols from the Moonstone Haven book.

Winthrop glided up the stairs behind Annie. The light flowed around him, giving away that he was having strong feelings about something. He settled into the chair Hank had placed at the end of the table opposite Helen.

He spoke first. "Sounds like you could use my help."

"Sounds like you would like to help," Helen countered with a *friendly but don't mess with us* tone.

Winthrop chuckled. "A perfect match then."

Angela let out an exasperated sigh and then turned red when she realized we had heard her. Winthrop gave her a wink.

"I would very much like to help," Winthrop said with a more polite tone. "If you would allow me."

"Please share with us what you know," Helen pressed, not quite ready to say yes to getting him involved.

Winthrop leaned back in his chair and steepled his fingers on the table. "Well, Angela sent me a few symbols she thought I would know."

"And do you?" Helen prompted when he paused.

"Yes," he replied. "But I'm also wondering how this group came across them."

"We will share that with you if I decide that you can consult on this project," Helen countered. "For now, I need to know if you have information that would be helpful."

It was like watching a ping-pong match. They were both volleying to each other and looked like they were enjoying it.

Winthrop's eyes narrowed, but he grinned, and the light pushed out from him, forming something like a spotlight around where he sat. "The symbols are used by a small group of individuals to indicate the species and abilities of otherworldly creatures."

Jordan looked confused. "There is already a taxonomy for that. Why use these symbols?"

Winthrop looked toward her, his eyes shifting to concern. "They are primarily used when you don't want certain people to know what you mean should they come across them in a communication."

"So spies use them?" I blurted out. Spying was on my mind, but that wasn't the right thing to say. Again my mouth was faster than my brain.

Winthrop took it in stride. "Spies, conspirators, secret societies bent on the consolidation of power, whatever you want to call them. Only one group I know of used these specific symbols, and they have been inactive for the last thirty years." He looked back at Helen. "They were not good people, and I know your agency would not have had dealings with them."

Helen looked panicked for a moment but hid it quickly, ignored Winthrop's statement, and shifted back to the topic at hand: "Can you tell us what one of the symbols is specifically?"

"A good-faith show of knowledge, sure," he said, pulling out his phone. He tapped it a few times and then turned it around to show an enlarged image of one of the symbols Angela had drawn out. "This is a symbol to designate a werewolf. Now, if there was another symbol next to it, it may indicate specifically what pack they were with."

We all exchanged looks. That particular symbol had been found several times in the book, and often other symbols followed it.

I watched Helen look at Jordan and ask a silent question. Jordan nodded. One by one, Helen made eye contact with each of us. We all knew what she was asking. When she got to me, I nodded: yes, I was okay with including Winthrop in this case.

"Okay," Helen said with one clap of her hands. "Winthrop, you can join us as a consultant on this case. Linda, you can show him the book and fill him in on *that*." The emphasis and her look made it clear that I could tell him about Moonstone Haven and the book but not about other projects, including the covert investigation and data mining we were doing at the Council offices.

"Understood," I said to confirm.

"Great," Helen replied. "I'll leave you all to that. Jordan, can you come make a phone call with me?"

Jordan nodded and stood. Based on my conversation with Jordan earlier, I assumed they were going to call Doria to see if they could get an address for the phoenix from her.

Helen and Jordan made their way to her office. I followed behind them to get the book from my desk so I could show Winthrop. Helen turned around to me before she closed the doors to her office. "Linda, we may need to make a house call this afternoon. Would you be free to come along?"

"Yes," I said without hesitation. I hoped she meant that I would get to meet a phoenix.

Back in the main room, I put the book in the middle of the table.

Winthrop looked at it skeptically. "So, that's the book that contains these symbols?"

"Yes," I said firmly. "We found it in a hidden room of a house that we are pretty confident was being used by a group that went by Moonstone Haven." I flipped open to a random page so that he could see the writing. "It looks like a log. There are letters we are pretty sure are initials and dates."

He reached out and pointed at symbols in a row. "And they used these symbols for each row."

"Yes," I said, getting more excited. "And if you are right in how they are used, then each of these initials is a person from the otherworldly community."

"Do you have a list of all the symbols?" Winthrop asked with excitement.

"Not yet," I replied. "There are a lot, and we've also been trying to research the initials and dates."

"We have printouts of the pages in the book that we can write on," Cam offered.

"That would be good," Winthrop said. "I can start filling in the ones I know."

Cam went to her office and brought back a binder that she had created with copies of the book. She handed it over to Winthrop along with a red pen. He bent his head over the binder of printed images and started to write out notes in the margin of the first page.

"When you finish that page, hand it over to us," Angela suggested. "Then we can start making an index so we can all help translate the symbols."

Winthrop hesitated for a moment. "This book and these notes will stay in this office, right?"

"Yes," I said firmly.

"Good. If someone was using these symbols for these people, either they were protecting them from something or they were involved in something that could cause tremendous harm."

"That's what we think too," I said, giving words to what I had feared from the moment I saw those logs.

We worked in silence for several minutes. Winthrop was making quick work through the pages. He grabbed a pad of sticky notes and marked a couple of pages with question marks for some symbols that he didn't know.

A door opening from the other side of the building alerted everyone. Helen and Jordan came into the main room, looking happy and in a hurry.

"Linda," Helen called out. "We're heading out. Are you ready to go?"

I nodded and fielded a confused look from Annie. I gave her the *I'll tell you later* face. The rest of the team returned to the pages in front of them to list the symbols from the book and match them to ones we knew. So far, only a few didn't have a translation.

JORDAN PARKED the car across the street from the house. It was not what I expected. No looming, ivy-covered Victorian mansion. It was big, like I had expected, but it was one of the new modern, boxy homes that were popping up all over Seattle neighborhoods. The house filled the space; hardly any yard was left. It was clad in tones of dark gray and wood. Large picture windows reflected back the tree-lined street it sat on.

The three of us made our way up the front walk. Helen led the way. She rang the familiar doorbell that was attached to a camera. Looking around, I saw other cameras tucked into the eaves pointing to all the entrance points. Such cameras were not uncommon to find on homes, but they were a clear sign that whoever was in the house was watching everything.

The strange feeling of someone on the edges of my vision was back, like I had felt in the Moonstone Haven house. I turned to check if anyone was on the sidewalk. It was empty. Looking up at the cameras again, I imagined someone sitting behind a computer, watching us standing on the front steps. That must have been where the watched feeling was coming from.

The door creaked open just enough for us to see an older man peek around it.

"Can I help you?" he asked with a slight shake to his voice.

"Yes," Helen responded clearly. "My name is Helen. We are with the OPT Agency and here to speak with Mr. Gray."

The man winced slightly when Helen said her name. I squinted to try to get a better look at him and what might lay beyond him in the house.

"Mr. Gray is not available," he responded, glancing nervously at each of us.

"And you are?" Helen asked in a way that he was not likely to refuse to answer.

"I'm Burton, Mr. Gray's house manager," Burton answered quickly, his eyes shifting between us.

"Burton, do you know who I am?" Helen asked, drawing his attention to her.

"Yes."

"Good." She slipped into the tone of voice that I'd heard her use many times to get what she wanted. "Can we come in and speak with you for a few moments?" she pressed more than asked.

"I suppose," Burton said with some hesitation, but he opened the door for us to enter.

We filed in and stood in a gleaming wood, glass, and metal entryway. It was minimalist and modern. Burton ushered us into a sitting room off to the left. The far wall was lined with bookshelves filled with books all in muted colors, as if they were selected for their aesthetics and not their contents.

"Thank you for speaking with us, Burton," Helen said

as we all got settled on the couch, facing him sitting in one of the two chairs surrounding a coffee table. "Is Mr. Gray unavailable for an extended amount of time?"

It took me longer than I'd like to admit to realize what she was asking between the lines. Mr. Gray was a phoenix, and he could be in a cycle. Jordan had filled me in a bit on the car ride over. It was what I would have expected: basically immortal and every few months they completed a cycle that included burning down to ash then being "reborn" from it.

"Yes, he is unavailable for the rest of this week," Burton said, still a bit warily. "Mr. Gray won't be waking up until late Sunday. He should be available next Monday."

"Would it be alright if we looked around the house?" Helen asked. "We are looking for an item that belongs to a client. We'd like to rule out Mr. Gray quickly."

Burton stared us down like he was guarding the gate of a fortress that held treasures, but it didn't take him too long to answer, "Yes, I suppose that would be alright. Mr. Gray would cooperate with the agency."

"Thank you," Helen said as she stood. "We appreciate your cooperation."

Jordan and I followed Helen's lead and stood up. Burton stood as well, a bit shaky on his legs.

"You can look around this floor," Burton said. "Let me know when you are done, and I'll show you the upstairs. There is one room that I can't allow you in."

"Understood," Helen responded quickly. Again, I read between the lines: the room we couldn't go into was likely where Mr. Gray was going through his regeneration cycle.

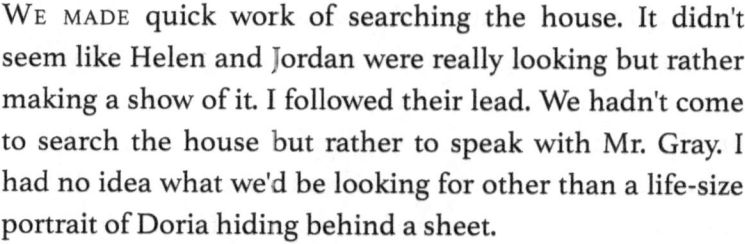

WE MADE quick work of searching the house. It didn't
seem like Helen and Jordan were really looking but rather
making a show of it. I followed their lead. We hadn't come
to search the house but rather to speak with Mr. Gray. I
had no idea what we'd be looking for other than a life-size
portrait of Doria hiding behind a sheet.

The style of the house was clearly professionally
designed but not the kind of place that I'd want to live in. It
felt too sterile. Like if you spilled anything, you'd be kicked
out or, at minimum, receive a public shaming. The whole
house was like the front room I remembered from friends'
homes, the one room in the house that we kids weren't
allowed in. It was kept pristine and ready for company at
any moment. My mom didn't have a room like that. Any
guests that showed up were immediately escorted into the
kitchen for tea or snacks, no matter its current state of
cleanliness.

Nothing jumped out at me as suspicious other than the
steel-reinforced door to the room we weren't allowed into,
but there was a good reason for that. If that was where Mr.
Gray combusted, turned to ash, and then was reborn, it
would need to contain the fire.

Back down in the foyer, Burton looked relieved for the
first time in the thirty minutes we'd been there.

"Thank you again for letting us look around," Helen
said. "We'll get in touch with Mr. Gray on Monday."

"You are welcome," Burton replied. "And I'll let Mr.
Gray know to expect your call."

Burton was quick to shut the door behind us. The three of us didn't speak until we were back in the car. The car doors closed, and I blurted out the joke that had been running through my head the whole time we were in the house: "So do you think the butler did it?"

14

The pen that would help me download data from the Council's computers was securely placed in my work bag. I had checked on it at least a dozen times from when I packed it to when I got off the plane and into the car headed to the Council offices. Cam had helped me practice how to use it several times the day before. I was nervous but ready. The first hurdle was to get through security with it.

"Good morning, Linda," Walter, the friendly werewolf security guard for the Council offices, greeted me like normal. "Starting the week late this time, huh?"

"Yes," I replied as if it was no big deal. "There was some work at my other job that I had to be in person for."

"Well, we're happy to have you any days we can get," he said as I scanned the blank solid-black card that served as my ID.

I placed my work bag on the conveyor belt that would send it through the X-ray machine to be reviewed. I then stepped through the metal detector and tried to keep my eyes off my bag. The machine made a beep that I hadn't heard before. Walter frowned at the computer he was looking at. I froze on the other side of the metal detector.

"Sorry, Linda," he said. "Let me put your bag through one more time."

Walter took the bag and moved it back to the beginning of the X-ray machine and then settled back behind the screen. It seemed as if time slowed as the bag moved through the machine, stopped inside to be scanned, and then exited the other end.

He looked up with a smile. "This has been temperamental the last few days, but you are good to go. Sorry to slow you down."

"No worries, thank you," I said as calmly as I could while I grabbed the bag and put the strap over my shoulder. It was a good thing I was wearing a jacket. Any longer, and I would have sweated through that too.

Getting to my desk took an elevator ride and a short walk down a hall. It was in a small maze of cubicles strategically outside Director Owens's corner office. The office was a stark contrast to the workplace I was in the other three weeks of the month. The walls, floor, and cubicles all melded into the same gray color scheme. Harsh overhead lights buzzed, and one flickered a bit in the corner of the large space.

Any windows were behind closed doors of conference rooms and offices that belonged to much more important people. The Council offices were three floors in the building, at least that I knew of, and each had the same setup.

The only place with any color was the kitchen, where employees could store their lunches in the fridge, use a microwave, make coffee from a pod, or grab a snack from the small supply of single-serve chip bags or trail mix.

It was in that break room the first week that I had tried to strike up a conversation with a couple of the witches who worked there—they seemed like the most approachable group—about what they thought about working at the Council and with Director Owens. They gave a handful of platitudes and nonanswers. When my face showed that I didn't believe them, one of them tilted their head and subtly looked up at a glass-domed device in the ceiling. It took a moment for me to see the blinking red light and realize it was a camera. Those glass-domed cameras were everywhere. Well, there weren't any in the bathroom, but there was one right outside the door.

A camera was also near my cubicle. My cubicle was an L shape with a desktop computer and a couple sets of drawers. The walls were high enough that when I was sitting, I could only see the tops of heads walking by. I had to stand on my tiptoes to see over them, and I usually just walked to the other cubes if I needed to talk with someone.

Like all employees at the Council offices, I didn't use a laptop, and I couldn't bring anything like that with me. My normal work laptop for the agency was being transported with my other things for the week to the apartment that I stayed in while I was in San Francisco. The driver, also arranged for by Helen and the agency, would leave them inside the door of the apartment.

The Council computer took a minute to boot up. I

checked my schedule for the week. There were a few meetings with Director Owens, during which I would shadow her. The rest of the time, I would continue to work with Willow on the coven records project. It was supposed to be finished that week, but Willow had already said we'd be granted an extension, so there was no need to rush.

My first meeting with Director Owens wasn't until after lunch. I cleared out a few emails and then messaged Willow to see if she was ready to start on the project. She messaged back immediately to say she was ready and to meet her at her cubicle.

I grabbed a notepad, my badge card so I could access the other floors, and a couple of pens, including *the pen*. My heart raced a bit more, and I started to rehearse how I could get Willow away from her computer so I could download her files.

Willow was on the other end of the floor from my cubicle. The records department took up most of the floor we were on. She was a senior clerk. Willow had told me that the records department was the second-largest department at the Council and that there were almost never open positions available. She felt lucky that she had been able to get a role in the department two years before. Prior to that, she had been an assistant to one of the managers who led a team of case agents in operations. She was one of the only witches on that team while she was there.

Case agents were all werewolves and they traveled in the field. Willow said she had spent most of her time hounding them about expense reports and then correcting them when they were wrong. She had let it slip to me that she thought case agents were mostly arrogant and that they thought their jobs were the most important at the Council. She had gone as far as to call them corporate bullies before she turned red, looked up toward a camera, and said they were actually important people in the Council. Her face may have looked contrite, but her eyes still had a bit of fire behind them.

Willow was at her desk with the spreadsheet already pulled up on one computer and the folder of coven reports on the other. Because I had joined the project, Willow was able to get a second computer set up in her cubicle so that I could help. It was more efficient, and I was surprised that she had to ask for it and that it took until my second week to get it approved.

"Good morning, Willow," I called out cheerfully as I stepped into her cubicle.

She spun around in her chair and smiled. "Good morning. We missed you yesterday."

"Yeah, I had to stay in Seattle on Monday for some work stuff."

"Well, you're here now. This goes way faster when you are helping."

I laughed a little. "That's good to hear. I worried a bit that I was slowing you down with my questions."

"Not at all," Willow replied quickly. "And it's nice to have the company."

I couldn't imagine sitting in a closed-off cubicle for eight hours a day with only short breaks to interact with anyone. Actually, I could. I'd had jobs like that. I had pushed those so far back in my memory it seemed like a lifetime ago. Working at the agency was so different. I reminded myself how lucky I was.

"So, what coven are we starting with today?" I asked. We had been going coven by coven along a map that Willow had in her head. I thought we were about two-thirds of the way done, if I remembered correctly.

"Let's see," Willow said, turning back to her computer to check where she had left off. "Oh, it looks like we are in your neck of the woods today. We'll be starting with the Seattle coven, and then if we get through that, we'll move on to Bellingham and then Vancouver."

My heart rate picked up speed, and I felt my vision start to tunnel. In my time at the Council offices, I hadn't had a vision, despite Director Cora Owens trying to help me force one. I didn't really want to have a vision at the office. I opened my eyes wide and took deep breaths, silently begging the vision not to come. Something worked, because I didn't lapse into one.

"Are you alright?" Willow asked. "Do you need some water?"

"No, I'm fine," I replied quickly. "Just a bit dizzy. I didn't get any breakfast this morning. It's catching up with me."

"Oh, that's not good. Do you want me to grab you something? I think there were bananas in the break room this morning."

I jumped on the opportunity to be alone at Willow's desk. I let myself look pathetic. "That would actually be great. Would you mind getting me a cup of coffee too?"

"Of course, milk and sugar?" she asked, and I nodded.

She got up and started toward the break room on the other end of the floor.

The coffee was in one of those pod machines. If I was lucky, it would be off and would need a minute to warm up. If I wasn't lucky, I still maybe had five minutes. The pen was fast, but the longer I could hold it in the port, the better.

I looked around one last time to ensure I wasn't within the eyeline of any cameras. I quickly took the cap off the pen and slid my chair closer to the computer tower under Willow's desk. There was a port on the front. As I had practiced with Cam, I pushed the end of the pen to extend the writing end and then placed it into the port, hoping that the promised magic was doing its job. The pen didn't do anything to indicate that it was working. That was on purpose. I wouldn't know if it was able to get any data until I got back to the apartment and docked it into my laptop.

I held the pen in my right hand and angled my body so I could see out the cubicle opening. The office was quiet, just the sounds of typing and an occasional cough. I would have been able to hear footsteps if anyone got close to where I was. My armpits filled with sweat again, and my mouth was dry. I wasn't sure what I could say to explain if someone saw what I was doing.

My steady counting to measure the time that passed was over three hundred. Willow should have been coming back soon. I probably got some data but decided to risk it and get more. The coffee pod machine was probably off when she got to the break room.

I was reaching six hundred when I heard footsteps. I

quickly pulled the pen out and rolled back over to my side of the desk. Willow walked in balancing a banana and two cups of coffee. The pen was tucked down to my side. I fidgeted with one hand to put the cap back on and tuck it under my leg on the chair.

"A second cup never hurt anyone," Willow joked.

I forced a laugh. "You are right about that."

She set a cup and the banana in front of me. "Take a minute to eat that, and then we can get started. Did anything interesting happen over the weekend?"

I peeled the banana. "No, just the usual. I was able to get all my laundry done."

"That counts for something."

"What about you?"

"Oh, I had to work over the weekend."

I perked up at that. In the few months I'd been coming there, I'd never heard of them working on the weekends. I wanted to learn more, but I had to be careful how I asked.

"That sucks," I said, trying to sound empathetic. "Anything crazy or just normal catch-up stuff?"

"Nothing crazy," she said and sipped her coffee. "The whole records department had to come in to review and summarize property holdings for all the North American packs. It sounds like there was a problem with some insurance stuff that Director Owens wanted to resolve quickly."

My mind raced alongside my heart. That was too much of a coincidence. If I remembered correctly, Director Owens had asked for details on one case during the review, the pack insurance holdings. I needed to let Helen know soon.

"That sounds like a lot of work," I tried to say neutrally.

"It wasn't too bad. With everyone working on it, we got through it so that it didn't mess up any other project's timelines."

"Well, good. Coven records are probably more interesting than pack holdings," I said jokingly.

"You are right about that. I'm still not sure we found what they were worried about."

I finished the banana and set the peel aside to throw away in the break room. It would be rude to throw it out in Willow's trash can and make her space smell like bananas for the rest of the day.

"Ready to get started?" I asked.

"Ready if you are."

The next two and a half hours were tedious, but we got through a lot. An hour in, I got up to use the restroom and threw away the banana peel. Willow also took the opportunity to go to the restroom. I was glad that the coffee request had worked. I had planned on trying to access the computer while she was in the bathroom, but if she only went when I went, then I'd never get that chance.

Several names were familiar from the Seattle coven's reports. I was carefully watching for a specific name: Rachel Bishop. I was curious how the coven would report on her and the shapeshifting ability that was so uncommon and often feared.

We were getting close to the end of the folder that held the documents we were going through one at a time. One document for each member. Rachel's document hadn't come up yet, even though her mom's document had been several back. I clicked open the last one. It wasn't Rachel.

"Does the coven report on every member in this survey?" I asked as nonchalantly as I could. Willow was used to me asking questions as we worked, so hopefully she thought it was just another random question.

"Yes," she said without missing a beat of her work. "They were required to report on every coven member."

"And every witch belongs to a coven?" I pressed gently.

"No, that's not required."

"So how do we catalog non-coven members?"

"They are registered directly with the Council. Kind of like the Council is their coven but only from a record-keeping perspective."

"Oh, that's helpful."

"Yes, and it's good for us. We don't need to review those reports. They get entered directly into the system."

"Makes sense," I responded quietly.

That meant that Rachel wasn't part of the Seattle coven, but her mom still was. I had no idea how common it was for family members to belong to different covens. All the records seemed to be filled with families. I filed it away as another thing to mention to Helen.

"I think this is a good stopping point," Willow declared as she leaned back and cracked her knuckles above her head. "Any plans for lunch?"

"I'm doing a working lunch," I answered. "I need to catch up on some work for the agency."

"You're lucky you live so close to the office," Willow

said. "I would love to be able to go home for my lunch break."

"It does have its perks," I responded as I stood up and carefully pulled the pen from under my leg without Willow seeing.

"Are you back with me after lunch?" she asked.

"Not right after. I have an hour with Director Owens, but then I'll be free to keep working with you."

"That sounds good. I'll see you around two then?"

"Yep, see you at two."

15

The walk to the apartment took less than ten minutes. I had an hour for lunch but needed to eat while I talked with Cam. The streets around me felt different from Seattle. There were a lot more people out, and I felt like I was being watched as I made the short walk. It was nice to get to the apartment and have that feeling fall away. The apartment door opened to a familiar view of the city with the water just beyond it. The agency didn't skimp on their employees' accommodations.

My bags were set by the front door as promised. I took my suitcase to the bedroom so it'd be out of the way. The bag that held my laptop and the docking station I would need was unloaded onto the kitchen counter.

I plugged in everything and settled into the barstool at the counter. By the time the video call with Cam connected, the pen was docked and downloading.

"How did it go?" Cam asked anxiously, skipping hellos

and going straight to the question. She knew I was going to try to get some data that morning.

"Good," I answered, still a bit out of breath from the walk back to the apartment and the nerves. "The pen is docked, and it looks like it got something."

"That's great." Cam sounded relieved. "If you are connected to the apartment's Wi-Fi, you can give me permission to access your laptop, and I'll pull the files over to our servers."

I clicked through the sequence that Cam had taught me to allow her to do that. "Done, you should have access now."

"Yep, got it," Cam said and then paused. "Wow, you were able to get a lot. Hopefully we'll find something useful."

"I hope so," I replied. "But I kind of doubt it. I don't think the director would let someone like Willow have access to the kind of information we are looking for. No offense to Willow, but she isn't high up enough in the organization for that."

"That's fair. Even if there isn't anything useful, it was a good test run for the pen."

"That's true," I said with a smile. "I'll be in Cora's office later today; if I get the chance, I'll see if I can get anything from her computer."

Cam looked worried. "Don't push it. If it's not the right time, we can wait."

Even if everyone was patient, I didn't want to wait. The director was suddenly changing things, and if it continued, who knew if we would get another chance? And if we didn't figure it out, others could get hurt.

"Alright, promise," I finally said to stop Cam from continuing to glare at me through the computer screen.

"I'll look through this data," Cam said. "But if you have the time, we have an update on Moonstone Haven house."

That perked me up. I still had at least thirty minutes before I needed to head back. I needed to eat, but this was more important. "Yes, I have time," I replied quickly.

"Okay, let me message Annie and Angela so they can join the call. They'll want to update you on what they found." Cam's eyes moved from the camera to another part of the screen. There were sounds of clicks and then the beep of two more boxes joining the conference call, with Annie in one and Angela in the other.

"Hey," Annie said. I could hear the echo through the video call.

Cam did too. "Annie, you are echoing. One of us needs to go into a room with a closed door or put on headphones."

Annie laughed and it echoed. "I can put on headphones."

That settled, I rushed to get down to business. "What's the update?"

Angela was the first to speak up. "We were able to translate about eighty percent of the symbols in the book."

"Eighty-seven," a voice behind her said.

"Is that Winthrop?" I asked, pretty sure I recognized him.

Angela gestured to someone behind the computer. "Yes, he's been here all morning helping with the translations."

Winthrop appeared on Angela's computer screen. He crouched down to be seen. "Linda, it's good to see you. You are being careful, right?"

"Yes, I'm being careful," I answered, amused at how he had switched to being overprotective of all of us as soon as Helen had said he could be part of the team for this case. It didn't register at the time to wonder why he was telling me to be careful; he wasn't supposed to know about the covert mission.

"Good," he said with a firm nod.

"As I was saying," Angela said to get us back on track. "We translated most of the book. The next thing that seemed easy was to make a list of all the initials with symbols that indicated they were vampires or associated with any of the vampire families."

I nodded my agreement. That was a smart move, seeing that we had a vampire on the case with five hundred years of memories.

"Winthrop was able to identify several of them. You were right that the initials were names," Angela said and then got serious. "As far as he knows, all of them were declared dead."

"Why would Moonstone Haven be tracking dead people?" I thought out loud.

"That's the strange part," Annie took over. "We checked several of them for the dates that they were declared dead. The dates in the Moonstone Haven book are all after those dates."

My mind quickly turned over what that could mean. It felt like the puzzle pieces were almost connected.

Cam knew my thinking face. "You'd probably come to the same theory we did."

"What's the theory?" I asked. We didn't have time for me to think about it if they already had one.

Everyone on the call paused as if unsure who should say it. Annie finally broke the stalemate. "We don't think they were really dead. We think Moonstone Haven was hiding them and made it look like they were dead so people wouldn't look for them."

"What people?" I thought out loud again.

"Two guesses," Cam said. "But you'll only need one."

There was only one person you'd want to hide supernaturals from. "The director."

"Exactly," Cam said.

"We need to check more initials for full names with other groups to see if the theory holds," Angela said practically.

Cam added, "We will ask Sarah if she recognizes any of the initials that use the werewolf or pack symbols."

I nodded my approval. If Cam trusted Sarah, then we could all trust her.

"What about the symbols we couldn't translate?" I asked. It felt important to understand the book fully.

"We know they don't belong to any group," Angela replied.

"All the groups were accounted for," Winthrop added. "They used the taxonomy symbol for symbol. So it's unlikely that it is a code for the individual's group or nature."

"Do you think the coven would know what those other

symbols are?" I asked. The Moonstone Haven house had been associated with the coven. They paid the taxes on it. And Enid, the witch who was murdered months before, was tied to the house.

"Possibly," Cam said. "But Helen doesn't think we should ask them anything about the book yet."

"I understand." The coven had been quick to call the Council when Rachel's shifting abilities and her involvement with Enid's murder had been discovered. It made sense that Helen didn't trust them.

Cam smiled. "We'll send you a list of the symbols we haven't been able to translate so you can have a look."

"That would be great." It sucked not to be in the office while something so important was going on, but I had something important to do in San Francisco as well. "Oh, speaking of, I have some updates that I need to get to Helen," I said, changing the topic. "Is she around?"

Annie shook her head. "No, she's out at Doria's house with Jordan."

"Well, I'll write her an email with all the details." I checked the clock. "I won't have time to email her until after the workday, so can you pass on a quick message?"

"Yes," Cam said.

Angela waved goodbye and closed her video feed.

"Oops, I forgot Winthrop was there," I said.

"No problem," Annie reassured me. "Angela's got you covered. What's the update?"

"Two things," I said. "First, the records team worked over the weekend to pull data and summarize the holdings of all the packs. Willow said it had something to do with an insurance problem they wanted to clear up quickly."

Cam connected the dots. "Wasn't the pack's insurance case the one that Director Owens wanted more details on?"

"Exactly. Seems like too much of a coincidence."

"I agree," Annie said, and Cam nodded.

"Second one," I continued. "We went through the Seattle coven's reports today. I didn't see a record for Rachel. Willow told me the covens had to report every member. Witches who don't belong to a coven must report directly to the Council."

Annie and Cam looked perplexed.

"It just seems strange that Rachel isn't counted with the Seattle coven," I pressed. "Her mom still is. It feels like something important, but I'm not sure why."

"Okay," Cam said. "We'll pass both those things on to Helen and let her know you'll send more information."

"Thank you," I said. It was just past twelve-thirty. "Anything else?"

"No," Annie replied. "We can do a call after work if any of us learn anything new."

"Great," I said, wrapping up. "Talk soon."

I had just enough time to scarf down a peanut butter and honey sandwich and some apple slices. Mrs. Clark would be disappointed to see my lunch choices. A friend of hers in the area stocked my fridge every week with ready-to-eat meals and salads, but those would all take more than the seven minutes that I had to eat.

∿

I MADE it back to the office with a minute to spare. The door to Cora's office was closed, so I stood awkwardly outside it, holding my notebook and pens. She didn't tell me what meeting I would be shadowing, but if it was like the others, it would be boring.

At one o'clock, there were five of us waiting outside her door: me, three men I didn't know, and John, a witch and the head of the records department. He didn't talk much and had a habit of pulling the sleeve of his shirt down to cover the tattoos that snaked up his arm. The other three men I didn't recognize, but two looked like werewolves with their symmetrical features and towering height. The other was a vampire; the light pulsed around him subtly and picked up speed when he looked my way. I was getting better at noticing the characteristics that would identify people, at least the big three: witches, werewolves, and vampires.

None of us knocked. I learned on day one that you waited until Cora called out that she was ready for you. We were also all quiet. There was no easy chatter or conversations about how people were doing. We just stood on shifting feet and waited for the call to come in.

"Ready," Director Owens called out, muffled behind the closed door.

The vampire in the group stepped forward and opened the door. The rest of us followed him in. I closed the door behind me. We all sat around a small conference table that occupied one end of the room. The other end of the room held an imposing desk with two wood chairs in front of it. The space was sparsely decorated. The only ornate thing in it was the ugly crown molding. A couple of abstract paintings flanked a set of windows, and a bookshelf held some leather-bound books and several awards of varying sizes.

"John, report on the status of the coven abilities project," Cora—or rather, *Director Owens* in this context—said.

I perked up. That was the project Willow and I had been working on. For once, I knew what we were talking about in one of the director's meetings. Still, I sat quietly with my notebook open to take notes for when Cora would ask me questions later to test how well I was paying attention.

"The team has completed seventy percent of the reports." John spoke quickly and clearly. "Current trajectory has the project completed by the end of this week, just as we had planned."

That was wrong. We were about seventy percent through the records, but unless more people were added or we worked overtime, the project would not be done by the end of that week. I tried to hide my confusion, but John must have caught my look. He subtly shook his head, so I let it drop. He probably knew something I didn't.

"Good," Director Owens said and then moved on. "Pierce, what is the status of the case agents' audit?"

Pierce, the scarier looking of the two werewolves, shuffled some papers around before he said, "I've completed the audit for all active case agents. I still need to review the few that are currently not active."

Director Owens looked stern. "Why isn't that done yet?"

"A few of the background checks took longer to gather than we had anticipated."

"That sounds like a problem with your team," she said. "Were the estimates they gave wrong, or were they incompetent in how they completed the project?"

Pierce stumbled over his words momentarily. "I-I believe the estimates were wrong."

"You'll correct them on that," the director said sternly.

Pierce nodded and wrote something on his notepad. "We are still within the original timeline," he said, defending his team.

Director Owens narrowed her eyes. "But you aren't within the expedited one that you reset."

"That was a stretch goal."

"Yes, and one that you should be capable of meeting."

Pierce just nodded again and wrote something else on his paper.

Director Owens tapped her pen on the table a few times and looked around. "Alright, let's move on to next quarter's projects."

For the next forty-five minutes, I struggled to stay engaged. The conversation was hard to follow with all the acronyms and code-word projects that were used. It was clearly a meeting of all the department heads. Based on what they were talking about, I wrote down everyone's name and what department they worked for.

"That's a good stopping point for today," Director Owens said, and I swore everyone sighed with relief. They had all been peppered with questions and pushed to bring in timelines to move faster and tighten up the budgets.

They all gathered up their things and filed out of the office with heads down and without saying goodbye to anyone.

Director Owens turned to me with a smile. "Good meeting, right?"

"Yes," I agreed quickly. "Really interesting. Thank you for letting me observe."

"Let's move over to my desk, and we can talk through what you learned."

I followed her over and sat in the hard chair in front of her desk with my notepad in my lap. The clock behind her desk showed that we only had ten minutes left of the scheduled time. I'd hoped we'd end on time, but we often went over.

Director Owens asked me a few questions about what was said in the meeting. I was able to answer them to her satisfaction.

"Remember," she lectured, "it's important to always push your people to give more than what they offer. If you don't push them, they will take whatever time or money they can."

I nodded along as she continued to lecture about how best to manage teams, but couldn't help but contrast her leadership approach to Helen's. Had I not just spent six months working with Helen, I might have thought that what Cora said was good advice. It fit with how other leaders I'd worked with had managed their teams. I hadn't known there was a different, or even better, way. But there was, and Helen's approach proved it.

The clock ticked past the hour, and I imagined there were people waiting outside the closed door to be called in. I began to get impatient about wrapping up. Being late to meetings was not something I liked doing, and I knew Willow was waiting for me. I also knew she would understand that my meeting with the director went over.

Twelve minutes past when we should have ended, Director Owens finally wrapped things up. "That's all for today," she said with a smile. "Have a good afternoon, and I'll see you tomorrow."

"Thank you," I said as I stood. "I hope you have a good day too."

"You can tell the people waiting that they can come in."

Two of the men from our previous meeting were waiting outside the office door. They both gave me a dirty look as I walked out and told them Director Owens said they could go in.

WILLOW WAS happy to see me, and we picked up on the records right where we left off. We were moving quickly when Willow suggested we take a break and get some coffee. The break room was empty except for the two of us.

"Can I ask you a question?" I ventured quietly.

Willow sipped her coffee. "Sure."

"I was just in a meeting with the department heads, including John." I continued to talk quietly in case someone walked by. "He mentioned that this coven records project would be done by the end of the week."

Willow smiled grimly. "Yeah, he came by and talked to me about that."

"So we will be done by the end of the week?" I was confused how that could happen.

"No," Willow replied. "He didn't want to tell the director in that meeting. He'll send her an email update at the end of today saying we hit a complication with some of the forms and need more time."

"What's wrong with the forms?" I asked.

"Nothing," she said calmly. "But it's better for the director to blame the covens than the records team."

"Are we moving slower than we should be?"

"No. We'll meet the timeline we originally gave. That timeline wasn't good enough, so we shortened it for a new one."

I was confused. "Why give a shorter one that was impossible to meet?"

"The director wasn't going to accept the original timeline, no matter how we explained it to her." She sipped her coffee and smiled weakly. "Better to just give her what she wants and then deal with an extension later. And there was a small chance we could have hit the shorter timeline, so it's not like we were lying."

The mental gymnastics the team was going through made me dizzy. The saddest thing was that they believed it was the best way for them to work and manage the director's expectations.

16

The next day at the Council offices was more of the same. Willow and I worked through the coven's reports. John stopped by just before lunch and told us the new timeline for completion. It was the original timeline that Willow had told me. We were both confident we'd be done by then, if not a few days before.

"Are you working during lunch again?" Willow asked as we neared noon.

"Yeah," I said with some fake disappointment. "This agency project is taking up a lot of my extra time this week."

"That sucks," Willow sympathized. "Hopefully we can have lunch together sometime this week."

I smiled. I really liked Willow and would like to have lunch with her. "I'll try to block out Thursday or Friday for that. I'll let you know."

"That'd be great."

We parted ways at the front entrance of the office building. Willow was going to grab a salad and head back to her desk to catch up on emails, while I was headed back to the apartment to check in with the agency.

I warmed up two pieces of lasagna and set up the laptop at the kitchen counter to join the video call. Cam, Annie, and Jordan were already on and waiting for me.

"Hello," I said cheerfully.

"Hi," Jordan said, matching my tone. "How are you doing?"

"Good, it was a long morning, but I'm excited to hear what updates you all have."

"Cam, do you want to start?" Jordan asked.

"Yes, please," Cam responded. "We were able to go through the files you collected from Willow's computer. There were several interesting projects. Nothing that looks obvious on the surface, but in the last year the records department has done a total recount of all the other-worldly populations."

"So like a census?" I asked. "That doesn't seem so odd."

"It wouldn't be odd if it was the normal census the Council does every ten years," Cam continued. "The last normal census was two years ago. This was like a census on steroids. They were asking some pretty intrusive questions. Especially around specific magical abilities of the witches."

"It's not only the covens that are being audited then?" I asked.

"Right," Jordan replied. "We're not sure what the reasoning is for it, but it could be important."

Cam nodded. "The other files on her computer were some budget-tracking spreadsheets."

"Seems normal, she is a senior clerk on that team and would probably help with budgets," I said in between bites of my lasagna.

"Yes," Cam said. "We had Angela take a look at them. She pointed out that there seems to be a lot of buffer in the budgets for unspecified expenses. She also found some deleted notes on some fields. Willow had some questions about the numbers, and someone named John deleted them with a comment saying that they were 'DCO approved.'"

"John is the head of the records department," I clarified. "And *DCO* is often used as shorthand for *Director Cora Owens*."

Cam smiled. "That's helpful. It does look like Willow only had records-department-related document access," she continued. "Do you think you can access other departments' computers or even a server room?"

"A server room may actually be easier than another computer," I said. "I may be able to find a way to get a look at one."

"That would be great, but don't push it," Cam warned. Everyone else on the call nodded in agreement.

"I'll be careful," I promised. "So, what's going on back home?"

Jordan spoke up first. "We've matched more initials in the book to missing and supposedly dead people."

"A few of them were even cases we worked on," Annie chimed in.

"I also reached out to Sarah," Cam said. "We gave her a list of initials with the werewolf or pack symbols. She recognized one right away. He was a young werewolf who went missing about four years ago. The pack had concluded that he ran away, but the dates match up with what is in the book."

"Did Sarah give any reason for why he may have run away or why he would need to be hidden?" I asked.

"No," Cam replied, shaking her head. "She asked if she could talk to Michael about it, but Helen doesn't want to involve too many people yet."

"At least not until we have more information," Jordan added. "We don't want to put anyone in harm's way."

"Fair," I thought out loud.

"We're going to deep dive into a couple of the cases," Annie said. "We're each taking one to see if we can figure out why they may have needed to be hidden. We'll save one for when you get back next week."

"Thanks." I smiled. "I'd love to help more when I get home."

I managed to eat my lasagna servings during the call. It was almost time to head back to the office, but I still had a few minutes. "Any updates on Doria's case?"

"Not much," Jordan replied, disgruntled. "We were able to talk with Burton again."

"About what?" I asked. Hearing his name again nudged something in my gut.

"We tried to get information about Mr. Gray's schedule."

The nudging was getting stronger.

"Burton wouldn't share any details," Jordan continued. "We didn't stay too long or press him, he seemed like he wasn't feeling well."

Suddenly all I could see was black and I thought I had lost connection to the video until I blinked away the tunnel vision and realized I was seeing a vision. There was a hospital bed surrounded by equipment, but the room didn't look like a hospital.

A man was in the bed. I could see the gray pallor of his skin from where I stood. I took a step forward and the man turned his head. The face was familiar but without hair it took me a moment to recognize Burton. He looked toward me and smiled.

Shocked, I shrank against the wall just in time for another man to enter the room. This man I didn't recognize. He was shorter and good looking, but his face was plastered with concern. He went straight to the bed and held Burton's hand.

They whispered to one another. The man laughed softly at something Burton had said. I strained to hear what they were saying, but the vision pulled away quickly. A whoosh in my ears cleared before I could hear Jordan calling my name.

Jordan leaned toward her screen, concerned. "Linda, where'd you go?"

I shook my head to clear my thoughts. "Sorry, I had a small vision."

"We figured as much," Annie said. "What was it?"

"It was Burton, he was sick," I answered, quickly recapping what I had just seen.

"Any clues on if it was past, present, or future?" Jordan asked.

"No, it was quick and I couldn't tell."

"And you didn't recognize the other person in the room?" Cam asked.

"No."

"Well," Jordan said. "We can let Helen know. Maybe Burton being sick relates to all of this. I'm just not sure how."

"If he's sick," I said slowly, not wanting to lead us down a wrong path, "could Mr. Gray want Doria's painting to help him?"

"That's an interesting theory," Jordan agreed. "I'm not sure how it would work with the painting, but we can ask."

I nodded; it seemed a stretch. "It may have just been that you mentioned he didn't seem well and my vision filled in something." When Jordan gave me an unconvinced look, I tried to change the subject. "Anything else on Doria's case?"

Jordan shook her head. "We are at a bit of a standstill until we can talk to Mr. Gray on Monday. We've been checking in with Doria twice a day. Other than being anxious—"

"Understandable," I said my inner thought out loud and winced at my rude interruption.

Jordan just smiled and nodded at my interruption. "Agreed. Other than that, she says she has noticed a few gray hairs and her smile lines are getting deeper. Helen told her to embrace aging and to be careful of injuries."

"Oh, how did she take that?" I asked.

"Mostly in stride," Jordan said. "But if her painting doesn't get found soon, I think that will change."

"How confident are we that the phoenix has it?" I pressed.

Jordan sighed. "We are looking for other leads, but nothing seems promising. If Monday is a bust, we may be starting back at zero."

"I have a good feeling we'll learn something on Monday," I said.

Annie leaned toward her camera, making her face bigger on the screen. "A *good feeling* or just a good feeling?"

I laughed. "Just a good feeling. But I'll let you all know if I get anything more than that."

We said our goodbyes and hung up the video call. I rinsed off my lunch dishes and put them in the dishwasher. Then I grabbed my bag and headed back toward the cold gray office cubicles of the Council.

THE METAL DETECTOR had stopped stressing me out; it was the fourth time I'd taken the pen through it without incident. I dropped my bag at my desk and headed down to Willow's cubical. My meeting with Cora wasn't until later in the afternoon, so we had time to work together until then.

Willow wasn't at her desk. I waited a few minutes for her, but she didn't show up, which meant she probably had left me a message or email about canceling our work time. I walked back up to my desk and woke up my computer. A message from her was waiting. She had gotten pulled into a meeting about next quarter's projects and would be in that all afternoon.

The only other assignment I had been given for my time at the Council offices was to read through Cora's work-in-progress biography. She was having it compiled by ghostwriters and thought it would be good for me to see the life history of another oracle. I held my tongue and didn't mention that I had lived most of my life with my mom, although I didn't know she was an oracle then.

At first I had been excited about reading the biography, but I quickly realized it was a glossed-over and sensationalized version of events. She had only mentioned her work at the OPT Agency in one paragraph. I knew she had helped found it and spent a significant amount of time there, but a naive reader would think it was just a blip on her journey. The bulk of the book was her childhood and adolescence, and then it skipped right to her time at the Council. There she spelled out in detail how she excelled and grew quickly in the ranks to become director.

Not wanting to read more about that, I decided to wander. I'd avoid the case manager floor. Willow was right; they were mean and not helpful at all when I tried to talk with them in the first week. The technical team was tucked into a far corner of my floor behind a windowed door. They had been nice when they helped set up my computer.

I knocked on their door and tried the handle. It swung open to reveal two techs sitting at their desks.

"Afternoon," the one closest to me called out. "Did you need help with something?"

I thought quickly on my feet and said the first thing that came to mind: "Director Owens has asked me to learn more about all the different departments." A little lie. "I've talked with some of the other ones already." Another little lie. "You were next on my list." A total lie. There was no list.

"Oh." He sounded surprised and a bit delighted. "We're usually not considered our own department, but we're happy to tell you about our work."

The other tech nodded in agreement and motioned to an extra chair behind another desk. I pulled it out and sat down.

"Maybe we can start with introductions. I'm Linda. I'm apprenticing with Director Owens."

They both smiled back. They probably already knew that, but it was not polite to assume you were so important you shouldn't have to introduce yourself.

"I'm Dave," the one who had asked if I needed help said. "I'm the lead IT support tech and a witch. I've worked for the Council for twelve years." He gestured to the other tech.

"I'm Kate. Also a witch. I'm a level-two support tech. I've only worked for the Council for three years."

Dave smiled at her, but Kate looked timid.

"Well"—I smiled at her too—"you've been working with the Council for way longer than I have and can probably help me learn a few things."

"Sure." She finally smiled back. "What do you want to learn?"

"First," I said and opened my notebook to start taking notes, "what is the IT support team responsible for?"

Dave motioned for Kate to answer. She cleared her throat and said, "We make sure that all the computers are set up correctly and help anyone who has a problem. We are also responsible for all the phones and meeting systems in the conference rooms."

She paused, so I asked, "Do you manage the security for the computers and data?"

"No," Dave said quickly. "That's owned by the security team. That team is also responsible for the physical security of the building like the metal detectors and monitoring system."

"Oh, that makes sense," I said as neutrally as possible. I paused. I hadn't actually prepared any questions to ask them.

Dave filled the silence. "We also manage the maintenance of the server rooms. That takes up a lot of our time. They have to be constantly monitored, and updates are really time-consuming when they are needed."

"Server rooms," I reiterated. "We have more than one?"

"Yes," Dave answered. "There are three in this building. One on each floor. The one for this floor is through that door. It's the biggest one, which is why our office is here."

I looked at the door he pointed to. It was a solid wood door with a number keypad next to it. It was likely kept locked, and needed the right code to get into it. I quickly glanced at the ceiling: no domed spy camera above the door.

"That's so cool," I said with real interest, just not the interest they would have thought. "Can I see it?"

Dave and Kate exchanged looks.

"Normally, we aren't supposed to," Dave said slowly. "But you are working directly with Director Owens, so it's probably okay."

He stood up and walked over to the door. I followed him. Kate gave me a quick smile and then turned back to her computer. Dave punched in the code. It was six digits, and I saw every number. I worked hard not to smile while I repeated the number sequence in my head.

Dave swung the door open and held it for me to enter first. The room was about twice as big as the small office space that Dave and Kate worked in. Racks of black boxes with blinking lights filled six rows, floor to ceiling. Cables were wrapped together with zip ties and hung between the boxes on the back of each row. It was noticeably colder in that room. Fans muffled the noise of our footsteps as we walked through on the concrete floor.

"This is really organized," I complimented Dave.

"Thank you," he said. "We do our best."

"So this would hold a third of the Council's data?" I asked, trying to sound curious but not overly pushy.

"No," he responded. "This actually holds all of it. We have a redundant system. The other floor's data rooms hold specific departments' data, but it all gets backed up here nightly. That way, if something goes wrong with one server, we don't lose the data."

"That's really smart," I complimented again.

"Thank you," he said and gestured to the door.

I followed him out of the room and back into the office space.

"Anything else we can help you with?" he asked.

"No," I said sincerely. "You've both been really helpful."

"Well, if you do ever need anything, you know where to find us."

"Thank you," I said and left their office space.

THE REST of the afternoon was boring. I walked around the office more but eventually sat down at my desk to read more of Cora's book to pass the time. On a whim, I used the pen to get the data off my computer. It would just be a few notes I had taken and a copy of the world's most boring book, probably not helpful.

My afternoon meeting with Cora was also boring. Angela would have loved it. The meeting was a financial review for the last quarter and a look at next quarter's budget requests. The head of finance passed around a printed packet of information that she'd be reviewing to Director Owens and the heads of departments that were there. She was nice enough to have one for me, even though the light shrank around her and she scowled at me a bit when she handed it over.

I made some notes on it as the meeting progressed. At the end, when we were gathering our things, the head of finance grabbed my packet of papers from in front of me.

Cora must have caught my confusion. "We don't allow

the financial reports out of the meeting. It's sensitive information."

"Oh," I said, trying to sound okay with it. "That makes sense."

The only person allowed to keep their packet was Cora, I guessed because she was the director.

Like normal I waited in my seat after everyone got up to leave the meeting. The head of finance and Cora stood at the door momentarily. I tried not to look like I was listening.

"When will the B report be ready?" Director Owens questioned.

"I'm having some trouble tracking down a few expenses," the head of finance said.

"Just send over what you have already completed," Cora demanded. "I'll review it and let you know if it's acceptable or not."

"I'll send that right over," she said and left quickly.

Director Owens walked back toward the table and offhandedly said, "It's so hard to find good finance people. She is my eighth head of finance in the last nine years."

"That must be hard." I tried to sound sympathetic.

"It is," she said dramatically. "Luckily, I'm good with numbers, so it hasn't been too disruptive."

She then proceeded to ask me questions about the meeting to see if I had been paying attention. I was able to answer them all and not look bored.

∽

THE FACADE I kept in the Council offices took a lot of effort and it was catching up with me. By the time I made it back to the apartment that night, I was exhausted. Jordan was my check-in person, and she noticed.

"Are you getting enough sleep?" she pressed as soon as we said hello.

"I think so," I said vaguely. I didn't want Jordan worrying about me.

"If you are still feeling tired tomorrow, we can do a checkup as soon as you get back," she offered.

I knew better than to disagree. "That'd be fine. How is Doria's case going?"

Jordan frowned at the change in topics; she knew what I was doing, but she let me get away with it. "I followed up on Burton's illness. I couldn't find any medical records locally. So I'm thinking it's either a future illness or it didn't happen around here."

"But you think it's related to the case?"

"We do, just not sure how yet. It's something we'll ask about when we interview them both on Monday."

"Alright, I'll try not to worry about it," I said. It was a lie; I would worry about it until I understood how it was related.

Jordan nodded and asked, "Any updates from your end?"

"A couple," I replied, happy to report on my progress. "I downloaded the data from my computer. I'll upload it after this call, and Cam should be able to access it. I don't think it will be that helpful."

"That's good," Jordan said. "Any data is good for us to have."

I decided not to tell them it would include Director Owens's work-in-progress biography. That could be a fun surprise for them to discover.

"Why the smile?" Jordan said with a laugh.

"No reason," I said quickly. "Well, you'll see when you see the data from today."

"Okay," she said slowly but didn't press me to clarify.

"Also," I said. "I found the main server room and learned the code for the door."

"That's good," Jordan said.

"It's going to be tricky getting to it without being noticed, but I'll figure something out."

"Just be careful," she said.

I'd heard that phrase more times than I cared for recently, but I knew it came from a good place, so I said what she wanted to hear: "I will, I promise."

I went to sleep that night running through scenarios in my head of how I could get into the server room. None of them worked out before I drifted off.

17

Aping from my phone woke me up before my alarm. I rubbed the sleep out of my eyes and nearly dropped the phone on my head when I saw Helen's message to contact her as soon as possible.

It took me two minutes to throw on a sweatshirt and open my laptop to message her. She quickly replied with a link to join a video call. As it connected, I ran a hand through my hair like it would actually do anything to make me look presentable.

"Good morning, Linda," Helen said. "Sorry to get you on a call so early, but we wanted to share some information we just learned."

The *we* from Helen's introduction turned out to be Jordan and Steve on the call as well. Their boxes also showed that they were in the office. It was either a really long night or an early morning for them.

"Morning," I replied, my voice cracking a bit with the

first words since waking. "It's not a problem. What's the news?"

"We got your message about Rachel not being listed with the Seattle coven, so we reached out to see if the coven knew what was going on," Helen said calmly.

"That's good. What did they say?" I asked.

"They said the Council told them that Rachel had requested to be in a new coven, so the Council helped to move her," she replied.

"I don't understand. Is that normal?"

Helen sighed. "This is the first time I've heard of this happening. And the coven was surprised about it as well."

"We also called Rachel's mom, Elsbeth, last night," Jordan added. "She hasn't heard from Rachel in months."

Helen looked grim. "We think Rachel is missing. We wanted you to be aware of this so you could look out for her name in other coven records."

"I haven't seen her name in any other records, I think," I said and racked my brain to think through them. Everyone on the call gave me a moment. "I'm pretty sure I haven't seen it."

"That's okay, keep your eyes open for it," Helen said. "And we'll look for her name in any documents you sent over from Willow's computer."

"I don't think Willow's computer would have the witches that aren't in a coven." I tried to remember what Willow had said about them. "I know we won't be reviewing those, so I'm not sure why she would have had them."

"That's alright, we'll keep digging on our side," Helen reassured me.

"I should have some more data for us today," I said. That settled it in my mind. Though I wasn't sure how I would do it, I would get into the server room.

EVEN THOUGH I was up early, I took my time getting ready and arrived at the office at the normal time. I had gone in early once and discovered nobody else was there. Everyone arrived on time and left as soon as five o'clock hit unless told they had to stay late.

I dropped my bag off at my desk and quickly checked my calendar. It was like almost every day there: working on projects in the morning and shadowing Director Owens in a meeting or two in the afternoon.

On my way to Willow's desk, I stopped by the break room and grabbed the trail mix she often snacked on. As I walked into her cubicle, she turned her chair toward me and said, "Good morning. How was your night?"

"Morning." I kept my tone cheerful and put the trail mix down by her. "I had a good night," I lied.

"Are you feeling okay?" Willow asked.

"Yes," I replied to the strange question.

"Oh good." She sighed with relief. "Apparently, there is a stomach bug going around. Almost half the office is out today."

"It did look like there were fewer people around. I

thought folks were just running late with traffic or something."

"Nope, they are all sick," she said. "Or they heard about it and decided to use it as an excuse to take a sick day."

"Are you feeling okay?" I asked, worried about her and not wanting to get sick myself.

"Yes." She laughed and pointed to a bottle on the desk. "But I did grab some hand sanitizer from the break room. I'd recommend using it frequently today."

"I will."

We got to work after that. It was routine enough at that point that my mind could wander. I had an idea of how to get into the server room that had kept coming up as I thought through it the night before. There was just one problem I couldn't get past, but with half the office out, the chances that it would work were higher.

About an hour into the reports and spreadsheets, I stretched and forced a yawn. "I'm going to go grab some coffee. Do you want some?"

"That would be great," Willow replied. "I'll double-check our totals while you are grabbing it. Unless you need my help?"

"I can get it," I reassured her. "You do the totals."

I overfilled both coffee mugs and carefully walked back to her desk. Willow was concentrating on the screen in front of her. Just inside the cubicle, I bumped into the side of the entryway and lurched forward. One of the mugs of coffee spilled over the computer tower for Willow's computer. The other one, the one I had carefully added cold water to, splashed down the front of my shirt.

"Oh no," I gasped.

Willow shot up and looked at me, horrified. I had dropped both mugs and was holding my shirt away from my skin.

"Oh my god," Willow exclaimed. "Are you okay?"

"Yes, I think so," I said quickly. I didn't want her to worry about me. "But I think I spilled on your computer too. I'm so sorry."

"That's alright,' she said. "I'll go see if Dave or Kate are around to look at it. You go clean up in the bathroom."

I smiled my thanks and hurried off toward the bathroom. Willow walked behind me toward the IT office, which was in the same direction.

"Are you sure you are okay?" she asked before we split off to our different destinations.

"Yes," I said, "I think there was enough cream in it to cool it down a bit."

Willow smiled with relief. "Oh good."

She continued on to get help for the computer, and I ducked into the bathroom. Fortunately, no one was in there; I quickly cleaned up a bit and counted in my head. I figured Willow would take only a few minutes to get their attention and head back to the desk. If I was lucky, either Dave or Kate, or both of them, would be out sick.

I pressed my ear against the bathroom door and listened. A few moments later, two sets of footsteps walked past in a hurry. I counted to sixty in my head to make sure they were out of view of the bathroom.

I left the bathroom and walked as quickly and quietly as I could to the IT office. Over and over in my head, I rehearsed what I would say if someone was still in there: *I'm looking for Willow.*

The door was closed. I knocked lightly as I opened it. The office was empty, and the door to the server room was closed. I scanned the ceiling to see if there were any cameras in the room. There weren't, just the one right outside the office door to their space.

I closed the office door behind me and walked over to the door with the keypad. The code had been seared into my brain from the repetition. I entered the six-digit code and held my breath until the red light turned to green. Something clicked, and I pushed the door open and let it close behind me.

My still-wet shirt and the cold air in the server room left me shivering, but it counteracted the hot sweat of nerves pooling in my armpits and under my bra. I pulled out the pen that had been in my pocket all morning and went to the nearest bundle of cables. Cam and I had practiced this part over and over again, but it was harder to do with cold and sweaty palms.

I pushed some zip ties apart to make a space where I could somewhat separate the cables. The one that would most likely be a data cable was in the middle. The pen lid punctured a small hole in the protective outside quickly, and I shoved the tip of the pen in and started to count in my head.

I strained to hear a noise outside the door. It was nearly impossible to hear anything over the sound of my racing heart and the fans in the server room. Not being able to rely on any sound to alert me, I decided to count to three hundred and then leave. That was enough time to fill the pen's storage. We wouldn't get everything—it was magic, but it couldn't hold a server room's worth of data—but we'd get something.

My count was at one hundred and seventy when I heard something big hit a desk outside in the office. I held my breath to try to hear more. There were some rummaging sounds and then a door closing loudly. Someone must have come back to grab something from the office, and hopefully they left again.

I finished my count, pulled the pen out from the cables, and pushed the zip ties back to where they had been. The cable with the hole in it was tucked back in the middle of the set where no one would notice it had been tampered with.

I froze at the door. That was the part that had always gone wrong when I played out the scenarios in my head. If there was anyone in the room past the door, I had no way to explain what I was doing and how I had gotten into the server room.

I turned the handle and waited for any sounds in the room. Nothing.

Trying not to make any noise, I opened the door a crack and listened.

Nothing.

I pushed the door open just enough to quickly slide out of the room and closed it behind me. My eyes swept the space. It was empty.

Realizing I was holding the pen out in front of me like a weapon, I shoved it back into my pocket, grabbed an extra keyboard from the shelf, and left the IT office. I needed anyone watching the camera outside the office door to think that the keyboard was why I went into that room.

I slowly walked back to the cubicle to give my heart some time to slow down. Kate and Willow were standing in the entryway to the cubicle.

"Linda," Willow called out when she saw me.

I held out the keyboard in front of me. "I grabbed a keyboard in case I also spilled on that."

"Oh, we won't need that," Kate said, and she took it to take back to the IT office. "You should be all set. But let me know if you notice anything."

"Thanks, Kate," Willow called out as Kate walked away from the cubicle.

"I'm glad I didn't break everything," I said sincerely.

"It looks like you were able to get cleaned up a bit," Willow said with a smile.

I had purposefully worn dark clothes that day, so I looked okay even though the cleanup was hasty. "I'll probably smell like coffee for the rest of the morning," I joked. "But I can change at lunchtime." I looked contrite. "How is the computer? Did I break it?"

Willow smiled. "No," she replied. "Kate was able to help me clean it up. We got most of the liquid quickly, and then she got an air canister and was able to spray off everything. Good as new."

"That's good," I said, truly relieved. I didn't want to break the computer, just buy myself some time.

"Yeah, it's a good thing," Willow said. "Dave is one of the

people out sick today, and he's the only one who could have gotten us a new computer if we needed it."

BACK AT THE apartment during the lunch break, the video call connected quickly and Cam's face filled the screen. I had already docked the pen and started downloading data from it. The call needed to be quick, and I needed a shower to get the leftover coffee residue off my skin.

"Hey, Linda," Cam answered. "You look happy."

"Happy and a bit sticky," I responded.

"What?"

"It's a long story," I replied quickly. "But first, I started a download of data. I was able to get into the server room. Not sure what I got, hopefully it's good."

"Wow, that's amazing." Cam's eyes went to the side, where I knew she had another screen. The click of her keys filled the speakers, and I used the pause to take a drink of water. Cam's eyes returned to the video call. "This is a lot of data. I won't know until we dig into it, but I have a good feeling that there will be something useful."

"Oh good." I sighed with relief.

"Makes sense why you are happy," Cam said, leaning in, "but why are you sticky?"

"I spilled coffee all over myself and a computer to get a chance at the server room," I said. "I guess it isn't a long story."

Cam laughed. "Not long, but good."

"I'll need to make this call shorter today to have time to shower."

"Sure, sure." Cam was distracted. I could tell she was looking at the files that were uploading to her computer. "Linda, you are amazing," she exclaimed.

"What did I do?"

"It isn't all the data, there's no way that the pen has enough capacity for that, but you were able to snag an index."

"What's an index?" I asked. "Like for a book?"

"Kind of. Someone must have created an index file to help speed up queries of the data stored in the internal network. So it shows all the files they have but not what is in them."

"Is that useful?" I asked, still unsure.

"It will be really useful," Cam reassured excitedly. "It looks like there is also some permission management in the index, so we can see who has access to what."

"That could help us target the most restricted files." I was finally catching on.

"Exactly. Now that I know how their access management is set up, I may be able to update the software on the pen to target file downloads based on access."

"I'm not sure I'll be able to get back into the server room," I cautioned.

"You could try any computer with this," Cam said with a smile. "If I can figure it out, we'll be able to bypass the restrictions and get to the files we want. You'll probably be able to do this from your own computer station."

"That would be great."

"Let me work on this for a bit," Cam said, already typing away. "Leave the pen docked, go take a shower, and I'll let you know if I'm done when you get back."

I said goodbye, closed the video call, and hurried to the bathroom. A quick shower and change of clothes made me feel back to normal, and it also helped wash away some of the nervous sweat. I took the soiled clotnes along with my other dirty clothes and started a load of laundry. Normally I'd wait and do laundry from the week at home, but I wasn't going to take coffee-stained clothes home.

It hadn't taken me too long, so I pulled a premade salad from the fridge and made a cup of tea. With lunch in front of me, I connected to the same video call. Cam was still on. I saw the side of her head and watched her profile as she typed and talked to herself.

"I'm back," I called out after she didn't notice I had rejoined the call.

"Good timing," she said and turned toward me. "I think I've got the programming updated. It should work from your computer and target the files restricted to the director and up to two other people. I'm hoping those are the important files."

"That makes sense," I said after swallowing a bite of my salad. "She likes to silo information, so stuff that's important wouldn't be widely shared."

"That's what I thought too," Cam agreed. "Also, I cleared out as much space as I could, but it may take a few times to get all the files. I'll narrow the targeting parameters after each set so we don't get repeats."

I thought through the rest of the week. "I'll only have three more chances to get data this week."

Cam sighed. "That's right, it's already Thursday. This week has flown by."

I sighed for a different reason. The week had dragged by for me. The weeks always felt longer when I was at the Council offices.

"That will be okay," Cam said. "I'll get the others to help me look through file names this afternoon, and we'll see if there are any specific ones we want to target. And if we don't get them all, there is always next month."

"Right." I didn't tell her that I was secretly hoping I wouldn't have to come back. If I could get the information we needed, then Helen could do something, and I could stop pretending to care about what Cora was trying to teach me. Although I would miss hanging out with Willow.

THE AFTERNOON WAS LESS stressful than the morning. I got back to the office before lunch was technically over. That plus the stomach bug that had taken out half the office meant that there was only one other person on my floor, and they were on the other side.

I used the opportunity to plug the pen into my computer port and download whatever it could. When that was done, I sat and thought through what I knew so far. I didn't dare write it down, even on paper, but I could organize my thoughts in my head.

First, I knew that I could get data from the server room if I could get in there again. Second, Rachel was missing, and I was pretty sure that the director had something to do with that.

There was a third something that tickled my head, something that felt off, but I couldn't put words to it yet. I thought back through conversations and meetings from the week. Then it hit me: the finance stuff. I could hear Angela's voice in my head telling me to follow the money.

The meeting with the head of finance had been the strangest of all the meetings I shadowed that week. They were so precious about the printouts and the information shared. The director had asked about a report that wasn't shared after the meeting had ended and everyone else had left. She also mentioned that the current head of finance was her eighth one in nine years. Even if Cora was terrible to work for—and I didn't doubt that she was—that still seemed like too high of a turnover. Something was going on with the finances of this place.

I didn't dare text Cam or anyone at the agency to guide them in the right direction for their search that afternoon. I bet they had already thought of looking for financial documents.

My shadow meeting with Cora was canceled about five minutes before we were due to meet. Almost all of the attendees were out sick, and from the sound of her email, she was not happy about it. Instead I spent the rest of the day working with Willow. She was happy to see me and had coffee waiting for me in a paper cup with a lid and a smiley face drawn on the side in marker.

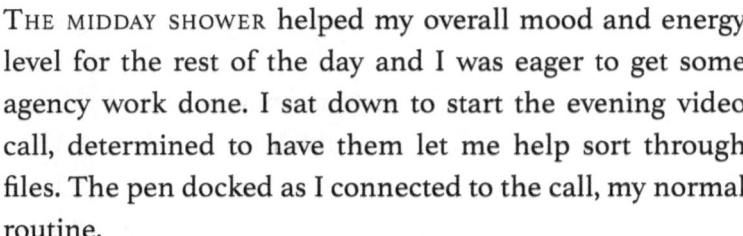

THE MIDDAY SHOWER helped my overall mood and energy level for the rest of the day and I was eager to get some agency work done. I sat down to start the evening video call, determined to have them let me help sort through files. The pen docked as I connected to the call, my normal routine.

Cam, Helen, and Jordan all joined the call that night.

"How was your day?" Helen started.

"Good," I replied. "Based on the smiles, I'm guessing Cam told you about my antics today."

"She did." Helen smiled. "It was a smart plan, and it clearly worked out."

"I'd say," Cam said. Her face was in profile as she typed and looked at her other screen.

"Anything good?" I asked.

"It looks like we got most of the files with the highest level of restrictions," Cam answered. "It will take us a while to go through them, but we've got a list of keywords and names now that we can search by."

"Sarah was able to confirm a few more names of missing or reported-dead werewolves for us," Jordan added.

Cam had her head tilted down, but I saw the subtle smile. She was still head over heels for her new girlfriend. Even the mention of her name made her smile. It was adorable.

"That's good," I said. "Any chance we got any of the financial reports?"

"Give me a second," Cam said. Typing sounds filled the space as we all waited for her. "Yep. We've got some, but I can't tell how complete they are. Angela could probably tell us if anything is missing."

The nagging thought from earlier was still there. "Have her check for financial records that have anything to do with B reports."

"Bee reports?" Helen asked.

"B, like the letter, I think," I confirmed. "It was something Cora asked the head of finance about. It seemed a bit secretive."

"Okay," Helen said. "We'll look for that. Anything else?"

"Not from my side," I answered. "Any updates on Doria's case or from the office?"

Jordan grimaced, and Helen didn't look happy either. Helen answered, "Doria cut her hand pretty badly this afternoon."

"Oh no."

Jordan shook her head and said, "I went and helped her. The cut needed stitches, and she was not as good a patient as you are."

I laughed at the inside joke. Jordan had patched me up a couple of times. I knew I wasn't a good patient, so Doria must have had a really hard time.

"She isn't used to dealing with injuries like that," Jordan said.

Helen added, "Understandably, she is now getting more anxious about the recovery of her painting."

"The cut should heal just fine," Jordan interrupted. "She probably won't even have a scar."

"I know," Helen said. Based on the tone of their exchange, they had already had this conversation. "You did great work, but like you said, this is new for her."

Jordan nodded and smiled weakly.

"You still think Mr. Gray may have it?" I asked to get us back on topic.

"Yes," Helen said. "I'm also confident that as long as we can speak with him on Monday, we should recover the painting."

"Why not just go search the house again with more people and take it back?" I asked.

Helen smiled softly. "I think the diplomatic approach would be better in this situation."

My checks went a bit red in embarrassment. I should have known that was how Helen would handle things. Maybe Cora's approach was rubbing off on me. That wasn't good.

"Well," Helen said and clapped her hands, "we have a lot of files to look through, and you have a long day tomorrow with your flight home in the evening."

Everyone nodded in agreement. We wrapped up the call, said goodbyes, and hung up for the night. Cam had promised to message me in the morning before I went into the office with any updates on the pen's programming. I slept more easily that night, knowing I would just need to have time alone in my own cubicle to get the data we needed. It's a good thing I didn't know what was coming.

18

F riday was my last day at the Council offices for another three weeks. Or, hopefully, forever. After work, I'd take the agency's jet back to Seattle and sleep in my own bed. That was the good news. The bad news was that I only had two more chances to get data from the office computers. I hoped it would be enough

I got into the office a bit earlier than normal so that it would be mostly empty. At my desk I quickly loaded up the pen with data from my own computer. Cam had let me know that morning that she had reprogrammed it to target the remaining restricted files and then fill up any additional storage with anything related to financial records.

My eyes and ears stayed glued to the entrance of my cubicle. I still hadn't come up with a good reason to explain why a pen was sticking out of my computer if someone saw it there. Luckily the floor remained mostly empty.

The morning dragged by. Willow and I were able to get through more of the coven records. Knowing that not every witch was represented in them, I started to notice the lack of any of the more dangerous abilities like shapeshifting. I made a mental note to bring that up with the team back in Seattle.

Eventually, it was lunchtime. I made another excuse to Willow for why I couldn't eat lunch with her. It made me sad to see her face drop, but I had to stop back by the apartment to clear out the data from the pen.

The pen was docked and downloaded. I connected to the video call and turned the laptop toward the kitchen so I could see it while I gathered some lunch.

"Hey, Linda," Cam called out.

I spun around from the open fridge. "Hey. Anyone else joining us today?"

"Yes," Cam said, already typing on her computer. "I know for sure Jordan and Angela. I think Helen was going to try to join too."

"That's good," I replied offhandedly and put some bread into the toaster. My stomach was gurgling and nothing sounded good. Toast with honey was a safe comfort food. Once I got that in my stomach, other food would sound more appealing.

Three other boxes joined the video screen before the toast popped.

"Good afternoon," Helen said neutrally.

Something was up.

"Afternoon," I replied and then waited for her to continue.

She started right in: "We were able to review the files you've gathered so far."

"That's good," I said, putting the toast on a plate and sitting down at the counter.

"Yes," Helen agreed. "For the most part, it is what we expected. We found several financial reports."

Angela smiled. "You were right about there being another set of reports. It looks like they have been keeping two sets of books. That's never a good thing."

"That's good for us, though," I countered as I spread a thick layer of honey on my toast. "If she has been mismanaging Council money, then that could be enough to get her in trouble with the Council Forum that she reports to."

"That's what I'll be looking for," Angela agreed.

"Right," Helen said, pausing to take a breath. "There was one file that we think must have had the wrong access permissions."

"What do you mean?" I asked and took a bite of toast. Usually Helen wasn't so cryptic.

"It was another index file. A list of names."

Helen's eyes swept around, looking at the faces in all the other boxes. I did too. They all looked grim. I kept eating, willing the toast to soothe the pit in my stomach.

She continued, "We were able to cross-match several of the names to people's initials in the Moonstone Haven book."

"That's good," I said, confused as to why everyone was so grim about it. This was the connection we needed.

Helen nodded. "There were a lot of names we recognized. And your mom's name was on that list."

I paused with my last bite of toast halfway to my mouth. It shouldn't have surprised me to find my mom's name in Council files. She was probably a registered oracle, and I had hoped to find information about her murder. However, actually hearing that we found her name made it real.

"Okay," I said slowly. "What does it say about her?"

"It doesn't say anything," Helen said, shaking her head slightly.

"It's an index file," Cam said softly. "Like the other one we found, it means that it was created to help someone easily search and return other documents."

"Then what do those other documents say?" I demanded with more attitude than the team deserved.

Helen leaned toward her camera, filling the screen more, and gently said, "We don't have those documents."

I sighed. "Right."

We were so close to some answers. It was almost more deflating to get so close than not finding anything at all.

"I still have one more chance to get files." I perked up. "Cam, can you target those files?"

"I can," Cam hesitated. "But I'm worried that they won't be on the server."

"Where would they be then?" I asked nicely that time.

Helen cleared her throat. "We think they are on Cora's computer."

"The index file points to two locations," Cam explained more. "One of them is the internal network, the servers that we've been accessing so far. The other is an acronym, *DCO*."

"Director Cora Owens," I interrupted.

"Exactly," Cam said. "If it's the same acronym that was used on the budget spreadsheets, it means they are probably on her computer."

"So I need to get to the director's computer this afternoon," I thought out loud.

Everyone was quiet. Their faces told me that they agreed but also that they were worried.

"We'll need to try to get to Cora's computer eventually," Helen said. "But you don't have to do it today or ever. We can find a way for me to get into her office and retrieve the information."

"But that could take weeks or months," I said, the frustration leaking through. I didn't want to wait that long or have to come back to the office.

"Better that it takes more time than you risk your safety," Helen said sternly. "I don't want you to try anything rash."

Everyone on the call nodded along with her instructions.

Helen continued, "We have to deliver the detailed report for the pack insurance case. I was going to just send it over in an email, but I think we can come up with an excuse for me to deliver it in person."

"That makes sense," I agreed, but I was still wondering how I could get to Cora's computer that day.

Helen must have read my mind, or my face betrayed me like it often did. "Linda, I need you to agree to not try to get the data from her computer today."

I nodded.

"We'll find a way to get it soon," she continued.

I nodded again.

"Linda?" Helen pressed.

"I agree," I said as convincingly as I could muster. "I won't try to get the data today."

THE TOAST ENDED up being my only lunch. After we hung up the call, I paced around the apartment a bit and then sat down at my laptop and looked at the most recent files. The financial records looked interesting, but I couldn't make sense of them. I had hoped for an obvious answer. At least we had Angela on our team. She'd find something.

The microwave clock finally said it was time to head back to the office. Before I undocked the pen, I checked Cam's message to make sure it was cleared and updated. It was ready to go. I shoved that and my notebook into my work bag and headed back to the office.

I was supposed to shadow another meeting that day, but half the staff was still out with the stomach virus. I'd likely get back and see a message that it was canceled. It was going to be a long afternoon, and I was grumpy.

A head with a slick blonde ponytail was peeking above my cubicle wall. I knew that ponytail; it belonged to Cora.

"Linda." She sounded a bit startled and turned my way as I walked into view. "I was just coming to find you."

I never left anything important at my desk, but a few papers had clearly been rummaged through. "Oh," I said, not giving away that I noticed anything strange. "Sorry, I'm just getting back from lunch."

"That's alright," she replied. "I wanted to let you know that the scheduled meeting is canceled."

I nodded. It was what I had expected, although it was strange for her to come to tell me in person.

"But," she continued in her fake sweet voice, "I was thinking we could use that time to talk about oracle stuff."

"That'd be good," I agreed and plastered a smile on my face.

"Great, come to my office once you've settled your things." She awkwardly patted my shoulder as she scooted past me to exit my cubicle.

Several deep breaths helped settle my nerves from the unexpected encounter. I set my bag in the bottom desk drawer, grabbed my notebook and the pen, and headed to Cora's office.

"I'm sure my biography has helped you learn a lot about a more traditional upbringing for an oracle where training is started at a young age if you have the potential," Cora started off with a not-so-subtle dig at me and my mom.

I shifted in the hard chair in front of her desk but worked to not let my anger show on my face. "It has been helpful," I lied.

"So, what questions do you have for me?" she asked.

I had not prepared any questions. My mind scrambled

through the ones that I really wanted to ask and landed on a safe option. "Can you tell me more about when you first started getting visions?" I asked, mirroring her overly sweet, *we're best friends* tone.

She leaned back in her chair and smiled. "Of course. I can see why that would be interesting to you."

I nodded.

"Like all oracles, I started to receive my visions around my mid-twenties," she said. "Although, I was a bit earlier than most. My first one was just after my twenty-third birthday."

She continued the story that I already knew from her book: There was a party that she was attending, and a few of the expected guests hadn't made it yet. She was worried about them and thinking about one of the guests in particular. Her vision blacked out—we had that in common—and she fainted. (I didn't faint. Point in my favor.) When she came to, she recounted what she had seen: about a mile down the road, there was a car accident with the guests. Several people left in cars to check it out. They found the accident and were able to help the people involved.

"At least two of the victims likely wouldn't be alive today if I hadn't sent help to them so quickly," Cora finished the story.

"That's amazing," I stroked her ego. "Have your visions continued that same pattern?"

"Saving lives?" she asked with a laugh.

"Sorry," I said, my cheeks going red. "I mean the blacking out and fainting."

Cora narrowed her eyes. "I can control when I have visions, so I make sure that I'm in a secure location to receive what I need to know."

She didn't really answer my question, but I didn't press her on it.

"Are most oracles able to control their visions?" I asked, changing the topic slightly.

We had danced around this question when we first started talking. Cora had asked me what I did to prepare for visions. I told her that they just came when they wanted to, so there wasn't much preparation. She looked shocked and told me that we'd work on control.

Cora squinted, considering my question. "The ones that aren't dangerous do," she said at last, with a hint of anger in her voice.

I took a deep breath and considered what to ask next. I wanted to steer clear of that conversation.

My vision started to tunnel, and I felt the pull in my gut that signaled an oncoming vision. I pushed back on it. I hadn't had a vision in front of Cora yet, and I didn't ever want to. However, as much as I pushed against it, the vision was coming whether I wanted it to or not.

I snapped into a cold building. There was a desk in front of me, like a hotel reception but not warm and welcoming. An unhappy-looking woman stood over a keyboard and hunched to look at the screen in front of her. Everything was white and gray. The floor was concrete. The cold from it seeped through my shoes. Footsteps from the left drew my attention, and I watched a man all in white and wearing a name tag walk down the hall.

He walked right past without giving me a glance. I let out the breath I was holding. The woman at the desk looked up at him.

"It took you long enough." She scowled. "We have a new one coming any minute for intake."

"I know, I know," he said back to her, matching her energy. "I'm here now, and they aren't, so it's fine."

The sound of a car pulling up made me turn. Two solid-looking doors with thick glass took up most of the wall. Outside the windows, I saw a black SUV with tinted windows pull up and stop. Two men dressed in black suits exited from the front seats. The men weren't familiar, but the suits they wore were. I'd seen those uniform-like suits in visions and when they came to the agency's office to take away Rachel five months before.

I was torn between watching the woman and the man now behind me and the scene that was happening by the car. I kept watching the car but felt like the two people were drilling holes through my back with their eyes. One of the black-suited men opened the back passenger-side door. He was blocking my view of who was back there. He seemed to be struggling with someone. After a few moments of struggle, he pulled a passenger out of the car and stood them up in front of him as he gripped their arm.

The passenger looked like she had been taken from her bed. She wore sweats, a T-shirt, and no shoes. Her long hair hung over her face, and her hands were bound in front of her. She swung her head up, clearing her hair from her face, and I locked eyes with Sarah.

I gasped and double-checked. That was Sarah, a

member of the Northeast pack and Cam's girlfriend. She looked away from me without any sign that she had seen me. I had to remind myself that it was a vision, and so far, the only person I thought had been able to tell I was present in their reality was my mom.

My eyes continued to be fixed on Sarah as the two men flanked her and guided her to the double doors. She had a cut on her left cheek, and her knuckles looked roughed up. She also had a large metallic collar around her neck. Dark red runes etched into the side of it seemed to glow. It felt evil. I wanted to rip it off Sarah's neck.

The doors swung open and startled me. I felt the whoosh of the vision ending. The pressure of the chair under me and the sound of Cora tapping her pencil brought me back to the present.

Cora's voice pierced the silence. "You finally had a vision."

I needed to think fast. I couldn't tell her what I had seen. I needed to buy some time to think through a plausible story.

My head was still down. I forced myself to breathe heavily and begged my skin to look pale. Slowly, I raised my head and tried to look as tired and haggard as possible.

Cora recoiled. "Are you okay?"

"No," I squeaked out in a whisper. "Do you have any water or a banana or something?"

Cora looked around, panicked, then walked over and opened the door. "Beth, I need you!" Then, "Shit," she mumbled, "Beth is still out sick."

She looked back at me. I tried to look even more pathetic.

"Shit," she said again. "I'll be right back."

She left and must have closed the door out of habit. I perked up and took my chance, even though I had promised Helen I wouldn't try anything. I could come up with an excuse. Right then, I had to see if I could get anything from Cora's computer.

Quicker than I thought possible, I was kneeling behind her desk and had the pen inserted into the port of her computer tower. My heart was pounding, and I tried to breathe quietly so I could hear footsteps outside the door. I counted in my head and tried to map out how far the break room was.

I didn't count well enough.

The door started to open. I yanked the pen out of the computer and flung myself around the desk as close to the chair as I could get. Sprawled out on the floor, I was hoping that it looked like I had fainted and fallen out of the chair.

"Shit, Linda," Cora called out when she saw me.

I sat up and shook my head. "Sorry, I'm okay."

"Are you sure?" she asked and passed me a mostly brown banana.

I took the too-ripe banana that I would have to eat and got back into my chair. "Yes, I just need a moment."

"Does this always happen?" she pressed and made her way around the desk to her chair.

"It's not always this bad," I said and then lied, "but I skipped breakfast this morning."

I would never skip breakfast. At least not anymore. Mrs. Clark would have strong words with me if she found out I was doing that.

Cora gave me a condescending look. "And that is why you need to learn control."

19

I kept the pen in the front pocket of my work bag. My hand kept going to it as I walked out of the Council's office building for hopefully the last time. The air had turned chilly, and the city was quieter than usual. Everyone seemed to walk with their heads down, hurrying to warmer places to escape into.

My warmer place would be Seattle. In less than six hours, I'd be home. First, I had to get my suitcase from the apartment and call the driver for a ride to the airport. That would have to wait five minutes so I could dock the pen and download the data. I texted Cam to let her know I'd be sending it. I didn't tell her what computer the data had come from. She'd probably figure it out.

The suitcase was packed and by the door. Sheets and towels were in the washer. Mrs. Clark's friend, who stocked the fridge and pantry for me, would come by and clean the apartment, readying it for the next person who needed to use it.

I received a text from the driver saying they were downstairs. Within ten minutes we were on our way to the airport. My work bag, with the pen in the front pocket, was on the floor by my feet. I didn't want to risk losing it, just in case it hadn't downloaded properly.

I got a text from Cam just before the plane took off.

Cam: I got all the files you downloaded

Me: good, have you had a chance to look at any of them

Cam: yes

The three dots of Cam's typing showed on the screen. I needed her to text faster. They wouldn't make me turn off my phone for takeoff, one of the perks of a private plane, but I would eventually lose service and the Wi-Fi was a bit spotty.

Cam: there is a lot of information

Cam: where did you get these

Me: don't be angry

Cam: no promises

Me: I had a chance at Cora's computer, so I took it

The three dots again. I bit my lip, anxious about her response.

Cam: I'm glad you did

Cam: but you are going to have to explain what happened to Helen

Me: do you think she'll be upset with me

Cam: maybe, but not for long, just be honest with her

Me: ok, I'll look at the files soon, anything I should start with

Cam: there's a folder that looks like it has the files for the name index, start there

Cam: but don't spend all night looking at it, you'll want to

Me: ok, I'll try

I wasn't going to make a promise I couldn't keep. If I stayed up all night, I could just sleep in. Other than some grocery shopping, there wasn't a lot I needed to do that weekend.

Cam: Helen's going to send out a message

Cam: she wants everyone who can to come into the office tomorrow morning

Me: I'll be there, even though I was looking forward to sleeping in

Cam: you'll want to come in once you see that folder

Me: cryptic

Cam: lol, yep

Cam: safe travels, see you soon

Me: thanks, see you soon

The pilot came on over the speaker, telling me to buckle up and that we'd be taking off. I did as instructed. A few minutes later, we were in the air. I pulled my laptop out and connected to the Wi-Fi. The message that Cam said would come from Helen about Saturday was in the chat. Everyone had already confirmed that they would be there. I added my confirmation too.

I opened the program that showed all the files I had uploaded from the last batch. Cam had left them on my computer for me. Normally she would clear out the files from my hard drive; there was no way everything I'd gotten over the week would fit on my laptop. While at the apartment, it was easy enough to access the agency's network to get to any file I wanted. The Wi-Fi on the plane would have worked, but it would have been agonizingly slow.

There were dozens of folders, most of them sounded uninteresting. A few stood out that I'd want to come back to, including operations, personnel files, and finance. Toward the bottom of the unsorted list, I saw the folder Cam had mentioned; it was simply named *Watchlist*. Not subtle, Cora.

I clicked to open the watchlist folder and gasped so hard I choked on my own spit. I coughed and reached for a bottle of water sitting to the side. Recovered enough, I looked again. The folder contained hundreds of documents, each one a name.

At the top of the file menu, I clicked the icon to sort the names alphabetically. They arranged themselves by first name. I scrolled through until I hit the *M*'s and found my mom's name, *Malinda Moss*.

For a brief second, I wondered if it was wise for me to open the file without any support systems around. Yes, the pilots were technically employed by the agency, but they weren't involved with investigations. And yes, the team was probably a single message away from chatting. Several of their names in the messaging app still had the active green dot. But if it was what I thought it was, I wasn't sure how I would react.

Six months of good examples and therapy had not yet improved my ability to make good choices for myself. I clicked the file name to open the document.

The document was several pages long and set up like a police record. A grainy color picture of my mom was in the top right corner. Basic information about her filled the first half of the page, including that she had a daughter, me, and that she was an oracle. There were several acronyms, some that I could guess, but many that I didn't understand.

The second half of the first page started what seemed like a timeline of entries. The first was in 1990, filled out by a name I didn't recognize. I skimmed through the entry. She had been in Montana. A werewolf pack alpha had provided a statement. They suspected she was an oracle. The entry recommended surveillance but deemed the oracle claim unlikely.

The entries continued. I wanted to read them all in detail, but I also wanted to get to the end of the report to see what happened. The latter choice won out, and I scrolled all the way to the bottom of the document. The last entry was short: *MSH confirmed. PI target. Elimination approved.*

A final statement at the end of the file read: *Case Closed, Deceased.*

I didn't read any more files after that.

My mom had been gone for three years at that point. For several months, we had a firm theory that the Council, specifically Director Owens, had been involved with her murder. I really thought I had come to terms with that. Proof would just be the final nail. But it was like the coffin lid that buried me with grief had just slammed shut all over again.

Unable to do anything, I curled up on the back couch of the plane. I layered three heavy blankets to put weight on top of me. I put on headphones with the volume as loud as I could stand, and I turned on an episode of my favorite podcast that I'd listened to several times. It took a while, but soon I escaped into sleep.

ONE OF THE pilots gently shook my shoulder. I couldn't understand him at first, but he repeated himself and said we'd be landing. I needed to sit up and put on a seatbelt. I nodded my understanding. He gave me a worried look but went back to the cockpit without saying anything more.

I rubbed the gunk out of my eyes and realized they were swollen. I had been crying in my sleep.

We landed. The pilots helped me with my things. The driver loaded them in the car. We headed to my house. I was a zombie. My mind was foggy and I moved as if the air was filled with mud.

The driver asked me if I was okay when she dropped me off. I said yes, but I didn't think she believed me. She helped me unload my bags and then got back in the car where she waited for me to get inside.

The house was glowing. The lamps were on timers and turned on at dusk so I wouldn't have to come home to a dark house. I unlocked the front door. Ilka was waiting for me. She blinked, meowed, and wrapped between my legs. Annie would have already come by to check on her like she did anytime I was away. The cat wasn't hungry, so maybe she sensed something was wrong.

I closed the door, barely noticing the tall woman in a

suit slowly walking down the sidewalk in front of my house.

I dropped all my bags just inside the front door. Normally I would put things away and shower before heading to bed. Not that night. I dragged myself upstairs to my bedroom. I shed my clothes and slept in my underwear; I had no energy to get into pajamas.

My last thought before escaping into sleep again was of the meeting the next morning. I set an alarm for eight o'clock. I wouldn't need it.

EVEN THOUGH MY brain still needed time to process, the sleep had helped my body deal with it. I was up and alert at five in the morning. I showered and put away my things. I even started to write up a grocery list. Ilka was upset that I had woken her up early with my chores.

After I took care of things to feel settled, I made some tea and sat at the kitchen table with my laptop.

I didn't open my mom's document again. I wasn't ready for that. Instead I went back and looked through the list of names. It was still sorted alphabetically, and it didn't take me long to find Annie and Angela. I resisted the urge to read their files. I wanted to get through the full list of names to see who I recognized.

Cam's name was down a bit farther, and then Enid's, the witch we knew the director had been involved with murdering. Hank, Helen, and Jordan were all there.

Even though I expected it, I almost choked on my

tea when I saw my name. That was harder to resist not opening, but I moved on. I paused when I saw my mom's name again. Rachel's name was listed, the young witch who had been manipulated into killing Enid.

Sarah's name on the list jolted my memory of the vision I had seen. With everything else going on around the files, I had let that slip my mind. I hadn't told anyone yet.

My eyes went wide with fear. What if that was happening right then? Or what if it had just happened and Sarah was in the hands of the Council?

I looked at the messaging app, hoping that Cam was awake and at her computer. She wasn't. I swore out loud and made Ilka startle awake. It was too important to wait. I grabbed my phone and dialed Cam's number.

It rang five times before a sleepy voice answered, "Hello."

"Cam, is that you?" I asked.

"Yes. Linda, is that you?" Cam's voice was starting to wake up.

"Yes."

"Linda, it's five thirty in the morning."

"I know, but this couldn't wait."

"Okay," Cam said, more alert. "What's wrong?"

"I'll explain everything," I said. "But I need you to call Sarah and make sure she is okay, right now."

"Call Sarah?" Cam replied. "What's going on?"

"Please just trust me and call her," I begged. "And then call me back."

"Okay, I will." Cam sounded worried. "I'll call you right back."

We hung up, and I counted out loud. The call couldn't take that long. Not quite two minutes later my phone vibrated on the table. I picked it up immediately.

"Is Sarah okay?" I asked.

"Yes," Cam responded. "Sarah's fine. She's at home. I told her to stay there and that I'd call her back when I knew more."

"Oh good," I said with relief. I wasn't too late. That meant what I saw was something in the future, unless Sarah had a past experience she hadn't told us about.

"So, what is going on?" Cam asked.

"I had a vision about Sarah," I said.

Cam sighed. "I guessed that. What was the vision?"

"It was of some kind of institute or hospital, it didn't look like a good place," I shared. "Sarah was being brought in by two people who looked like they worked for the Council. Sarah was roughed up, and it looked like they had dragged her out of bed."

I paused to give Cam time to take it in.

"Okay," Cam said after she had taken a couple of deep breaths. "Sarah is okay right now. I'm going to call her back and tell her to go stay with a friend. We both should try to get some more sleep, and we can share this with the team and figure out a plan in the morning."

"Okay," I agreed. I didn't tell her that I had already been awake for almost an hour and that there was no chance I was going back to sleep.

COFFEE MUGS, plates with cinnamon rolls, and open laptops sat in front of everyone at the conference table on the second floor of the agency's office just before nine on Saturday morning. I smiled upon smelling the cinnamon rolls when I opened the front door. Mrs. Clark knew they were my favorite, and I chose to believe that she made them specially for me that day.

There wasn't the easy chatter that usually preceded our morning meetings. This wasn't a usual morning meeting, though, and not just because it was the weekend.

Winthrop caught my eye at the end of the table where he sat. He kept his face neutral, but I almost felt sympathy behind his expression. It was the soft pulse of light pushing in and out around him that gave away his nervous energy. He must have caught me noticing because he steeled himself and steadied the pulses.

Helen walked from her office and everyone got quiet. She brought a stack of papers and her laptop. Annie moved the coffee and plate that she had set out for her so that Helen could put the papers down.

"By now, I think you've all seen the list of names and at least some of the files associated with them," Helen said calmly. "We have a lot to talk about today and then plans to make. I want to remind everyone that we've already had a difficult week, and the coming days won't be any easier." Her gaze landed on each of us in turn as she gave out instructions. "We'll work only half a day, have lunch, and then everyone will take the rest of the weekend off to recharge. We need clear heads for what is coming. Understood?"

We all nodded. She was right, and we all knew it.

Appeased that we all agreed, she continued, "Jordan, will you start us off?"

"Yes. Thanks to Linda's efforts," Jordan began and gave me a sideways look, "we have obtained a cache of files that provides proof of a detailed surveillance, confinement, and elimination program conducted by Director Owens with Council staff."

I winced at her use of the word *elimination*. That was the word used in my mom's file, and it sounded like it was also found in other files.

"We've been able to link several theorized cases to the surveillance files," Jordan summarized and then looked to Steve.

"Additionally," he picked up the thread, "we know that each of us and several of our close associates are in the watchlist files. I'm still working through the details in each one and determining the threat level."

I looked around the table to see if anyone's reactions could tell me what *threat level* meant. There were no hints, and it didn't feel like the right time to ask. I made a note for myself to come back to that.

"For now, I have confirmed that everyone's security systems at home and the system at the office are functioning appropriately," he concluded and then looked at Annie to continue.

"We have also cross-listed the initials found in the Moonstone Haven book to names found in the surveillance files," she said, looking at me. I hadn't realized that they had already started on that. "There is a lot of overlap; so far, about four in five suspected names are matches to the names in the files."

The team had clearly been busy while I was at the Council office, so I had a lot of catching up to do.

Angela picked up the update thread from Annie. "We also received a lot of financial data. It is clear that Director Owens was keeping two sets of books for the Council's financial records." Winthrop smiled toward Angela; he looked so proud of her. She smiled back and continued, "I need to work on it more, but so far, I've found several discrepancies that would point to embezzlement. Based on the accounting records, I also think there may have been several incidents of blackmail."

Jordan added, "We're hoping that some of the watchlist records can confirm that and help us find the blackmail victims."

Helen nodded. "Let's talk about next steps."

"Sorry," Cam interrupted and looked my way. "I think Linda has some information to share."

"Right," I said, giving Cam a grateful smile. I hadn't been sure how to bring it up. "Friday afternoon, when I was with Director Owens, I had a vision."

"What?" Jordan blurted out. Helen looked upset, and the rest of the team looked concerned.

I decided it was better to just keep going. I explained

what had happened and that I saw Sarah being taken into custody.

"She was wearing a metal collar that had glowing runes," I added, trying not to look at Cam. That detail had not come up when I had called her.

Cam took a deep breath. "The collar was probably being used to prevent her from shifting. We've had suspicions that the Council has combined technology and magic to suppress gifts, but I haven't been able to confirm it."

"Is Sarah okay right now?" Helen asked.

"Yes," Cam answered. "I called her as soon as Linda told me. She is safe, and she is going to stay with friends for now."

"Good," Helen said. "That's good. Linda, anything else we should know?"

I thought for a moment. "I think the vision was triggered by Director Owens talking about dangerous oracles. But I'm not sure how that is related to Sarah."

Hank cleared his throat and offered, "Maybe your vision was trying to show you how the director wants to deal with any individual she deems dangerous."

Everyone around the table paused. Hank was not one to throw out random thoughts. If he offered up an idea, he had already thought it through a lot. That theory was one that had been shuffling around in my head, but I hadn't wanted to give a voice to it. I smiled at him and mouthed, *Thank you.*

The rest of the morning was subdued. Helen got us

back on track, and we divided up tasks to start on Monday. She reminded us that we also had Doria's case, and on Monday, we should be able to talk to the phoenix, Mr. Gray. It was going to be a long weekend trying to listen to Helen's advice and relax ahead of a big week.

20

I was in the office for ten minutes Monday morning before Helen and Jordan found me at my desk to go to Mr. Gray's house. The boxy modern house and the street it sat on were both quiet that morning. Jordan parked the car across the street again.

"I want to try to interview both Mr. Gray and Mr. Burton," Helen said, turning to face Jordan and me in turn. "Let's see who answers that door. If it's Mr. Burton, we'll talk with him first."

We both nodded in agreement.

At the door, I stood back a bit so Jordan and Helen could take the lead. While waiting, I looked around. The steps we were on had some leaves. The grass of the front lawn was a little overgrown, and the plants that had started to grow buds looked sadly crowded by some weeds. I didn't remember the yard looking like that the last time we were there. I started to share my observations with Helen and Jordan, but before I could, the door opened.

The door swung open wide and a handsome, shorter man stood framed by the light coming in from windows at the back of the house. With dark hair and a large bright smile, he looked mid-thirties, but I was bad with age. Something about him was familiar, but I couldn't quite place him.

"Hello," he said cheerfully. "How can I help you?"

"Mr. Gray?" Helen asked.

"Yes, that's me."

"I'm Helen Pendleton, with the OPT Agency."

"Oh, yes. Burton mentioned you'd be stopping by today." He moved slightly and gestured into the house. "Come on in."

We followed him into the same living room where we had talked with his house manager. The room was the same but had some clutter on the tables: a few colorful books stacked with bookmarks sticking out, a cup of half-drunk coffee, and some tissues that hadn't made it to a garbage can. It wasn't dirty but rather looked lived in compared to the sterile environment from our last visit.

The three of us sat together on the couch and Mr. Gray took the chair across from us.

"So, what can I do for you?" he asked politely.

"Do you know an individual named Doria?" Helen asked neutrally.

"Yes, I do," Mr. Gray responded, still smiling. "She is a longtime friend."

"A friend?" Helen pressed.

"Well"—he laughed softly—"a type of friend. We have a friendly rivalry."

"What does that rivalry entail?"

He chuckled. "Let's see. The last thing Doria did was mail me a box of butterflies. Burton opened the package inside the house. It took us weeks to catch them all and release them outside."

He laughed again. The three of us sat silently. He was a strange man, and he still felt familiar.

"I, of course, retaliated by having all the pizza delivery shops in a ten-mile radius deliver pizzas to her house at the same time."

I couldn't help but smile. Seattle had a lot of pizza shops, so there were probably a lot of pizzas.

Mr. Gray looked at me and smiled back. "I heard that she ended up donating the bulk of them to a homeless shelter. Apparently, it's turned into a monthly occurrence now at that shelter."

"Those sound like pretty harmless pranks," Helen said.

"Yes," he said. "The prevalence of more delivery options has progressed our pranks in the recent decades."

"Do you ever take each other's things as a prank? Even temporarily?" Helen asked casually.

Mr. Gray's smiling face transformed into something scary, his eyes flashing orange for a brief moment. "No. We have our boundaries. Why?"

Jordan leaned into me to help me steady myself under his gaze.

Helen took a deep breath and answered, "Doria is missing something that is important to her."

Mr. Gray narrowed his eyes and asked, "Her painting is gone?"

"You know about that?" Helen asked, letting the surprise slip through slightly.

"Of course," he said with a smile coming back to his face. "Doria thinks it's a big secret, but I've known about that for the last century."

I couldn't keep my face from looking shocked, but I recovered quickly. It was still wild to hear otherworldly people talk about time frames like centuries. No one looked like they were hundreds of years old.

Helen was unfazed and continued on, "Do you have any ideas of where the painting could be?"

Mr. Gray leaned forward with his elbows on his knees, his fingers templed under his chin. "No, but I will help find it."

The state of the yard and the house had been nagging at the back of my head since we sat down. It finally came to me why I thought it was strange.

"Is Burton around?" I asked during the pause in conversation.

Helen and Jordan were used to me doing that and they went with it.

Mr. Gray tilted his head and the smile fell away. "No. He needed some time off. I let him take a break starting on Friday when I woke up."

"Friday?" I asked. "Burton had told us that you'd be waking up late on Sunday or this morning."

"No. I follow a regular schedule, it is always Friday morning."

"So Burton has been gone since Friday?" Helen said, picking up the thread that I had started.

"Yes."

"When is he due back?"

"The end of this week."

"Do you know where he has gone?"

"No."

"Can you get in touch with him if you need to?"

"Of course."

"Has Burton been acting out of character at all recently?"

Mr. Gray narrowed his eyes again. "No."

Helen didn't respond. She let the silence hang in the air.

Mr. Gray sighed. "Okay, maybe. He's slowing down, but that happens when humans age. It's why I agreed to such a long vacation. I'm going to have to start looking for a new house manager soon."

He looked my way and raised his eyebrows as if asking if I wanted the job. I was shocked at the suggestion and shook my head. Mr. Gray laughed softly. The laugh was the last clue I needed: he was the man from the vision who was in the room with Burton when he was sick.

Helen ignored his antics. "Can we see Mr. Burton's rooms?"

"Sure," he replied and stood to lead us to them.

We had already looked at Burton's rooms the last time we had come to the house. The only room we hadn't searched was the room behind the solid-steel door. I thought Helen would have wanted to see that room, but I had learned to trust her instincts. She trusted mine.

The space we were led to was three rooms: a sitting room, a bedroom, and a bathroom. Mr. Gray hovered in the doorway as the three of us spread out between the three rooms. I stayed in the sitting room to look around.

I walked the perimeter of the room to see if anything would jump out at me. A small couch sat in front of a coffee table and TV. Bookshelves filled one of the walls with an old-fashioned roll-top desk nestled between them. The desk was closed. It had been opened when we came through the last time, but I didn't remember anyone looking at it closely. It was too small to hide a painting in.

When I got to the desk, I looked back at Mr. Gray, watching his face as I opened it to see if he would object to what I was doing. He shrugged.

The desk was organized. Letters, papers, pens, and other random things filled all the little cubbies. I reached out to pull some letters out of a cubby when my vision tunneled.

It was dark. A single lamp lit a small corner of the room. I recognized where I was: the sitting room that I was just in before the vision started. I looked around. The room was much the same but it was nighttime. Sounds of footsteps from the bedroom caught my attention.

Burton walked out of the bedroom, hunched and coughing. Slowly, he shuffled into the sitting room and grunted as he knelt down at the edge of the rug. He peeled back the corner of the rug. I moved closer so that I could see better.

He pulled out two boards from the wood floor. I

couldn't see what was under there. Burton looked around the room and then toward the door that went out to the rest of the house. He took a deep breath and pushed an arm down into the gap in the floor.

His body went rigid and his face contorted in a silent scream. I sucked in a breath and held it. Before I started to go lightheaded, his face relaxed, and I let out my breath. He pulled his arm out of the gap, put the boards back, and replaced the rug. He stretched his arms above his head and cracked his back from side to side. Then, like a man twenty years younger, he sprang up from the floor and smiled.

He walked toward me. I took a step back, but he stopped at a trash can to the side of the desk. His hand opened to reveal a clump of feathers. He sighed sadly and then crushed them between his fingers. Turning his hand over the trash can, ashes fell out where the feathers had once been.

My vision tunneled again, and I let out a small gasp. The letter that I had been holding scraped along my finger, leaving behind a paper cut. I put the finger up to my mouth to soothe it while I thought about what I had just seen.

I replayed the scene in my head. It was obvious that he was hiding something under the floor. The feathers were like the ones we had found outside Doria's house. I couldn't make sense of what he was doing with them. Also, why would he have Doria's painting? We didn't know if it would have worked to heal Burton.

The paper cut hurt and I was feeling lightheaded from the vision. Something about the letters I was holding also seemed important. They had triggered the vision.

Mr. Gray, still standing in the doorway, cleared his throat. He gave me a worried face when I looked over to him.

"Paper cut," I said as an excuse.

He nodded but didn't look convinced.

I picked up the letters I had dropped. They were already opened, so I didn't feel too bad about pulling the contents out of the envelopes. They were full of medical bills. The name they were addressed to was one I didn't recognize. I couldn't make sense of what the bills were for —they were full of medical terms and jargon. But there was somebody in the house who would know.

"Jordan," I called out. "I've got something you should take a look at."

Jordan and Helen both came out through the bedroom door.

"What did you find?" Jordan asked.

I didn't say anything; instead I handed over the bills I had found. Jordan scanned them quickly and furrowed her brow.

"There's more," I whispered and snuck a glance at Mr. Gray still in the doorway. "I had a vision."

Jordan and Helen both widened their eyes.

"There is something under the floor in this room that is helping Burton. It looked a lot like the feathers we found at Doria's," I whispered.

Helen straightened up and looked thoughtful for a minute, and then it was clear she had made a decision. "Mr. Gray," Helen said, turning toward him, "we need to look under the floor of this room."

He shrugged again and looked unbothered by all of it. "Okay."

I moved toward the place where Burton had lifted up the rug in my vision. Following his moves, I knelt and folded back the corner of the rug. I pulled at a couple of the boards before finding the ones that lifted up easily. Once the boards were removed, Helen leaned down and shined the flashlight from her phone into the space. We all jumped when a set of eyes glowed back at us.

Recovered from the scare, we leaned down and could see that it was a painting—Doria's painting. There were also several clumps of feathers tied together and sewn onto strips of cloth.

We tried to remove some more boards to make it easier to retrieve the contents from under the floor. They wouldn't budge.

"Do you have a hammer or a crowbar?" Helen asked Mr. Gray.

"Yes," he said calmly. "I can get that for you."

He left the doorway, and both women turned toward me.

Helen asked, "What did you see in the vision?"

"I saw Burton come to this area of the room and open this compartment," I said, gesturing toward the hole in the floor that we were kneeling around. "He was looking really frail, and then he reached into the hole and seemed to get younger."

"Doria's painting shouldn't have worked for him," Jordan said, confused.

"That's what I thought," I added.

Helen pulled a set of the feathers out of the hole. "But these do look familiar?"

"Yep," I agreed.

Jordan added, "Phoenix feathers."

Mr. Gray's voice from the doorway startled us. "Phoenix feathers can only be found during our transition cycle."

Helen stood up and held the feathers out to him. "Do you know why Mr. Burton would have these feathers?"

Mr. Gray frowned. "He shouldn't have them. They are all supposed to burn with me."

"Looks like we have some things to talk about," Helen said.

Mr. Gray looked worried.

We used the hammer and crowbar that Mr. Gray brought to pry up more of the floorboards. The painting was still in its frame and looked undamaged. The painting, feathers, and medical bills were all brought out into the living room.

"Did you know anything about any of this?" Helen pressed Mr. Gray.

"No," he said sadly and shuffled through the papers. "I know he had been feeling poorly, but he assured me he was okay."

Jordan took one of the bills off the coffee table. "Based

on these, and assuming that the name on them is a fake name Burton has been using, it seems that Burton has pancreatic cancer. It has a high mortality rate," she said softly. "He likely only had a year with treatment, maybe less."

Mr. Gray looked shocked. "Why didn't he tell me?"

We let Mr. Gray have some time to process what he had just learned, but we still had questions we needed answers to.

Helen calmly asked him, "Why would Mr. Burton have these feathers?"

"It's not common knowledge," Mr. Gray hesitated, "but phoenix feathers have healing properties."

"Oh," Jordan let out uncharacteristically. We all politely ignored her.

"Our small community has done our best to hide that and squash any rumors," he said, the sadness shifting to anger. "A very long time ago we were hunted for our feathers. Our population used to be much larger. Taking too many of our feathers during our transition cycle can be life-threatening."

"Would the feathers have been able to heal his cancer?" Jordan asked.

"No, not permanently," he answered. "They'd help with the symptoms, but they would keep coming back, and you'd need new feathers once you've depleted the magic from them."

"Burton probably wanted to find another way to get better," I thought out loud. "He didn't want you to die. Maybe he thought if he could change the painting, it could help him."

"That wouldn't have worked," Mr. Gray said regretfully.

Helen smiled sadly at him. "Desperate people do desperate things."

He nodded. "What happens now?"

"Well," Helen answered, "Doria tasked us with recovering the painting. We've done that. As the other wronged party, I'm going to leave it up to you on how you want to deal with Mr. Burton."

JORDAN and I wrapped the painting in a blanket that Mr. Gray gave us. We loaded it into the car as Helen spoke with Mr. Gray on the front steps. They shook hands, and then Helen joined us at the car.

"Did he say what he was going to do?" I asked.

"He's going to hire a home nurse for Mr. Burton and keep him as comfortable as possible," Helen said and turned to Jordan. "He asked if we had any recommendations."

Jordan nodded. "I'll get him a list. There are several who work with supernatural clients but could also provide end-of-life care for humans."

My vision of the hospital bed in a not-so-hospital place came to mind. Burton would be well taken care of, and Mr. Gray would be at his side.

"That would be good, thank you," Helen said. "Let's get this painting over to Doria, and then we can return to our other project."

The other project involving the director and her watchlist files had completely left my mind during the morning. It was nice to have a break from it, but I wanted to get back to it as quickly as possible.

DORIA OPENED the door as if she had been waiting just on the other side. The huge, blanket-covered thing we were holding made it obvious that we had her painting. She smiled and ushered us quickly inside.

"You found it," she said as soon as the front door had closed.

Jordan and I took the blanket off to show her the painting.

"Wonderful," she said softly. "If you could just lean it against that wall, I'll put it away after you leave. Come sit and tell me where it was."

We left the painting where she had indicated. I looked at Jordan, wondering why she hadn't touched it yet to heal. Jordan didn't seem to know either.

Sitting in the living room, Helen started to share the story of what happened, "It was at Mr. Gray's house—"

"I knew it," Doria said under her breath, interrupting.

"But," Helen said, "it wasn't Mr. Gray who took it."

"Oh."

"Mr. Gray's house manager, Burton, took the painting. We recovered it hidden in his rooms."

"Why would Burton take it? He's such a sweet man."

Helen cleared her throat. "Mr. Burton has pancreatic cancer."

"Oh no."

"We think he hoped to find a way to save himself."

"That poor man," Doria said with tears in her eyes. "Is he doing okay right now? Can the doctors help him?"

Helen looked toward Jordan to answer.

"Well, he wasn't at home," Jordan said. "Mr. Gray says that he is on vacation. So we don't know for sure what his current state is. Pancreatic cancer is aggressive, and the mortality rate is high."

We all paused to let Doria absorb the information. It was obvious that Doria, Mr. Gray, and Burton had an amicable relationship, although one that included elaborate pranks.

Helen leaned forward slightly toward Doria. "I hope I didn't overstep, but considering Mr. Burton's condition and some other circumstances that Mr. Gray can reveal if he chooses to, I've left the decision on how to deal with Mr. Burton's thefts to Mr. Gray."

Doria narrowed her eyes. Helen let the silence hang.

"I suppose I only asked you to return the painting," Doria said and looked out toward where it sat in the foyer, "and you did that. So, that's okay with me."

"Thank you." Helen sounded relieved. I released the breath I had been holding.

"Now that that is settled," Doria said with a shift in tone, "I have something to share with you. One moment."

The three of us exchanged confused looks as Doria got up and walked out of the room. We didn't have to wait too long before she walked back in holding an old-school composition notebook that had clearly been used a lot.

The edges on it were ragged. The cover was torn in one corner with doodles all over it.

"I've decided that you should have this," Doria said, and then she surprised us all when she handed it to me.

"What is it?" I asked before I dared open it.

"Malinda trusted me with this right before she died," Doria said, her voice cracking on the name.

"Malinda?" I gasped. "You mean my mom?"

"Yes," she said. "Your mother and I had been friends for years."

I looked at Helen to see if she knew that. She shook her head and looked sad.

Doria leaned back in her chair and continued, "Malinda recorded several related visions that she had in that notebook."

I cracked the book open and saw my mom's familiar, messy handwriting. She must have been writing quickly, as it was hard to read some spots. There were notes in the margin that looked like they had been added after the initial writing. Some words were scratched out, and others underlined. I wanted to read the whole thing right then.

Helen put her hand out onto the notebook, closing the cover and holding it shut. She narrowed her eyes toward Doria. "Why did Malinda give this to you?"

"Helen, don't feel hurt." Doria tried to smooth things over. "I know you and Malinda were once close and she told you everything. Well, almost everything."

Helen pushed down harder on the notebook. Her jaw clenched.

Doria continued, "You'll see when you read the visions.

Malinda told me that she saw in the first vision that someone at your agency was going to be working for the Council."

I took a sharp intake of breath and tried to catch Helen's eyes. That must have meant me. Helen wouldn't take her eyes off Doria.

"The visions in that notebook are all about something the director is going to do," Doria explained. "Malinda didn't know if she could trust it with you knowing that one of your people would be working for her."

I tensed again and tried to explain, "But I'm only—"

"Not now," Helen uncharacteristically hushed me and then turned back to Doria. "But why you? Malinda had a lot of friends who weren't connected to the agency."

"She did." Doria smiled. "But I'm the only one the director wouldn't be able to spy on with her oracle gifts."

Helen glared at Doria. Jordan's eyes darted between the two of them. My eyes were glued to the notebook Helen held closed on my lap.

"Take the notebook," Doria insisted. "I've watched you all work these past two weeks, and I believe I can trust you with this right now."

"Thank you, I guess," Helen said, still sounding frustrated and confused by what had happened.

"You're welcome," Doria said. "I'm not sure what it is, but I think you are going to need whatever that notebook can tell you."

"You haven't read it?" I asked.

Doria broke eye contact with Helen and smiled at me. "No, Malinda asked me not to. So I didn't."

Helen stood abruptly. "We should go."

Jordan and I followed her lead. I clung to the notebook, and we moved quickly to the front door. As we left, Doria held the door open.

Doria called out one last cryptic instruction as we walked down the front path: "You call me when you decide to make a move."

21

At the office, the team was sitting around the kitchen table; they had just started to eat lunch. Helen, Jordan, and I grabbed plates of food and joined them. We updated them on what had happened at Mr. Gray's home and how Doria had reacted when we returned the painting to her. When Helen got to the part about the journal, all eyes turned to me. I looked down in my lap, where I had placed the notebook.

Annie was sitting next to me and whispered in the silence that followed, "What does it say?"

Everyone had heard her ask the question they were all thinking.

I looked up at the group around me and answered, "I don't know yet."

Helen cleared her throat and gave me a sympathetic look. "You'll have time to read it after lunch. Then Annie and Cam can scan it so it will be easier for more people to review."

I nodded my head, grateful that Helen had made it clear that I was going to read it first. Everyone ate in silence for a few moments.

"So the butler really did do it?" Cam joked.

Chuckles and groans filled the table.

"I heard Linda make the joke first," Cam laughingly defended herself.

Jordan pointed her fork at Cam. "He technically wasn't a butler."

The joking had the much-needed effect of easing the mood. The team knew how to deal with serious situations; well-placed humor was one of their favorite coping mechanisms.

"We'll meet this afternoon," Helen said as people were finishing up their lunches. "Linda, once you look at the notebook, let me know how much time you think you'll need to read it. Based on that, I'll send out a meeting invite for everyone."

People started to get up and take their plates over to the sink. They then wandered away in pairs to their offices or labs to continue the work they had started that morning. Soon Annie and I were the only two at the table.

"Are you going to be okay reading your mom's visions?" Annie asked softly.

"I think so," I said but didn't even convince myself.

"I'm here if you need me."

"Thank you," I replied automatically and then paused. "Can I come read in the living room?"

My office was exposed more than other rooms, and anyone needing to talk with Helen would have to walk past me. I wanted a quieter place to read, and there was the added bonus of being near Annie if I fell apart.

"Of course," she said. "You go get settled and I'll make you a cup of tea just in case you need it."

Annie took my plate with her as she got up to clear her own dishes. I gave her a smile and then gripped the notebook as I walked to the living room. There was a set of chairs in front of the window. They were cushy and big enough that I could sit in them with my feet tucked under me.

I settled into one of those chairs and finally cracked open the notebook again. The page was the same mess of hurried writing that I had seen at Doria's house. Helen was waiting for an estimate of how much time I needed. I took a deep breath and flipped through each page.

"What?" I accidentally said out loud.

"What?" Annie echoed as she walked into the room holding two mugs of tea.

"The notebook," I said and flipped through the pages again, counting. "There are only fifteen pages of writing."

The blank pages after that were numbered by hand in small writing on the top outside corner of each page. Every page, even the blank ones, looked like it had been flipped through several times. The pages were worn, and some had fingerprint smudges.

"Oh," Annie said and set down the tea on the side table. "Is that bad?"

I sighed. "I guess not. It just wasn't what I was expecting."

"Have you read any of it yet?"

"Not really," I admitted. "I'm having a hard time getting started."

"You can do hard things," Annie reminded me of our mantra.

"You're right," I said and sat farther back into the chair.

"And if it gets too hard, that's why you have all of us."

I smiled and took a deep breath so I wouldn't cry. "You're right again."

"You've got this," she said and patted my knee before she walked over and sat at her desk across the room.

I flipped through the notebook one more time to make sure I hadn't missed anything. I hadn't. There were fifteen pages of writing. That would probably take me an hour to read and reread a couple of times. I sent Helen a message telling her that. A few moments later, my phone pinged with a meeting scheduled for two thirty. She had cushioned my time estimate by half an hour; that worked for me.

There was nothing left for me to do but start reading.

I had noticed it before but hadn't made sense of it: the first several lines were crossed out in the notebook. I squinted at them to see if I could figure out what they were. They weren't sentences, but rather bullet points like a list. Then it hit me: it was the start of a grocery list.

My mom had a habit of using anything she could find to write grocery lists. She wrote them when the thought hit her. She likely bought the notebook for another purpose and was just going to use a page because it was convenient.

Similarly, I bet she had just grabbed the notebook after the first vision because she felt compelled to write it down.

I knew everything that was in our shared home. A few months after my mom's death, I went through her room. There were no vision-filled notebooks anywhere in the house. Maybe she had more vision notebooks secreted away with other friends.

I let that thought go and moved on to the lines that were not crossed out.

Dark office. After hours?? Large desk.

Computer, not a laptop. Something feels off.

Several moments pass. Someone comes into the office.

Not sure who it is, don't see a face. They feel familiar.

Kneel behind computer. Gets up, leaves.

The writing continued like that: short clips of what she saw or felt in chronological order. A small note in the margin pointed to the line *They feel familiar.* I had to squint again at the small writing, but I thought it said *OPT agent.*

The first entry talked more about how she was waiting in the office. Light eventually filtered in and she had assumed that meant it was morning. She heard noises outside of the office, and then she woke up.

She woke up. It was a dream she had. Were all her visions dreams? Helen had told me that some oracles had dreams instead of waking visions like I had. I had thought that I was like my mom when it came to visions. Maybe we weren't the same.

I moved on to the second entry. She was back in an office space, but not the same office as the first dream. It was a "sea of cubicles," as she put it. The picture in my head of the Council offices fit her description, but I didn't want to assume. This time, she was watching someone type on their computer. She was just seeing the back of their head but she made the same note, clearer this time, *OPT agent* pointing to the line describing the person.

The next two entries were much of the same. Both ended with *woke up*. I was beginning to wonder why she had felt compelled to write down these visions. I must have been missing something. Or she didn't write down what was obvious to her.

Five pages in and I finally got to something that seemed important. She was back in the first office, but there was a conference table instead of a desk. Six people were sitting around it and talking. She had one name written: *Cora*.

That had to be Director Cora Owens. In her retelling, Cora was leading the meeting and she was angry. She demanded to know why they couldn't find someone. A note in the margin just said *who* and was underlined three times.

The next several pages were more mundane visions in the office cubicles, watching over the shoulders of different people as they typed on computers. She never said what they were working on. The person she thought was an OPT agent showed up a few more times, always with a note in the margins calling that out.

I was coming up to the last pages, and I was getting frustrated. The notebook was supposed to be useful for us, and so far I'd only learned that my mom thought someone from the agency was working for Director Owens.

Doria had already told us that.

After taking several deep breaths, I was ready to be

done with what had so far been a disappointing read. The first line made me sit up straighter. She wasn't in the office this time. The place she was describing seemed familiar.

White and gray room. Cold. Intake desk.

Hurried, frustrated woman behind the desk.

I hear typing. She's hunched, looking at a screen.

Two doors with barred windows. Concrete floor.

Eerie long hallways.

I had seen that place in my own vision. The vision I'd had in Cora's office. The vision where they had taken Sarah. I raced through the next part, where she talked about seeing someone being led through the hall. She didn't recognize who it was, but in the margins she wrote, *drugged?* Then I saw the strangest thing in the whole book.

The last line she had written.

Linda, close your eyes.

On instinct, I did as the notebook instructed me. I felt the familiar pull in my gut of a vision. When I opened my eyes, I was standing in that building. I could feel the cold through my shoes again. I wrapped my arms around myself to ward off the chill. The smell of fresh paint tickled my nose. That was different. No one was at the desk. The monitor was on and cast a glow on the wall it faced.

I waited a moment, but nothing happened. Then I felt like someone was behind me, watching me. I'd had that feeling several times the last couple of weeks. Holding my breath, I turned around slowly, not expecting to see anyone, like all the other times.

Light brown eyes and a face surrounded by a halo of

wavy hair met me. A tear slid down my cheek. My mom smiled back at me.

"Linda," she said softly.

"Mom?" I asked back in a whisper.

"Yes," she answered and choked back a sob. "We don't have a lot of time, and you need to know something important."

I swallowed hard to hold back the tears and nodded.

"A lot of people are in danger, and you need to help them," she whispered, but the words still echoed off the sterile walls.

"Who?" I asked. "And how?"

"People who are special," she said and then looked sad. "People like you. You are special."

My heart knew the answer, but I asked anyway, "What do you mean, special?"

"Magical and otherworldly," she whispered. "I'm sorry I never told you. I thought I was doing the right thing."

I let the tears fall. A mix of sadness and anger. Why had she kept this from me?

She continued before I could ask her: "You need to find a woman named Helen Pendleton."

I smiled through the tears and laughed softly at the irony. "I know Helen."

"You do?" She was surprised. "Good. I'm sorry I can't help you more."

We both turned at the sound of footsteps coming down the hall.

She looked nervous. "Check page thirty-seven. But you need to open your eyes now."

"Page thirty-seven? What do you mean? You didn't tell me what is going on," I pleaded. "What am I supposed to do?"

"You already know," she said.

"I don't."

The footsteps were getting closer.

"Three seven. Open your eyes, Linda," she demanded. "Now!"

My eyes shot open.

The chair was soft under me. A warm sweat covered my body from the drastic change in temperature. I looked up to see Annie staring at me with worry in her eyes.

I flipped to page thirty-seven in the book, sure that I wouldn't find anything. Everything past page fifteen had been empty. I had checked twice. I found the page numbered thirty-seven and almost dropped the book.

An address filled the middle of the page. It wasn't my mom's handwriting like the rest of the book, but it was familiar. It was like the handwriting in the logbook from Moonstone Haven house. It was Enid's handwriting. The address was somewhere in California.

"I need to talk to Helen," I said and leaped out of the chair, gripping the notebook.

Annie followed me up the stairs but didn't come into Helen's office with me. I left the door open.

"Helen, sorry to interrupt, but it's important," I said.

Helen looked startled but recovered quickly. She eyed the notebook I was holding and gestured for me to sit down.

I set the notebook on the desk in front of me and

flipped it open to page thirty-seven. Helen leaned forward to see what was on the page, then looked up at me confused.

"Do you know this address?" I asked.

"No, why?"

"My mom told me to find you, and then she told me to check this page in the notebook," I said, talking quickly and not making sense.

"Sit down and start from the beginning," Helen said calmly.

I sat down and took a deep breath. "I was reading through the notebook. It had some interesting things but nothing that seemed new. At least until the last page."

"And?" Helen prompted when I paused to think through what had happened.

"And she talked about a vision in a hospital-like place. It seemed like the same place from the vision I had on Friday, the one with Sarah," I said and tried to slow down. "Then, at the end of that last entry, it said, *Linda, close your eyes.*"

Helen looked worried and like she wanted to say something, but I ignored her and continued, "So I did, and then I was in a vision. It was the building from Friday's vision. And my mom was there."

"Oh," Helen let out softly.

"We talked," I said and swallowed back tears. "She said there were people in danger, we need to help them, to find you, and to check page thirty-seven."

"This page with the address?" Helen said, pointing to the book.

"Yes," I said. "But that address wasn't there when I first checked the book. It was only there after I snapped out of the vision."

I paused and gave myself some time to catch my breath and think. Helen was thinking too. I stared at the book when something strange caught my eye. The number on the page had a slash between the three and the seven. The other pages weren't numbered like that. It felt intentional, but I wasn't sure what it meant.

I could see the wheels turning in Helen's head. "We need to figure out what is at this address?"

I smiled, and it felt right. "Yes, I think so."

We both sat in silence for a moment. A cough from the doorway made us both turn and look.

Annie peeked her head in and asked, "Do you want me to gather the team?"

"Yes, please," Helen answered.

MY HANDS WERE SWEATING. I took them off the notebook sitting on the conference table in front of me so they wouldn't leave a mark and placed them in my lap. We were just waiting for Cam; she was down in the basement and taking the longest time to get up to the conference room.

"I'm here," she huffed out as she cleared the last few stairs and came into view. "Sorry, I had to finish something I couldn't stop in the middle of."

"That's alright," Helen reassured her as she took her seat at the table.

The table was full. Even Mrs. Clark and Winthrop had joined. That was always a sign that something serious was going down.

"We've got a lot to cover," Helen started the meeting. "I know many of you have updates, and we have some new information that we need to act on quickly. We're going to start with that." Helen turned toward me and gestured for me to start.

"I read through the journal," I said. "Cam and Annie, you can have it after the meeting to scan so everyone can read it."

"Great," Cam said. Annie knew there was more coming, so she didn't say anything.

"There wasn't a lot that I got from most of it," I said grimly. "Maybe some of you will catch something I didn't. But it was clear that she thought someone from the agency was working at the Council."

"You, right?" Steve said.

"I think so," I answered. "She either wasn't able to or chose not to describe them in detail, and she didn't use any names."

I scanned the table for other questions. There weren't any.

"Most of the entries are visions that are placed in an office; I'm pretty sure it's the Council offices in San Francisco." I cleared my throat, which had suddenly gone dry. Annie stood, grabbed water from the sideboard, and passed it to me. I took a quick drink, careful not to choke on it. Everyone waited patiently for me to be ready to continue.

"The last entry was at a different location," I said, ready to continue. "I think it was the same building that I saw in my vision on Friday. The last words of the entry said, *Linda, close your eyes*."

Everyone leaned in with wide eyes. I shared the encounter in as much detail as I could. It was more than I was able to tell Helen. I caught her making some more notes as I recounted the story. My eyes filled with tears but they didn't fall. No one interrupted me.

I concluded with the theory that had settled firmly in my head about the reason the page number thirty-seven was different: "Today is March fourth, I think something is going to happen at that address on Thursday the seventh."

22

Helen clapped her hands to silence the side conversations that had broken out after my proclamation. "Okay," Helen said when everyone quieted down and turned toward her. "I know this gives us an accelerated deadline. Let's continue with the updates and decide on a plan. Hank, can you start a whiteboard for us?"

Hank nodded and rolled over a whiteboard. He wrote *Mystery Building* and *Thursday* in the middle and drew a box around it.

"Annie, let's start with you for an update and anything relevant, and then we'll go around the table," Helen instructed. I let out a breath. That put me last to go if I didn't count Helen, which would give me time to process more of what had been happening.

Annie nodded and started, "I've been working on matching the initials of people in the Moonstone Haven book to names on both the watchlist from the director's computer and our own cases. There were a lot of names between the book and the director's files. Without a way to narrow them down, we were only able to match six names so far. All of them were missing person cases."

"I'm working on a program to help with the matches," Cam added. "But it's taking a bit of time, sorry."

Annie smiled sympathetically. "That's alright. We'll keep matching by hand until you get something ready. It's working so far, just slow."

"At this point," Helen added, "it's most important to have enough cases to confirm our theory. We'll match up everyone eventually."

"Agreed." Annie nodded.

"For the update, I don't think we have time to go through all of them," Helen said.

"The summaries of the four I've gone through are already in the case file," Annie offered.

"Great, folks can read them when they have time for the details and add comments," Helen instructed. "Do you have any patterns or specifics that you want to share now?"

Annie's eyes sparkled. "Yes, we think that the Moonstone Haven book used a code of letters added on to someone's initials to indicate that they were there multiple times."

"Interesting," Cam let out. We all nodded in agreement.

"The book didn't have any repeated initials, but they started going from two letters to three," Annie explained. "One uncommon set of initials, XT, was in the book four times with a different third letter added for each instance after the first one. We matched those initials to a witch named Xander. The timelines of the Moonstone Haven book correspond to run-ins he had with the Council from the director's file."

"That seems pretty conclusive for your theory," Steve said, impressed.

"I agree," Annie said. "If that is the case, then Xander was in and out of Moonstone Haven house over the course of three years. He never stayed longer than three months, and it was several months between each visit."

"What did the file from the director's computer say about Xander?" Helen asked. She had said we wouldn't review the details, but we were all invested and wanted to know, so no one stopped Annie from answering.

"He was deemed a priority-one target and was put on the surveillance program prior to their first mention in the Moonstone book. After the date he was mentioned in the book, the director's watchlist report says that he was missing and priority to locate. Shortly before the last entry in the book, the report says that he was approved for elimination."

Angry heads shook around the table. We all knew *elimination* meant Director Owens wanted that person killed.

"I know," Annie said, catching the reactions around the table. "But then the next entry said *elimination deferred, intake approved.*"

I blurted out the connection I had made in my head: "Intake was a phrase my mom used to describe the desk in the building."

Helen nodded and turned to Annie to ask, "Was there anything in the report after that?"

"No, that's where it ended," she answered.

"Okay," Helen said and looked over at the whiteboard. I followed her gaze along with the rest of the team and saw that Hank had filled in a lot of new circles in a spiderweb of information. The picture was starting to become clear.

"Jordan, anything to add?" Helen asked.

Jordan looked over at Angela knowingly. "I think Angela should go next."

"I've been looking over the financial reports to find where the money was going," Angela said. "We know that the two accounting books were different. It looked like Director Owens was showing a larger operating cost in the main books than was true. She padded each department with a lot of expenses, all in nondescript categories. Not enough in each one that someone would think it was that strange. But when you add it all up it's a lot."

"Do we know what she was doing with that money?" Helen asked.

"Originally, I thought it was just classic embezzlement," Angela answered. "But the second set of books shows a major project. The total in padding from the main books matches the funding of that project. I found some contractor invoices that tied back to that project. At first, I thought it was for a house the director was building for herself with Council funds. But now I think it may be a project to build a place like the one Linda described."

Every set of eyes focused on Angela, and she shrank back a bit at the reaction. Winthrop gave her a proud smile of encouragement. She sat up straight again and looked resolved.

"It's just a theory," Angela continued. "But it would make sense. And now that we have an address, I can see if that matches any of the contractor invoices."

We all watched Hank add that new information to the board.

Angela raised her hand to get attention back. "I'm also still looking into the potential blackmail—there are several incoming streams of money that don't make sense."

Steve volunteered, "Let me know if you need help with that, I've dealt with blackmail cases in the past."

"I will," Angela answered and then gestured that she was done.

"I know I said we'd go around and get all the updates," Helen said. "But it seems like we've got a pretty clear theory coming together. Does anyone have anything to add to this theory?"

Everyone shook their heads.

Jordan spoke up. "I think we all need a bit more time to review the information that we have."

"That's fair," Helen said and looked around the table. "Does anyone have anything to suggest we are heading in the wrong direction? Anything? Even a feeling or a hunch?"

Again everyone shook their heads.

"Okay," Helen said and clapped her hands together. "Let's divide up some work streams and tasks."

We all opened up our laptops, ready to take notes.

"Angela, do you need help with any of the financial stuff related to the potential building?" Helen asked.

"Yes, I could use some help going through the files."

"Winthrop and Hank, can you help her?"

"Yes," they said in unison.

"Annie, I think we should confirm your theory about repeat guests to Moonstone Haven house on a couple more cases if we can," Helen proposed.

"I agree," Annie said. "Jordan and I have been working on it so far. If she doesn't have anything else, I could use Jordan's help more."

Jordan smiled. "I can help you with that."

"Great," Helen said. "Jordan, I'd also like you to look at the journal when you have a minute." Jordan nodded. "Steve, I'd like you to review the journal as well."

"Will do," Steve replied.

When I went to pass the journal across the table to Steve, Cam raised her hand. "I can get that scanned really quickly so that everyone can access the images. That way, the journal won't be a blocker."

"Right," I said and passed her the journal instead. "That's a good idea."

Helen looked at Cam, concerned. "Cam, I know you've got another project you need to finish. Do you have time to scan that?"

Can nodded. "Yes, it won't take me very long. If Linda can help organize the files in the case folder, that will speed it up."

"I can do that," I offered quickly. That might give me a chance to ask her what her other project was.

"Okay," Helen said. "After that, Linda, there are a lot of case notes from last week that you should catch up on."

"Will do," I promised.

The working groups split off with the understanding that we'd meet back up at four o'clock to review what we found and make plans for the next day. I followed Cam with the journal down to her lab in the basement.

It was only the third time I'd been down there. It was a mix of tools and electronics. She had a bank of 3D printers in racks along one wall, several of them spitting out half-formed shapes. In another corner of the room was a free-standing chamber that looked like it could withstand a bomb. She had told me the first time I'd seen it that it was an RF chamber. It sounded important, but all I knew was that you couldn't get internet or cell service when you were in there with the door closed.

On her main workbench, a project was laid out in pieces. It looked somewhat familiar. I kept looking back at it as Cam started to scan the journal pages.

"Cam, what are you working on?" I finally asked.

She looked over at the pile of parts on the workbench and winced. "I'm trying to recreate the suppression collar that we think the director has."

"Why?" I asked with more force than was warranted. As someone with a magical gift, I was repulsed by the idea we'd have something that could restrict that.

Cam looked at me thoughtfully. "I need to know how it works if I'm going to figure out how to counteract it."

I sighed. "I'm sorry. I should have known that's why you'd be doing that."

"It's alright," she said with a sad smile. "But please don't mention it. Helen doesn't want it getting out just yet."

That seemed strange, but then I realized why. "She doesn't want Winthrop to know about it?"

Cam nodded. "We don't know what it would do to him or really what it would do to any otherworldly person's immortality."

"That's scary," I said. I hadn't thought about it that way.

"Yeah," Cam said, continuing to scan the journal. "I'm going to destroy the device as soon as I have a counter device created. That's not something that should be in the world." Cam handed me back the journal. "I got every page, even the blank ones. They should be in order, but if you could double-check when you organize them into the case folder, that would be helpful."

"I'll do that," I said and then turned to leave. "Good luck with your project."

"Thank you." Cam was already back at her workbench and looked a mix of sad and frustrated.

BACK AT MY DESK, the scanned pages of the journal came together quickly. They were in the correct order and every page seemed to be there. I clicked through all of them to check. I did a double take when I got to page thirty-seven. It was blank.

I opened the notebook and flipped to page thirty-seven. The address was there. That was strange, but I didn't have time to dwell on it. Instead, I made a comment on the page thirty-seven document with the address that was in the physical copy of the book.

That done, I settled in to review what Annie and Jordan had put together. The two had written up summaries of the cases that matched all three places: the Moonstone Haven book, the director's watchlist files, and our case files. The pattern was pretty clear.

All of those people had timelines like the one Annie had laid out for us. They were first being looked into by Cora and her people. Then they started to show up in the Moonstone Haven book. Sometimes months, sometimes years later, they were a missing person case at the agency. All of them were unsolved, except for one that had been found. Dead of natural causes. At least that's what the case file said. It didn't sit right with me.

The names rattled around in my head, but I didn't understand anything. Frustrated, I switched over to Angela's reports. The group working on those was all typing in the summary document. I decided to give them more time to finish up what they were doing, and then I'd take a look.

The missing address on page thirty-seven of the journal scans caught my attention again. I wondered if there were any other discrepancies between the physical copy and the scanned version. Since there wasn't a lot of information, I decided to go through each page and compare them.

As I was doing that, I started to wonder about the word choices that my mom had made and the way she grouped words together. It wasn't very consistent between rows. Some lines in the notebook only had a few words. Other lines had words scrunched onto the end.

I was reading the last entry again, the one that described the building from our shared vision. Then it jumped out at me. It was like those acrostic poems you wrote about yourself in elementary school—the ones where you write your name down the left side of the page, one letter per line, and then on each line you list something about yourself that starts with each letter in your name.

The first letter of each row was a last name that I had just seen, White. That name was one of the cases Annie and Jordan had pieced together.

I grabbed a sticky note and a pen, wrote the name out, and stuck the note to that page. Starting back at the beginning, I looked for the same pattern.

Not every row contributed a letter, but most entries had at least one name. I got excited when one of them toward the middle matched a name from Annie and Jordan's review; the rest didn't sound familiar yet. My heart sank when I got to the second-to-last entry and found the name *Sarah.*

I filled out a sticky note for Sarah's name and bookmarked that page. Taking the tabbed journal with me, I went to go find Annie and Jordan. They were in Jordan's office with heads bent over their laptops. The door was open, so I knocked lightly to get their attention and then walked in.

"I think I have a clue about what names to look for," I said, placing the notebook on the desk.

Annie looked impressed. "What did you find?"

I flipped the notebook open to the first tabbed page.

"The entries have names embedded in them." I pointed out the first letter of each row from a section that had a name.

"Interesting," Jordan said softly.

I flipped to the entry with the name we had talked about in the meeting that afternoon and pointed to each letter. "Here's another one that we know is related to what is going on."

Jordan and Annie looked at each other and then back at the book. Jordan put the pieces together first. "These names could be pointing us to the ones we need to look into."

I nodded. "That's what I think too. I think my mom left us these as clues."

"How many names are there?" Annie asked.

"I didn't have time to count them," I admitted. "But dozens." I flipped to almost the end of the entries and pointed out the name there. "Also, I found Sarah's name."

"Oh no," Annie said under her breath.

"I think she is in real trouble," I added. "This, along with seeing her in the vision I had, is too much of a coincidence to ignore."

Jordan cleared away a catch in her throat and then said firmly, "Let's hurry and write out a list of all of these names so that Annie and I can start using them to filter our search. Then, you need to go talk to Helen about Sarah. I think it's time to get her pack alpha, Michael, involved."

Annie and I nodded in agreement. I read out the names as Annie wrote them down on a paper provided by Jordan. Jordan typed them into the computer as well. She wanted to have a redundant list.

That done, I took the notebook and went to find Helen. Her door was closed, but this was important, so I knocked. A muffled "come in" came quickly.

I pushed the door open. "Sorry, but I need to show you something I found."

"Come in," Helen said eagerly. "What did you find?"

I set the notebook down on her desk again. She raised her eyebrow at the tabs that dotted the edges. Quickly flipping to a few entries, I pointed out the names that were hidden there.

"Annie and Jordan already have the list of names and are checking the files for matches," I said quickly.

"Good, that's really good. It'll go quicker with names rather than initials. Cam needs to focus; if this helps narrow down the search, we can hold off on the matching program we need from her."

I nodded but didn't admit that Cam had told me about her secret project.

"There's something else," I said and turned to the right page. "I found Sarah's name."

Helen leaned back in her chair and let out a worried sigh. I tilted my head in understanding. I was worried, too, but I gave her the time to process.

"I think we need to get Michael involved now," Helen finally said.

I smiled sadly. "That's what Jordan said too."

Helen nodded. "Jordan has good instincts. We've been holding off getting any otherworldly people involved until we knew more, except for Winthrop of course, but I guess it's time to start gathering allies."

23

I stood up to leave when Helen reached for the phone to call Michael.

"No, stay," Helen said and gestured for me to sit. "I'll put it on speakerphone; he might need details that would be better coming from the source."

I was the source. I had tried so hard not to let my visions become the center of any investigation. They had helped point us in the right direction, but we always got the evidence. It was still hard to come to terms with being so important to the team. It was like some kind of supernatural imposter syndrome.

The phone rang a few times, and then a gruff voice picked up. "Hello, this is Michael."

"Michael, this is Helen. I have you on speakerphone with me and my EA, Linda."

"Helen and Linda"—he lost some of the gruffness—"to what do I owe the pleasure of your call?"

"Not a pleasure, I'm afraid," she said calmly. "You need to be aware of something, and I need your help."

"You always have my help," he said, and then we heard some commotion in the background. "Let me move to somewhere quieter. We were just finishing up a pack meeting."

"Maybe have them stick around. You may want to talk to them when we are done here," Helen said.

"Okay," he said, slowly drawing it out. He muffled the phone, but we could hear him calling out to someone and then telling them to keep the pack around until he was off the phone. Michael came back on, a new urgency in his tone. "Helen, what is going on?"

"It's a long story, but I'll give you the short version so I can get to the main point."

"Fair enough," he agreed.

"We've been investigating Director Owens," Helen said, her calm slipping a bit. "We believe that she has been using her Council resources to abduct and murder people."

"That's a big claim," he said, but something in his voice didn't sound surprised.

She looked at me and raised her eyebrows. She had heard his lack of surprise too. "We've been able to collect some evidence from various sources."

"Good."

"Good?" Helen asked back at him.

Michael cleared his throat and then quietly said, "I've had my suspicions, too, but that's not something you throw around without evidence. How can we help?"

"First," Helen said and looked worried, "you need to

know that some of the evidence that we learned about very recently pointed to Sarah being at risk."

A low growl came through the speaker, and every hair on my body stood on end. Images of huge werewolves in their wolf form sprang to mind. I had only seen them once, but it was an image that was easy to conjure.

"I appreciate you letting me know," Michael said, the control back in his response. "She was at the meeting tonight. We'll get her to a safe house and watch over her until you tell me it's all clear."

"How would you feel about you and her coming here instead?" Helen threw out.

He growled again but not as much.

Helen persisted. "I know you don't like being away from your pack, but I think we're going to need you here to make some big decisions along with the other community leaders."

"Can I read in your local pack's leadership to the situation?" he asked.

"That's your call," Helen said. "I trust your decision."

"I'm going to want the long version of all of this, and I want to see the evidence you have."

"Of course," she said and then asked, "You'll come?"

"Yes, of course, I'll come," he said with only a little exasperation. "And I'll bring Sarah. If she's at risk, I want her near me, and I know your office is safe."

"Speaking of the office, you can plan to stay here. We'll get our guest suites ready for you." Helen nodded to me, and I nodded back that I understood I would need to work with Mrs. Clark to get the rooms ready.

"Okay, at least I'll get some of Mrs. Clark's food by staying there," he joked but sounded committed. "I'll message you our flight details. We'll try to be there by the morning."

"Thank you, Michael," Helen said. "Stay safe."

"You too," he said and then hung up the call.

Helen looked at me and let out a sigh. "Well, I've started the dominoes now, whether we are ready or not."

I tried to give her a reassuring smile. "We'll be ready."

She smiled back. "I think so too."

"How can I help?" I asked.

"Talk to Mrs. Clark—we'll need to prepare to house and feed around twelve visitors. I also want the team to be able to stay on agency grounds if it comes to that."

"That's more people than rooms we have," I thought out loud.

Helen smiled knowingly. "Tell Mrs. Clark that we'll be initiating fortress protocols. She'll know what to do and will fill you in."

"Okay," I said. I shouldn't have been shocked that the group had something like that.

"I'll make a list of the guests and get it to you when I've got confirmations," she said, starting to write on sticky notes, peeling them off quickly and lining them up on her desk. "For now, I need to make some phone calls."

I picked up the notebook, not wanting to let it out of my sight, and got up to leave.

"Oh," Helen called out before I walked out the door. "You can let folks know about the visitors, but we'll talk about it in thirty minutes at the four o'clock meeting too."

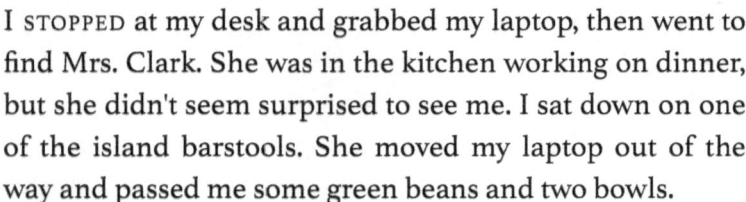

I STOPPED at my desk and grabbed my laptop, then went to find Mrs. Clark. She was in the kitchen working on dinner, but she didn't seem surprised to see me. I sat down on one of the island barstools. She moved my laptop out of the way and passed me some green beans and two bowls.

"So, what do we need to do?" Mrs. Clark asked calmly.

I started to snap the green beans, putting the ends in the smaller bowl and the good pieces in the other. "We are going to have visitors for a bit. Helen didn't say how long. But she said it could be up to twelve and she wants the team to be able to stay here if we need to."

Mrs. Clark nodded and continued to peel potatoes. "Good."

I tilted my head; she wasn't surprised or flustered by the request.

"She also said that we should initiate fortress protocols?" I asked more than said.

"That makes sense," Mrs. Clark answered.

"What are fortress protocols?"

She looked up from the potatoes and smiled back at me. "We have a plan to house and feed large numbers of people at the agency grounds for an extended period of time in case of a siege. I can send you the document that has all the protocols and tasks that we'll need to do. We'll probably need Annie's help with people arriving tomorrow."

I hadn't told her that people would be coming then, but I let that slide. Mrs. Clark just seemed to know things.

"We have the meeting at four o'clock," I said. "Maybe the three of us can meet after that and work out what we need to get done."

"That sounds great, dear."

Mrs. Clark called other people *dear*, but this was the first time she had used that term of endearment with me. I smiled back at her.

She didn't react and continued, "Why don't you go let Annie know and I'll see you in the four o'clock meeting?"

I nodded. She took back the bowls of beans that I had snapped as we talked. I was surprised to look down and see that I had gotten through all of them in our short conversation.

Laptop and journal in hand, I went back upstairs to Jordan's office, where I knew Annie would still be. They were just where I had left them, heads bent over their laptops and piles of notes to the side.

"Linda," Jordan called out as she noticed me walking in. "The list of names from the journal matches up perfectly with the initials in the Moonstone Haven book and names in the director's watchlist file. Most weren't in our case files, so we wouldn't have found them without that list."

"That's good," I said. "But I have something else I need to talk with Annie about." I sat in the chair, and they both looked confused. "You're both going to hear about this in about fifteen minutes, but I'll need Annie's help after the meeting."

"Okay," Annie said, closing her laptop. "What's up?"

"Helen called Michael and told him what's going on," I

said quickly. "Michael and Sarah are coming here tomorrow morning."

"That's good," Jordan said. "Cam will be happy to see Sarah and have her nearby."

I nodded and continued, "It sounds like it isn't just them coming. Helen asked me to work with Mrs. Clark to prepare the fortress protocols and get ready for a dozen people, plus the team, to stay at the agency."

"Fortress protocols?" Annie asked. Jordan didn't seem confused.

I raised my eyebrows at Jordan, and she answered my unspoken question: "We have a protocol if we need to shelter in place with a large group of people."

Jordan had used the term *shelter in place*, Mrs. Clark had called it a siege, and Helen had just said we needed to house and feed people. Something was going on that I wasn't fully aware of.

Annie spoke up before I could put words to my confusion. "Cool. I can help with that. We're almost through the list from the journal."

"Oh good," I said. "You, me, and Mrs. Clark will meet after the four o'clock meeting."

"Speaking of which," Jordan said, "we might as well head out to the conference table—it's almost time."

CAM WAS ALREADY at the conference table. She was huddled over her laptop, working on something. I went and sat by her. She looked up at me, confused that I wasn't in my normal seat.

I lowered my voice to a whisper. "I didn't want you to be surprised. We found something else that pointed to Sarah being at risk." Cam stiffened, and I hurried to continue, "Helen called Michael. Sarah and Michael are both coming to the office. They'll be here tomorrow morning."

She let out a sigh of relief. "Thank you for letting me know."

"Helen is going to update the whole team," I added.

She nodded her understanding. I got up and went back to my normal seat. All the other seats filled up quickly. Helen, as usual, came in just as everyone else also joined and got settled.

"From the updates I've been getting, it sounds like everyone had a productive afternoon," Helen started off. "We've still got a lot to do, so I'm going to summarize and talk next steps. Please interrupt if you need to add anything or have questions."

I prepared to take notes. Helen could be hard to keep up with when she got in the zone, and based on how her face was set, she was ready to pull all the threads together.

"We have all the evidence we need to make a move against Director Owens," she said firmly. I noticed that she had begun to call her Director Owens more often, rather than Cora.

Even though I knew that this was the outcome we were working toward, it felt weird having it said out loud.

"Now is the time," she said and looked over at Hank. "With

the address from the journal, Hank was able to determine that the building is in use. We aren't sure how many people are being held there or what exactly is happening. Also, I received an email from Director Owens this afternoon." She paused and looked at all of us. "Director Owens has demanded that the agency cease operations, effective immediately, pending a thorough investigation of our processes and premises."

The table erupted in angry chatter. Helen gave us all a moment to express our anger and then cleared her throat to return our attention to her.

"Obviously, we aren't going to do that," she said with a sly smile. "But I think this is a sign that the Director either knows or suspects that we are investigating her. So we need to move fast."

Everyone nodded along with her proclamation.

"To make a move, we need allies. I've already called the werewolves', witches', and vampires' regional leadership. They will be sending representatives tomorrow. I still have a few phone calls to make."

"Did you tell them what it's about?" Steve asked with concern.

"Only the werewolves' leadership," she answered. "The other ones, well, I had to pull some favors to get them to come without giving them a reason."

"Good," Steve said. "I'm not sure who we can trust yet."

"I agree," Helen said. "But we'll need to convince them about what is going on. So, Jordan, Angela, and Winthrop, I will need the three of you to work with me on compiling the case."

They all nodded. Winthrop had a wicked grin, and the light pulled around him like a spotlight.

"Linda, Annie, and Mrs. Clark are going to prep the office for our visitors," she continued. "We are initiating fortress protocol."

Steve and Jordan nodded sternly; they must have been the ones who already knew exactly what that meant.

Helen explained, "That means that, starting tomorrow, I need all of you—including you, Winthrop—to stay at the office for an indeterminate amount of time."

Every face around the table looked resolved with a touch of nerves.

Helen softened. "I know this sounds scary, but we have a plan for this type of situation. Go home tonight, pack for at least a week's stay for you and any pets you need to bring to the office, and coordinate with Linda if you have any special needs or requests."

Special requests I could handle. That was one of my talents, and I loved when I could help the team feel taken care of.

Jordan raised her hand to get Helen's attention and then asked, "Who are we expecting to come as representatives?"

"Michael for the werewolves, but he may include the local pack as well," Helen said and looked toward Cam. "Sarah will be coming with him for her safety."

Thank you, Cam mouthed.

Helen continued, "The witches and vampires both needed to discuss. They'll be getting back to me this evening with their representatives' names." Helen looked down the table at Winthrop. "I suggested you as a representative."

Winthrop gave a sharp nod. "I'll make a phone call and ensure that is the case."

Helen smiled her thanks. "I'm going to ask Doria to serve as the representative for the demons. They usually aren't included in conclaves like this, but I think it's time that they were."

Plus, I knew that Doria had told us to call her when we made our move. This seemed like the kind of move to call her about. Jordan's face told me that she was thinking the same thing.

"I still need to get in touch with the sirens' leadership," Helen concluded.

I raised my hand. "What about the rare supernaturals, like Mr. Gray?" *And me,* I thought but didn't say out loud.

Steve answered, "Like the demons, they usually don't participate in conclaves."

"But shouldn't they have representation in this? They are being targeted as well," I questioned. "Maybe Mr. Gray could be their representative?"

We all looked toward Helen. She looked thoughtful for a moment and then said, "I agree. They should be represented, and I think Mr. Gray would be a great choice for that. I will call him."

Mrs. Clark cleared her throat and gave a look toward Helen.

"Right," Helen said. "Per the fortress protocols, you'll all have a list of responsibilities we'll need you to take on while we have guests. Those are listed in the document that Linda will send out to you all after this meeting. Please let her know if you have any questions."

I made a panicked face toward Mrs. Clark; I still had no idea what they were talking about. She just smiled back at me. Her face told me that I'd learn soon.

The meeting wrapped up. Steve, Hank, and Cam followed Helen to her office to review the security plan. Jordan led Angela and Winthrop to her office to outline the case that we'd present to all the conclave representatives. Annie, Mrs. Clark, and I went down to the kitchen to talk about our tasks over treats.

Mrs. Clark floated around the kitchen, pulling out cheese, crackers, and tea for us. She also made a tray for the other two groups. "The document is in your inbox," she told me. "Send that out to the rest of the team while Annie and I deliver these snacks to the others."

"I will do that," I said, popping a piece of gouda in my mouth as they left the kitchen.

The document was ten pages long and mostly bullet-point lists. It spelled out preparation items and daily tasks during the active days. The list also included each person on the team, not including our consultant Winthrop. Someone had been keeping it updated.

I skimmed the document and then sent it out with a reminder to let me know if there were any questions. I probably wouldn't know the answer, but I could find the right person to ask. A round of thank-you emails came back, confirming that everyone had received it.

Halfway through a more thorough reading on the second page, Annie and Mrs. Clark came back. We moved our treats and laptops to the kitchen table, where we could more easily talk and snack.

"I guess because we don't have a lot of time to prepare, we should start with that list and make sure we have it covered," I suggested, looking around for agreement.

Annie smiled. "That sounds like a good idea."

"Mrs. Clark, there is a whole section on food," I said. Starting there seemed like the easiest thing to check off. "Do you need any help with that?"

"No," she said calmly. "I'll make a supply run tonight for a few things, and may need to do another trip in the morning, but we stay pretty well stocked."

"Great," I said and made a note for myself on my notepad. "The other big section is on sleeping arrangements. It looks like we'll need the full list before making the room assignments, but I think I can get started on that. Mrs. Clark, I'd love for you to check that over for me before it's finalized."

"Of course," she said. "Also you should plan on the two guest rooms in my cottage and the sofa bed if it's needed."

"That still doesn't sound like enough rooms," Annie said what I had been thinking.

"I know." I sighed. "I guess we'll have to double up in rooms."

"Or," Mrs. Clark offered, "we could open up the bomb shelter bunk rooms for the team to use."

Annie and I stared at her. I found my words first. "We have a bomb shelter?"

"Yes," she said nonchalantly. "Basement floor three, the door is hidden in the wood paneling in the foyer on that floor. I can show you. Plus, the extra bathrooms and showers down there in the gym will make it more comfortable as a place to stay. The bomb shelter only has two bathrooms, but it does have beds for all of us."

"Okay," I said and made another note for myself. "Sounds like we know where the team will stay."

"Include Helen in that," Mrs. Clark said sternly. "She'll want her suite to go to one of the guests."

"Got it," I said. She was right, that's what Helen would want. She wasn't the type of boss who wanted special treatment.

"And if you need it, I can clear out my room for a guest," she added.

"I'm not sure we'll need that. But either way, it sounds like every room is going to be used," I said, making the list on the paper. "That's four rooms on the third floor, one room on this floor, the two rooms in your cottage, and then the bomb shelter for the team." I looked at Mrs. Clark and Annie. "Anything I'm forgetting for sleeping arrangements?"

"Oh," Annie said. "The vampires won't need to sleep. They can go several weeks without it. They'll probably just want a dark space to retreat to if they need privacy and then a place to freshen up."

"We could set up the back parlor for them," I suggested. "And there's a bathroom back by it that they could use."

"That should work," Mrs. Clark confirmed.

I was feeling better about the sleeping situation.

"Annie, let's go check all the rooms," I said. "We can do

a quick refresh if needed and remove any personal items that shouldn't be there."

"Every room should already have fresh linens and towels," Mrs. Clark said. I smiled at her; it was like she knew this was coming, but then again, she always ran a tight ship.

"Thank you," I said. "I'll put together the room assignments as soon as I get the list from Helen."

"We can get this done tonight," Annie said encouragingly.

"Yes, we can," Mrs. Clark added. "You two go check the rooms while I make my shopping list, and then I'll show you the basement bomb shelter."

Annie and I exchanged excited looks. I'd never seen a bomb shelter before, but I bet ours was fancy.

24

I stared at my bedroom ceiling the next morning. It was too early to get out of bed, but my mind was spinning. We had stayed at the office until eight before Helen forced us all to go home and insisted that we didn't come back to the office until after eight the next morning.

Annie, Mrs. Clark, and I had prepared all the spaces. Mrs. Clark picked some greenery and small purple blooms from the garden for each room. She was disappointed that it was still too early for a proper flower arrangement.

We had gone down to the third floor of the basement to check out the shelter where the team would be staying. The door was well hidden but Mrs. Clark found it easily. Based on the state of it, she must have regularly come down there to dust and refresh the room.

It had two large spaces and two smaller bathrooms. The first large space had couches and a large table, a small galley kitchen on one wall, and racks of bins lining the other wall. The other room was smaller than the first and had queen-size bunk beds built into the walls on two sides. The bathroom doors were at the end of the room. It was more utilitarian than the rest of the office but still had nicer things than most hotels.

Helen sent me the final guest list around seven that evening. I went over the sleeping arrangements again in my head. There were ten people in total, plus our team. They would start arriving at ten that morning, and everyone should be in by lunchtime.

I had already assigned rooms to Michael, Sarah, Doria, and Mr. Gray I had already assigned rooms. I figured they would be on the list before I got it from Helen. Sarah would be in the room that Helen used on the third floor. Michael would be in the room across from it so he could be close to her. Doria would be in the guest room on the main floor; it had the most built-in security, and Steve insisted on that room for her. Mr. Gray would take one of the rooms in Mrs. Clark's cottage.

The witches were sending Hazel from the local coven, and Ivy would be coming in from a coven in the south. There was a note that they were good friends and offered to share a room. Mrs. Clark suggested that they would be most comfortable in one of her cottage rooms.

The vampires had agreed on Winthrop but would also be sending over Ms. Wadsworth from the local family to "balance the reaction," as they put it. I talked with Winthrop and he agreed that our plan to give them the parlor as a private space and the adjacent bathroom would be comfortable for them.

The sirens were also sending two representatives, Mira and Ara. Both were local because sirens didn't like to travel far from their homes. They requested separate rooms and bathtubs. Luckily, the third-floor bedrooms all had bathtubs and freestanding showers.

The team was okay with the sleeping arrangement in the basement shelter. It was clear from the reactions that everyone except Annie, Angela, and I had known about the shelter in the basement. Even Winthrop seemed to know, which unnerved Steve.

I rolled over and decided that six o'clock was late enough in the morning to get out of bed. I stood in front of my bathroom mirror, giving myself time to wake up. Something felt off. The strange feeling was back. More than ever, it was like someone was just outside of my field of vision, but every time I moved to see, they weren't there. It tickled the edges of my brain. I realized that it felt kind of like when I made contact with my mom in the last vision. Smiling, I let myself remember *Linda, close your eyes.*

I closed my eyes to recapture the feeling of seeing my mom. Instead of seeing my mom, I found myself in Cora's office. It was darker than normal; the harsh overhead lights weren't on. A soft sound of breathing drew my attention to the desk. Cora was sitting there with her eyes closed, hands braced flat on the desk in front of her. She was muttering something I couldn't make out.

Holding my breath, I willed the vision to end. I didn't want to be there. It didn't feel like a normal vision. I watched Cora carefully. The moments dragged on. Then suddenly her eyes snapped open.

"Interesting," she said, the coldness in her voice making me shiver. "I was wondering where you went."

She was clearly talking directly to me. I didn't respond.

"Can you hear me?" she asked, a mix of curiosity and concern.

I froze in place. She looked confused. This was new to her too. She stared at me and then suddenly lifted both hands and slapped them back on the desk. I didn't flinch.

She got up and walked over to me. "What are you seeing?" she mumbled.

I didn't move. I kept my breath steady. I wanted it to be over.

An evil grin filled her face. "Are you trying to spy on me? Helen has gone too far. You're all in trouble now."

I was frozen in fear, unsure how much longer I could stay still. I didn't know what to do. My mom's voice came into my mind: "Open your eyes, now!"

The whoosh was sudden and left me nauseous. I gripped the bathroom counter and gave myself a few minutes to steady. Cora had talked to me in a vision. She said she wondered where I went. Had she been watching me? Shit. Every time I felt someone watching me just out of view, was that her? What did she know?

I needed to get to the office.

I TOOK a quick shower and threw things in the bag to finish preparing for the week. I had avoided Ilka's things. She had never stayed away from the house, and while she was used to seeing my things packed up, I had no idea how she would react to having her things packed up. There wasn't time to worry about that anymore.

Turned out, I didn't have to worry. Ilka sat at attention and supervised me as I took her food, toys, litter box, and dishes. As I was zipping up the bag of her things, she walked over and put a paw on her favorite blanket. I followed her instructions and brought that too. When I pulled out the cat carrier that I used to take her to the vet, she walked right into it and laid down. She was a strange cat.

I sat in the dark, waiting for my ride, willing myself not to have a vision and not to do anything that Cora could see and use against us. It was 7:45 when the car I had arranged to take me, Ilka, and all of our stuff pulled up to the office. Lights were on, and I was relieved that I wasn't the first one there.

Annie met me at the door. "Almost everyone is here. I'm having folks take their things straight down to the shelter."

"Do you know if Helen is here already?"

"She's upstairs." Annie looked at me, worried. "Are you okay?"

"I don't know," I answered truthfully. "Can you watch Ilka? She's asleep, so just leave her in her carrier. I need to talk to Helen."

"Of course," Annie said. I was already walking away.

Helen was in her office, luckily not on the phone. "Linda, what's wrong?"

I wasn't surprised that she could tell I was upset about

something. Sitting on the edge of the chair in front of her desk, I quickly told her about my morning and my fear that Cora knew what was going on.

Helen looked stoic. "I was afraid of that. We have wards on your home. But she's had a lot of contact with you and that may have helped her get past them."

"So she knows everything," I lamented.

"No," Helen said. "Not necessarily."

"But she knows something," I countered. "She was really angry with you."

Helen scoffed. "It wouldn't be the first time. And she probably doesn't know that we know that she knows."

"I'm sorry for all of this, I should have been more careful."

"You don't need to be sorry. None of this is your fault."

I nodded, but I wasn't sure I believed her.

"But," Helen continued, "we have learned something new."

"What's that?" I perked up.

"Based on how you described it, I think you were able to make contact with Cora in your vision because she was actively trying to have a vision about you."

"Oh."

Helen smiled. "That may be useful in the future."

"That's good, I guess."

"It is good," Helen said cryptically. "For now, you should be okay here. The wards are stronger. Don't worry about it right now. Go help with preparations, and don't tell anyone about this just yet. We'll talk more later."

"Okay." I said and left, happy to have something to focus on that wasn't Cora spying on me.

Back downstairs everyone was busy. I found Annie and shook my head. "I knew I should have come earlier."

"You're not the last one." Annie laughed. "Most of us came because we couldn't sleep."

"Do you know if Mrs. Clark got what she needed?" I asked.

"Yes," she answered. "But she and Steve took the van to Costco to get another load."

"Is Costco even open right now?"

"Helen made a phone call," Annie answered.

"Of course she did." There was no end to what Helen was capable of. I wanted to be her when I grew up. It also made me wonder if Costco had otherworldly connections. "Do you think anyone would have a problem if I let Ilka wander around the house?" I asked. "I don't think she'll like being kept in a room."

"No, I don't think anyone would mind," Annie said. "The only other pet that will be coming is Hank's cog, Juniper, and she's so chill. I bet they will get along."

"He's not here yet?"

"No, he'll probably come right on time." Annie smirked. "He's a rule follower."

I laughed and bent down to let Ilka out of her carrying case. She stretched on her way out and then walked right over to rub against Annie's legs.

Annie bent down to give her some scratches. "Oh, I've missed you too."

"I'll go take my things downstairs," I said, grabbing the

bags. "Can you keep an eye on Ilka to see how she settles in?"

"Of course," she answered and picked her up. "The two of us will go check the guest rooms again. That way I can give Ilka a tour of the building."

"Don't let her onto any of the beds," I said. "I'm not sure if anyone is allergic to cats."

Annie giggled as Ilka snuggled under her chin. "No one on the team is, but I'll check with our guests as they arrive."

"Ask them about dogs too."

"Will do."

They walked away up to the second floor, and I made my way toward the back of the house where the elevator to the basement was hidden. I passed Jordan on my way.

"Good morning," Jordan greeted me with her usual cheerfulness.

"Morning," I said, trying to sound cheerful. Helen didn't want me telling anyone yet and there was no sense worrying everyone. "How is the presentation coming along?"

I knew that they had worked on it until Helen kicked us all out to go home. I'd planned on taking a peek at the presentation that morning after I knew we were ready but before our guests started arriving.

"It's good," she said. "I think it's really solid. The only part that might get heated is what we should do about the situation."

"I don't think I thought that far ahead," I admitted. "What is the proposal?"

Jordan frowned. "We don't have one yet. That's the

problem." A commotion from the kitchen drew our attention, and Jordan grimaced. "I think they're back from the store. I'm going to go help them unload."

"Sounds good. I'll drop my stuff off and come back to see if you all still need help."

Jordan gave my arm a friendly squeeze and then headed to the kitchen. I opened the door to the elevator, punched in my code, and loaded my things to head down to the basement. There was no way I was dragging those bags down three flights of stairs.

The door to the shelter was propped open. A couple of bags were on the couches in the living space. Back in the bunk room more bags were on the floor and some on beds. I found a bed that looked empty of things and set my bags on it. We'd reshuffle beds if needed once everyone got there.

Based on the count of beds with belongings on them and accounting for Mrs. Clark staying in her cottage instead of down there, two of us were not there yet. I knew one of them was Hank, and I guessed that the other was Cam.

Cam's lab was on the second floor of the basement. I decided to stop by to see if she was there and had just gone straight to the lab instead of taking her stuff to the shelter. She was really stressed about figuring out the suppression device so that she could counteract it.

The lights in her lab were on. I pushed the door open and called out, "Cam?"

"Over here," she answered, standing in front of an open cabinet.

"You *are* here," I said and walked into the lab. Cam looked a bit ragged. I was worried about her. "I didn't see your stuff down in the shelter."

Cam gestured over to a pile of bags by the door. "I didn't make it that far."

"Is there anything you need? Have you had anything to eat yet this morning?"

"No." She sighed. "And no. But I'll come up soon and get some breakfast. I'm so close to figuring this out."

"Okay, don't forget to eat," I gave one last attempt and then headed upstairs to see where I could be helpful.

THE KITCHEN COUNTERS were filled with food and drinks, and more was coming in loaded up in Jordan's arms and a cart pulled by Steve. Mrs. Clark walked around the island with a clipboard, checking off items on it. It looked like enough food to last us a month. I almost teared up when I saw a bag of cat food, the expensive brand my mom had gotten Ilka hooked on, sitting on the floor by the island.

Mrs. Clark caught my reaction. "Just in case," she told me. "We can't have our most special guests going hungry."

As if she knew we were talking about her, Ilka strutted into the kitchen with Annie following behind.

Annie laughed at the sight of the kitchen filled with food. "This looks like enough. Where are we going to put it all?"

Mrs. Clark huffed, a little affronted. "We'll find room."

"There are some empty bins in the basement," Jordan

offered. "We can fill those and then store extra stuff down there."

"Oh, I also plugged in the extra refrigerators down in the large pantry," Mrs. Clark said and went back to checking off items on her clipboard.

I turned to Jordan. "We have extra fridges? And a larger pantry?"

"Yes," she answered. "We don't use it much, but it's part of the fortress protocol."

"That was not on the document," I mumbled to myself. "I'll get it added for next time."

Jordan laughed. "You'll probably be adding a lot of stuff, but hopefully we won't need this protocol again."

Jordan, Annie, Angela, and I each took an armful of items that we were told needed to go into the basement refrigerators. There were five in total in a small room that also had empty shelves. The two large refrigerators and two equally large freezers would hold food. The smaller refrigerator was waiting for the supplies the vampires would need. Hank was making that supply run that morning.

After dropping off the food in cold storage, we grabbed some empty bins and headed back upstairs. Mrs. Clark sorted the items into bins and labeled each one with tape that had a date on it. She asked us to put the bins on the shelf in order so they would be easy to find.

Steve finished unloading the van, and then he helped us sort and move everything to where it needed to go. It went quicker with his help and the cart he had that could hold heavier bins.

Soon we were back to a normal kitchen and the smell of bacon frying and croissants baking. The coffee Mrs. Clark had started was ready and we all grabbed a starter mug to take a break.

Steve looked my way as we all sat at the kitchen table. "So, what else do we need to do before people start arriving?"

"Well, the rooms are all ready," I answered as I thought through the list in my head. "We know who will be in which room. Mrs. Clark has all the food under control. We've got drivers arranged to pick up everyone who's coming in from out of town. And you've got security handled." I looked around the table to see if anyone had anything to add. They didn't. "I think we are ready."

The doorbell rang ominously as if in response to my declaration.

I looked at the clock on the wall. "We weren't expecting anyone this early, right?"

Angela shook her head. "It's not Winthrop, he would have just come in."

Steve looked at his phone and stood abruptly, knocking the table and making all our cups rattle. "Stay here," he told us all.

"Does anyone else have the doorbell camera feed on their phone?" I asked as he ran out of the room.

Jordan was already pulling out her phone. "I do."

We all looked her way and gave her a moment to pull up the app.

She took in a sharp breath. "It looks like it's someone from the Council."

"It's not Cora, is it?" I asked.

"No," Jordan answered. "I don't recognize them, but based on their outfits, they are either from the Council or missionaries. They look too much like werewolves to be missionaries."

Several of us let out a nervous laugh. We heard the front door close. Jordan narrated what she was seeing on her phone: "Steve went out on the porch to talk with them. They are handing him some papers. One of them is saying something to Steve. Steve does not look happy. They are walking down the front steps."

The front door opened. We all tried to look inconspicuous as Steve walked back holding a stack of papers.

Jordan asked what we all wanted to know: "What did they want?"

"They came to make sure we received the orders to shut down operations," Steve said. "They also seriously implied that they will be watching the office to make sure we comply."

I made a worried face. "I think they may notice the parade of otherworldly leaders who will be coming to the office today."

"Who will notice?" Helen asked as she came into the kitchen.

"The Council's werewolf thugs," Steve said and handed her the papers.

I raised my eyebrows at Annie; that was the most unprofessional thing I'd ever heard Steve say. She made a similar surprised face back at me.

Helen skimmed through the papers. "I think we are going to need a new plan. Give me ten minutes."

We all sat wondering what was happening as she turned on her heel and headed back upstairs.

"I guess we have breakfast and see what she comes back with," I said to the confused table.

Mrs. Clark, with impeccable timing, sat a stack of plates down on the table. "Eggs will be ready in five minutes. Come grab the other things."

Everyone got up and brought something back to the table, setting it with utensils and plates of food. We were all there, so it was easier to eat family-style.

"Should we grab Cam?" I asked.

"I'll go get her," Annie offered. "We should also call Hank and see how close he is."

Steve pulled out his phone. "I'll call Hank."

A loud meow sounded from the front of the house, and then the front door opened. Annie laughed as she got up. "I think Hank just got here. I'll go get Cam."

Five minutes later, all of us, including Cam and Hank, were eating eggs, bacon, fruit, and croissants at the kitchen table. We had filled the two of them in on what had happened. Everyone ate slowly. Juniper and Ilka had become fast friends and were curled up on a dog bed that Hank had brought in and put in the corner. The cuteness of it helped distract us all until Helen came back down with a satisfied smile.

"Okay, I think we have a new plan," she said, sitting down in the empty chair at the table.

We all gave her a moment to catch her breath.

"Doria has agreed to help us," she said with a smile.

Steve voiced all of our confusion: "How?"

"It turns out that Doria still has an open portal," she said with a grimace. "It's in her basement."

I blurted out what first came to mind: "We're going to another dimension."

"No," Helen reassured me. "Doria can point the portal to a space in this dimension. We just need a location that doesn't have radio wave interference."

She looked at Cam. It took Cam a moment, but then she perked up. "The RF chamber in my lab."

"Exactly," Helen said with a smile. "You'll have to relocate some of your projects. But we can use the RF chamber to create a portal entrance. We'll have to reroute our guests to Doria's home, and then she'll shepherd them here."

"I'll call the drivers," I offered.

Helen smiled in my direction. "That would be great. I'll call the local folks. Steve and Jordan, can you call Doria so she can give you instructions on what you'll do on our end to help her?"

They both agreed, but Steve looked skeptical.

"Cam, do you need help clearing out your lab?" Helen asked with a worried look.

"No," Cam answered. "I only have one active project, and it's almost done. I can finish it and then store it."

"Oh," Helen said, surprised. "That's great." Helen turned toward Angela. "Can you call Winthrop and have him come soon? He can skip the portal. I have a feeling the Council people have been watching our office for a while.

They'll be used to seeing him around and it shouldn't raise any red flags."

"I'll do that," she answered.

"Great, then you can both come help finish up the case presentation. Everyone else, keep doing whatever we need to get done to be ready," she said and stood up to leave. "Keep Linda in the loop and let her know if you have any questions or concerns."

Mrs. Clark handed Helen a plate of food as she left the kitchen. "You heard her," Mrs. Clark rallied us all. "Let's get things ready, and if you don't have anything to do, you can help me peel and cut vegetables."

Mrs. Clark may have thought she was threatening us, but everyone at that table would have gladly helped her prepare vegetables for lunch.

25

The portal being created in Cam's lab was too interesting to resist. Once I called to reroute the drivers and made sure everything was as ready as it could be, I stopped by to see if Mrs. Clark needed any help. She didn't, so I went down to the lab to see how it was going.

Steve stood in front of the closed door to the RF chamber, blocking the view of what was going on inside. Cam was at the workbench clearing away the rest of the project she'd been working on.

"All done?" I asked her vaguely when I caught her attention.

Cam smiled back. "Yes. It's not tested, but I think it's done."

"Both versions?" I tried to find a way to ask about the counter device without spilling the beans to everyone else in the room.

"Yes," she confirmed.

"So you've destroyed the bad version?"

"Not yet," she answered and then quickly went back to work putting things away in bins.

I knew Cam was at a breaking point and was still worried about Sarah, so I didn't press the issue with her. Instead, I walked over to Steve.

"Everything going okay over here?" I asked quietly, not wanting to startle him.

He turned toward me, smiled, and replied, "Yes, and I think you are just in time."

"In time for what?"

He motioned toward the RF chamber. Past Steve, I could see Jordan through the small window in the closed door and a dark swirling void filling the back of the chamber in front of her. It played tricks with my eyes. At times, I thought I could see flashes of faces or views into rooms, like looking through a window being blasted with a stream of water. It reminded me of when my visions were blocked and I couldn't see them clearly. I didn't have long to think about that before a hand very clearly popped out of the middle of the swirling void.

I took a step back. Steve stood still. Jordan, in the booth, moved forward and reached both hands out to grab the hand sticking out of the void. Jordan pulled and leaned back into the corner of the chamber, pulling whoever was in the void with her. I watched as the hand became an arm, then a shoulder, then a head, followed by a body.

Doria stood in the open chamber and tilted her head side to side to crack her neck. Jordan knocked on the door. Steve and I both backed up as she swung the door open.

"Phew," Doria exclaimed. "I haven't done that in a while. Glad it worked."

"Glad it worked?" Steve echoed. "What would have happened if it hadn't worked?"

Doria patted him on the back. "It doesn't matter now. It worked, and it seems stable."

Jordan chuckled. "I think it's cool."

"It is cool," Doria agreed. "Remember, I'll need someone down here just in case. But I should be able to walk through now with our guests."

"*Our* guests," Steve corrected.

"That's what I said," Doria answered with a smile.

He shook his head. "Do you need anything else?"

"Nope," she answered, not losing her cheerfulness. "Just let me know when you want me to bring folks through."

I cleared my throat in the background. "They should start getting to your house in about fifteen minutes."

"Cutting it close then," Doria said.

"I staggered the drivers, so you should have at least ten minutes between each one. There are eight in total, not counting you. Here's the list."

I handed her the list we had created of who should be coming. Helen, Steve, and I'd had a somewhat heated conversation about trusting Doria to greet and shepherd people on her own. I reminded Steve that outside of the agency's wards, the director could hone in on any of us to get a view of what we were doing. She couldn't do that with Doria.

Helen agreed it was worth the risk to keep the director in the dark about what was happening. Also, she added that if we were trusting Doria with the portal, we should be able to trust her with the first step of getting the people there.

"Cool," Doria said and took the list. "I'll head back home and wait for *your* first guest."

"Thank you," I called out as she walked back into the chamber and closed the door. It was strange to see her disappear through the void.

"Annie is going to come down, and we'll take care of the handoff," I said to Jordan and Steve. "Helen asked me to have you both head up to her office once the portal was done."

"Yeah," Jordan agreed. "We need to finish the proposal presentation."

"Any decision on what to do with the director?" I asked.

"Not yet," she said.

Steve added, "We have a few options. We could present those and see what the group thinks."

"We still need to write them up," Jordan answered before I could ask. "You can check them out before the meeting with the full conclave at two o'clock."

It had been decided that it would be best to get everyone settled and fed before breaking the news to them that the director of the Council, whom they trusted to uphold the peace and order of all the otherworldly communities in North America, had actually been abducting and murdering members of those communities.

～

THE PORTAL WORKED FLAWLESSLY. Annie and I greeted and ushered our guests from the portal in the basement to their rooms, where they could freshen up. We got a few shocked looks when they realized there was a basement to the agency's mansion-turned-office. Luckily for us, most of them were still reeling from the trip through the portal and didn't have the emotional or mental space to take in the weirdness of our basement.

I messaged Cam when we were expecting Sarah. She was waiting as Doria pulled Sarah through the portal. Cam rushed over to her, and I had to turn around so that I wouldn't cry watching the reunion.

Everyone settled into their rooms and had a wonderful lunch of soup, salad, and sandwiches. I was eating my lunch upstairs at the conference table when Annie came through the double doors of my office with a cart full of chairs. She must have used the elevator to bring them up from the basement.

"Steve and Hank are on their way with the table," Annie said as she started to unload.

I hurried to eat my last bite and then jumped up to help her. "What's going on?" I asked.

"Helen decided that this would be the easiest space to fit everyone."

"That's what I thought too," I replied. We had talked the night before about how we were going to fit all nineteen of us in a room. The winning idea had been to set chairs around the edges of the large conference room downstairs. We couldn't fit everyone around that table, but the room would hold us.

That decision had clearly been changed last minute.

I looked around the space that we were adapting to fit our needs. "Do we need to move anything else to make room?"

"We're going to shift the table a bit so that we can double it up and extend it," Annie said with her hands on her hips, taking a breath after unloading the extra chairs.

"I think we should move the sideboards on one wall," I offered.

"Good idea. I'll help you. We can put them in the office closest to them."

Annie and I got to work scooting the sideboard cabinets to whichever office was easiest to put them in. In the middle of moving the last one, Steve came into view from my office with some table legs in a cart.

"Great idea," he encouraged us when he saw the space we were making.

The three of us moved the conference table over and then set up the legs just in time for Hank and Cam to come in with the two top pieces and other metal parts.

"What else do we need?" I asked the group.

Cam peeked from around the table where she was crouched down tightening fasteners. "The TV on the stand in Helen's office. We are going to use that for the presentation."

"I'll grab that," I offered. "Annie, I've also got the packets printed, but they need to be sorted and put into the folders. Do you have time to help me with that after?"

"Of course," she said.

I checked my phone for the time. We had about an

hour before the meeting would start. I still hadn't had a chance to read the full proposal.

THIRTY MINUTES LATER, the conference table was set up, the TV was in place, and packets were set at each chair along with a notebook, pen, sticky notes, water glass, and a small bowl with treats. We had also decided to assign seating. Hank hand-wrote each name card; it turned out he knew calligraphy and kept a fancy pen set in the office. The name cards were lovely.

I snuck away to my office to read as much of the proposal as I could before the meeting started. I knew much of the setup, so I skipped to the end. Helen would have the joint conclave review the evidence of Cora's crimes and take a vote of no confidence, then they would discuss three proposals for how to proceed.

The first was to leave punishment up to the Council Forum. Even though Director Owens was a member of that forum, they technically were supposed to oversee each other, but that clearly hadn't been happening. I wasn't fond of that option.

The second option was to keep her under house arrest within either vampire or pack territory. Those two groups had the best abilities and the needed resources to contain her.

The third option was to use the building that the director herself had been working on to confine others. The new director would need to oversee that confinement.

The last option threw me. I flipped back several pages and found the section where the proposal recommended that a new Council director be appointed and that the Council undergo reform.

A pull in my gut fought the anger in my head and won. A whoosh and tunnel vision pulled me into a vision. The anger came with me.

The room I was standing in was familiar but with some changes. It took me a moment to realize that I was standing in Cora's office in San Francisco. The room was lighter, with plants on the shelves and a bowl of candy sitting in the middle of the conference table. The big desk was the same, but the hardwood chairs in front of it had been replaced with soft-looking mid-century modern chairs. A new couch and chairs had been set up like a sitting room in the middle of the room.

The door to the office opened. I moved out of the way even though they probably wouldn't see me. Four women walked into the office. The two I recognized were Helen and Cora. The other two were clearly supernatural, a were-wolf and a vampire.

All four walked over to the small table and sat down. Cora's back was to me so that I couldn't see her face. Helen, whom I could see, was smiling and talking to the group.

It wasn't clear when the meeting took place, but my gut said it was in the future. My gut was also angry with what I was seeing. If we didn't make the right decision, then Director Owens would stay right where she was, and nothing would get better, and more people would be hurt. And, somehow, Helen would be wrapped up in all of it.

Angry tears began to fall from my face in the vision. I closed my eyes to try to stop them. When I opened them back up, a quick whoosh rang in my ears, and I was back at my desk in the office holding the stack of papers. A few teardrops left marks on the top paper I had been reading.

The proposal to keep the Council running had to be wrong. If we did that, then my vision would probably come true, and nothing would have changed except for a few plants and a couple of chairs. That wasn't going to happen if I had any say in it.

A ping from my phone gave me a ten-minute warning that the meeting was going to start. I didn't have time to talk with Helen. Steve and Jordan were probably busy too. I didn't know what I was going to do, but right then, it was time to go to a meeting.

MRS. CLARK and Annie set up the last drinks and snacks on the table. I felt a little guilty; I should have helped them. They both just smiled at me and finished up what they were doing.

"Any final things I can help with?" I asked.

"Nope," Annie said cheerfully. "Everything is ready to go."

It was good timing because folks started to come into the space and find their places at the table. I was in my normal seat, but because of how the conference tables were set up, Annie was to my right instead of across the table from me. Jordan was sitting at the top of the table next to Helen. The rest of the team was scattered among the community representatives. Helen and Mrs. Clark had been particular about who would be sitting where.

Although most of the representatives didn't know exactly why they were there, everyone settled in and chatted easily with those sitting close by. I tamped down the anger I was still feeling about the proposal to keep the Council and the vision I had seen.

Annie tapped my arm and whispered, "Are you okay?"

"Yes," I lied. "I think it's just nerves about this meeting."

"That's fair," she said. "At least with us sitting next to each other, we can pass notes."

I smiled and thanked the universe for a friend like Annie.

Helen came in and sat down at the head of the table to my left. We still had a few minutes until the meeting time. She let everyone finish up their conversations, and the room naturally settled into a ready silence.

"First," Helen started with a smile, "I want to thank everyone for coming on such short notice and for trusting me regarding the importance of the meeting even though I wasn't able to give you details."

Several heads nodded, and a few folks let out a small chuckle. Helen looked around the table, and I tried to follow her eyes. I noticed that no one had opened the folder in front of them yet.

"Many of you know each other, but I'd like to start with a round of introductions," Helen said. "I'll start."

Helen introduced herself and then gestured to Jordan to go next so we'd introduce clockwise around the table. The introductions quickly went through Michael and Sarah, who represented the werewolf packs. Steve sat next to them. Then came the sirens, Mira and Ara.

I looked closer when I heard Mira introduce herself. The voice was familiar and I realized that she was the other woman in the vision I had at Doria's house. Doria and Mira didn't seem to know each other. Maybe it was a vision of the future. I let it go and tried to concentrate on the other introductions.

Hank sat between the sirens and the witches, Hazel and Ivy. Mrs. Clark and Cam sat at the end of the table. Ms. Wadsworth and Winthrop were next on the other side.

Mr. Gray's introduction caused a bit of a stir, but he handled it well and ended with a reminder for everyone: "Thank you for including me as a representative of the rare otherworldly community members. We may not be a homogeneous group, but put together, we are the largest group among the communities represented at this table. I appreciate Ms. Pendleton for having the foresight to include us."

"Please call me Helen," Helen responded with a smile. She shared her smile with the rest of the table, giving everyone the message that this would be how things were done from now on if she had any say in it.

The stir Mr. Gray caused was nothing compared to Doria's introduction. I realized why Mrs. Clark had sat the two of them sandwiched between the bulk of the team on one side and Angela with the vampires on the other side.

Also, it made sense that Helen had gone clockwise, leaving Doria for near the end.

"It's a pleasure to be here," Doria started, the crackling echo of her voice barely detectable. "And I'm glad that the portal worked so well for everyone."

Several people leaned forward and seemed mostly curious, except for Hazel and Ivy. The two witches looked pissed.

Mira's melodic voice interrupted, "I hope you'll tell us more about the magic used for that. I didn't realize the witches of the Seattle coven had access to a portal."

"We don't," Hazel, the local coven member, said firmly.

Half the table looked confused, and side conversations broke out. The witches weren't answering any of the questions being shot their way. They both were glaring at Doria. Doria was smiling, trying to look innocent, and failing miserably. She looked pleased with the commotion.

Helen let the reactions go on for a moment and then cleared her throat. It took longer than normal, but it was a big group. Soon enough, everyone settled down and looked toward her.

"Doria"—she gestured in her direction—"please continue."

"The portal belongs to me," Doria said calmly. "I'm here representing the demons."

All hell broke out again, no pun intended. After all, demons weren't actually from hell. The witches were loudly asking why Helen had invited a demon into the agency. The sirens were trying to get the attention of the two witches, asking what they knew about demons. Ms.

Wadsworth was having a heated whisper conversation with Winthrop. Mr. Gray was trying to tell everyone that it was only fair to include the demons. Michael and Sarah weren't saying a word but they both looked ready to defend Helen if words turned to action.

I caught Helen rolling her eyes, which was very uncharacteristic of her. She leaned over and whispered something to Jordan. Annie slipped me a note that said *good start* with a smiley face. I elbowed her and suppressed a giggle.

Helen didn't respond directly to anyone but she let the side conversations and exclamations of concern go on a bit longer that time.

"Okay," she finally said loudly and clapped her hands together. The table went silent quicker than before. "Much like Mr. Gray representing the rare otherworldly communities, I decided that it was important for the demon community to be represented as well."

"But they aren't otherworldly, right?" Ara, the other siren, asked without malice.

Helen smiled politely at her and her genuine question. "They are technically the most otherworldly."

Doria smiled at that.

"But most importantly," Helen continued, "they have been outside the community for too long. Mostly due to misunderstandings and, if we're being honest, prejudice."

It was pretty clear who was already on Helen's side of the argument. Winthrop must have explained it satisfactorily to Ms. Wadsworth in their whispered exchange. She was sitting stoically in agreement. Michael and Sarah seemed to have already known about Doria as well. They both nodded along with Helen's statement. Mr. Gray, sitting next to Doria, had reached out and patted her arm. We already knew that they were longtime frenemies, but currently, they were more friends than enemies.

That just left four people undecided about what to do: the witches, who looked angry, and the sirens, who looked curious.

"Before we move on," Helen said, looking toward those two groups, "I need to know that everyone at this table can accept Doria and the demons' involvement going forward."

26

I tried not to breathe too hard as Helen stared down the other side of the table. She wasn't joking when she said she wouldn't move on until everyone agreed with Doria and the demons' involvement in the conclave. The silence that I was used to hung heavy in the air. I was debating who would crack first.

"I'm good with that," Mira's melodic voice answered. Ara, sitting next to her, nodded in agreement and sent her long hair floating behind her.

Helen smiled at them both and then turned back to the two witches with a neutral face.

"Fine," Hazel said in a tone that did not sound fine.

"Fine?" Helen asked back.

Hazel sighed, and the other witch, Ivy, nudged her with her elbow.

"Yes," Hazel said more convincingly. "We agree to Doria and the demons' involvement in the conclave."

Helen smiled. "Great, let's—"

"But," Hazel interrupted and looked at Doria, "I want your assurance that you'll commit to whatever the group decides on. There must be a reason Helen has been so insistent to get us here and it must be important."

Doria smiled. "I will." The crackle of her voice was prominent, and I noticed a few people recoil slightly. Doria either didn't notice or didn't care.

"Okay," Helen said slowly and looked around the table. "Any other questions or comments before we move on?"

She made eye contact with each person, and most shook their heads in response. I gave her an encouraging look; even badass bosses like Helen needed encouragement sometimes.

"Let's continue. Annie, please."

Annie introduced herself and then looked toward me.

I took a deep breath and followed the standard introduction that everyone had been giving. "I'm Linda Moss."

A few heads turned, and I thought I heard a sharp intake of breath from down my row. I clenched my fists under the table and continued. I couldn't think too hard about why my name created a stir.

"I'm Helen's EA and I've been working at the agency for the last six months," I finished in a rush and then looked at Helen. She smiled at me comfortingly. I smiled back and then looked down at the table.

Some low chatter had broken out in a few groups. Like before, Helen let it go on for a moment before I watched her make eye contact and make a *do you have a question* face at a few people.

Hazel raised her hand and waited for Helen to

acknowledge her. She glanced my way with an unclear expression, back to Helen, and then back my way before she asked me, "Are you Malinda's daughter?"

"Yes."

"Oh," she said, surprised, and looked back at Helen. I didn't see Helen's face but saw Hazel's expression falter and then set in a practiced-looking smile. "That's lovely."

Winthrop cleared his throat loudly and pulled the light in to spotlight himself. "I think it's time to move on to the meat of this meeting. Of course, if you are ready for that, Helen."

"I agree. Thank you for getting us back on track." Helen paused, closed her eyes for a moment, took a deep breath, and then started to explain, "We are faced with a pivotal moment to make a decision and act. The sad truth is that our communities have been targeted by the very person who has been charged with keeping us safe.

"We all know of friends, family, and acquaintances who have gone missing. Or who have died under mysterious circumstances. We now have evidence. We now know what has been going on. We can no longer sit by and let our communities remain afraid. We need to come together. We need to act. We need to remove Director Owens from the Council and ensure she can no longer harm anyone."

The room was silent. Faces were blank with schooled expressions to not reveal what they were thinking. I was angry that they weren't angry.

Helen, ever diplomatic, continued with the plan: "If everyone can turn to the first page in the folder in front of them."

Folders opened and pages ruffled as we all followed her instructions.

"There is a lot of information to go through and process," she said, getting everyone's attention back to her. "We felt that it would be easiest to have everyone read a summary of the evidence and charges, and then we can work through specific questions before moving on to decisions and a vote of no confidence. Any questions?"

Some of the folks around the table had already started reading. Others shook their heads and then followed the example of those who had started to read.

Mira let out a gasp. "I don't understand. The director has been abducting and murdering people for decades? Our people?"

Helen looked at her thoughtfully. "I know it's a lot to take in. Please keep reading, and you can write questions on the document or on the notepad in front of you. There will be plenty of time for discussion."

Mira nodded and went back to reading. It only took that one instance and Helen's calm but insistent answer to quell any other questions before the reading was completed. Several folks took Helen's suggestion and were writing. I had already skimmed the intro, but everyone on the team was reading it, so I put my head down to read it thoroughly as well.

The document was well written and easy to understand. They hadn't minced words and clearly laid out what was going on. Footnotes and references to appendices were added at specific points to provide more information or a piece of evidence. People would flip through the pages of the folder when they got to a point they wanted to know more about.

Mr. Gray started using the small sticky notes to tab specific documents. Soon, everyone around the table was doing the same. Annie slipped me a note around the ten-minute mark of reading: *This is going well.*

I wrote back, *Is it?*

I had no idea how long it was supposed to take. Since I'd already seen all the evidence, it didn't take me long to read through the document. I even took time to tag several of the points I thought were strongest.

Everyone had their heads down. My mind was wandering and I looked around, seeing if I could gauge any reactions. I noticed the lamps blinking slightly, dimming and then coming back to their full light. No one else seemed to notice.

Something drew my attention to the stairs going down to the first floor. A strange shadow rippled up the stairs and then painted the walls until it got to my office doors, where I lost view of it. Again, no one else seemed to notice. Maybe my mind was playing tricks on me. It had been a long day and my emotions were running high.

I was just going back to reading the document when I felt the presence of something on the edges of my view. I looked around the room, moving quickly side to side to try to catch what was there. A whisper of "close your eyes" startled me. The whisper wasn't the gentle sound of my mom. It was Cora. I snapped to attention, blanking out my mind. Helen caught my eyes. I probably looked terrified. I knew I felt that way.

Helen mouthed, *Are you okay?*

I nodded. The wards had to be working. The lights and shadow ripple seemed to mean that Cora was trying to push through. I had to hold her off, which meant not letting my mind wander and accidently inviting her in.

Another ten minutes passed. I kept my mind clear. The agency team looked restless, but the rest of the group was still reading intently and studying the materials we had provided. Jordan gave me her *have patience* look. I scrunched my nose back at her quickly in protest.

Another ten minutes passed. The reading, tabbing, and note-taking seemed to be slowing down. Helen must have thought so too.

She cleared her throat gently to get everyone's attention. "Let's take five more minutes and finish up where you are. Then we'll have a quick break to grab a drink, snack, or use the bathroom."

Mrs. Clark got up from the table quietly and motioned for Annie and me to join her. I happily got up and followed her downstairs to the kitchen.

She started to pull precut fruit and cheese from the fridge. "Can you two help me set up these snack trays and take them upstairs?"

We did as we were asked and started to arrange the cheese and fruit.

I let out a sigh and whispered to Annie, "It was smart to make them read the information rather than have a presentation that is interrupted every minute, but sitting that long in silence was brutal."

Annie and Mrs. Clark laughed quietly so the sound wouldn't travel upstairs to the still-reading group.

"Not as brutal as it could have been," Annie leaned in and said. "We learn from our mistakes. Last time we had a big meeting like this, it took an hour to get past the first three slides."

"And that topic wasn't even about overthrowing the director," Mrs. Clark teased as she set crackers out onto the trays.

Annie and I both laughed a bit uncomfortably at Mrs. Clark's joke. Then we all worked in silence for a few moments. I couldn't take any more silence.

"How do you think it's going?" I asked.

Annie shrugged. "No one has walked out yet, so they are at least considering it."

It took a few minutes before the trays were ready. The sounds of low chatter and chairs scraping meant that the group upstairs had paused for a break. The three of us each took a tray and headed upstairs.

Small groups had separated, and I overheard conversations about what they had just read. Everyone seemed to have come to the same conclusion: Director Owens was bad news, but they didn't know what to do about it.

Hank walked toward me and caught my attention. "I wanted to let you know that Ilka is in my office with Juniper. I just checked on them, and they are both sleeping."

I smiled at Hank. "Thank you, I was just going to go look for her."

"I'll let you know if I see her leave my office," he offered and then walked away to get some cheese and crackers.

I went in the opposite direction to join a conversation that Annie and Jordan were having. Jordan leaned toward me as I walked up. "What's the vibe you are picking up?" she asked.

"Good, I guess," I said quietly. "It seems like everyone is taking the evidence seriously."

"Agreed," Annie added. She paused and gestured over my shoulder with her head. "Looks like someone is coming over to talk with us."

Hazel and Ivy walked up, and we opened our circle to let them join.

Hazel, the more vocal of the two witches, looked my way. "We wanted to come say hello and introduce ourselves."

I reached out and shook the hands that were offered to me. "It's nice to meet you," I said.

"We knew your mother, Malinda," Hazel said with a sad smile. "She was a great woman."

"Thank you, I agree."

Ivy spoke quietly but asked, "If it's not too personal, I was wondering if you have your mother's gifts?"

I smiled and quickly thought of how to answer. Even if it wasn't explicitly in the documents we shared with them, it wasn't like everyone wouldn't find out at some point during the meetings.

"I do," I answered. "But I'm not sure if it's exactly the same."

"Oh, it never is," Ivy said. "You get the gift you need, not the one you want."

I wanted to ask her what she meant by that, but Helen clapped her hands together and asked everyone to take their seats so that we could get started again. Everyone sat quickly and settled back into the serious conversation that we needed to have.

"Thank you all for reading through the information. We thought it best to start by getting everyone the same context," Helen said and then gestured toward the TV that had been rolled over and plugged in during the break. "Jordan is going to walk through a summary, and then we'll start with questions and discussion."

Jordan stood with a clicker in hand by the TV. Chairs scooted around so that everyone had a view.

"As you read in the documents," Jordan started off with practiced ease, "we have three sources of evidence that we brought together to support our theory."

Jordan clicked through slides about the Moonstone Haven book. She shared the truth about how we had found it. Well, the truth without my visions. Throughout that section, glances were thrown toward Hazel and Ivy.

"Any questions about the Moonstone Haven book?" Jordan asked the group.

"Hazel and Ivy," Michael asked them, "were either of you aware of Moonstone Haven and can you corroborate this information?"

I made a hopefully subtle face toward Annie. Why was Michael trying to punch holes in our case? Did he not believe us?

"Yes," Hazel said after some hesitation. "Helen and her team are correct. We recently became aware that some witches within the covens and a few select other people have been running a network of people and locations to help conceal any otherworldly member who needed protection."

Michael smiled knowingly. I felt bad that I had doubted him. He was asking the questions that would help bolster our case, not hurt it.

He asked gently, "Who did you believe they needed protection from?"

Hazel and Ivy exchanged a worried look. "From the director," Hazel answered softly.

Mr. Gray, three people down from me, began to look red in the face and put off heat. He leaned forward and glared at the two witches across the table. "You knew what the director was doing," he accused.

"We didn't know everything," Ivy defended but sounded sad. "The witches involved thought it was just witches, so we kept it to ourselves. We didn't think anyone would help us or even believe us."

Ivy looked at Hazel for help. Hazel nodded and added, "But then they started to hear about other people, so they helped them. It still seemed like one-offs."

"How long?" Mr. Gray asked. His skin had started to return to his normal color, and the heat was no longer noticeable.

"About thirty years," Hazel answered.

Several people gasped around the table. Mr. Gray let

out a sigh of steam that could be seen dissipating in front of him.

"To be fair," Winthrop said, focusing the attention on him, "at least some of the vampire families have suspected as well. I won't speak for Ms. Wadsworth or the Seattle family, but my family has been keeping tabs on the Council's misdeeds for the last century and, more recently, Director Owens specifically."

More angry heads shook around the table. Winthrop held his ground and continued, "Similar to the witches, we at first thought it was isolated to the vampires. It wasn't until recently that we learned other groups were being impacted."

"There is a pattern here," Helen said calmly. "Even before Director Owens, the Council worked to keep each group isolated from each other so we wouldn't challenge their authority. Director Owens took it a step further and escalated to murder."

"And it worked," Michael added. "But thanks to Helen and her team, we won't be isolated again. We need to work together."

"Thank you, Michael," Helen said, and the group began to settle down. "Jordan, let's continue on."

Jordan nodded and clicked to the next slide. "The other important evidence is the journal of visions from Malinda."

We didn't even get to the journal summary before Mira had a question. "And the journal was being held by Doria, right?"

Doria smiled politely. "Yes, Malinda entrusted me with

the journal for safekeeping until it was the right time to share it."

"I don't mean this to be rude," Mira hesitated. "But why you? Malinda was known to hang out with the coven, and she was friends with Helen. Why didn't she trust them to keep it?"

Doria kept her smile plastered on her face, but thoughts were dancing behind her eyes. "I have a special talent," she said slowly. "Malinda knew that oracles cannot sense me or anyone I have physical contact with."

Mira still looked confused. "I don't understand why that is important."

Doria looked in my direction. I answered, "Director Owens's oracle gift allows her to think about someone she knows and have a vision of what they are presently doing."

"Oh," Mira said, surprised. "I thought she just had visions of the future like Malinda."

Others around the table reacted similarly. I hadn't realized that the director's oracle ability was not common knowledge. I didn't think it was a secret; it would have come out when her autobiography was published for the otherworldly community.

"Wait," Ms. Wadsworth said abruptly, "so Cora could be seeing this right now?"

Chaos erupted around the table. Only the agency team and the witches sat calmly. I wondered why Ms. Wadsworth had called her Cora when we'd been referring to her as the director the whole time.

Helen quickly stood and held up her hands to stop the concern. "No, she can't," Helen said firmly.

The group settled down.

When it was quiet again, Mrs. Clark added from her end of the table, "There are wards protecting this office and the grounds. No magic can have access unless it is invited."

Hazel and Ivy gave Mrs. Clark a knowing look. The rest of the table looked appeased and didn't question it further.

Across the table from me, Michael was flipping through pages of the packet in front of him. It looked like they were copies of my mom's journal with the annotations that we had included. A smile grew on his face.

"Malinda was smart," Michael said quietly, but the whole table turned in his direction. "She knew what she was doing, and her visions were always meant to help." He held up the papers of the visions. He looked pissed, but there was sadness behind his eyes. "This is enough for me and the packs to take action. We can't allow other werewolves to continue to work for the director and help attack our communities."

Helen nodded in his direction and gave him a sad smile that I didn't understand. "Thank you. But it's not the only information we have. Jordan, let's move on to the director's files."

Unlike the journals, we hadn't printed out any examples from the watchlist files that the director had. The primary documents had described them, but there had been concern about sharing a specific file as an example because it contained so much personal information.

Hazel spoke again before Jordan could even start. "How exactly did you get these files?"

Helen and I had discussed how much of that we wanted to share, so we decided to go with radical honesty.

"I got them," I answered quickly. "I have been apprenticing with the director, a forced apprenticeship." I felt the need to clarify. The faces I saw had an understanding reaction. "During my time spent at the Council offices, I used a device developed by Cam to get information off of computers. I was able to get access to the director's computer. That computer had these files."

The explanation was short and honest. I left out how I only got the access because I had a vision and pretended to be on the verge of fainting.

Everyone around the table looked impressed, and I let that bolster me. We hadn't gotten to the hardest part yet.

"Will we get access to those files?" Ms. Wadsworth asked. A few heads around the table nodded. They also wanted access.

"The files contain a lot of personal information," Helen said. "Long term, we'll work with each group to share the watchlist files for their community members."

That seemed to appease the group. Helen gestured for Jordan to continue.

"The other pertinent thing to discuss is the building being used by the Council to confine people," Jordan said as she flipped to a slide with an overhead view of the building that Hank had gotten from one of his sources.

"We believe that the director is using Council resources for this," she said. "And that she is hiding this from the Council Forum."

Angela leaned forward so that everyone could see her

and said, "Appendix 12 shows the evidence of two accounting books. You can see where I've annotated the differences between the two."

Papers shuffled as everyone turned to appendix 12 in their packets.

"We believe that the director created this building to hold people she deems dangerous and that she is actively holding people there now," she finished.

I waited for the side conversations to start. They didn't. Everyone looked sad and worried. It was like a blanket snuffed out the room.

"So it's happening again, and by one of our own this time," Mira said softly, breaking the silence.

"Yes," Helen replied. "I believe that Director Owens is trying to bring back forced institutionalizations."

27

"You'd think an oracle would know better," Hazel said to Ivy. We all heard her and they both looked my way with guilty faces. I looked back at them, confused.

"I mean the director," Hazel said quickly. "Not you."

Ivy explained, "A long time ago—well, long for humans—it was common for our people to get institutionalized, alongside some unfortunate humans, because we were different or dangerous. We were drugged, experimented on, and often killed. We worked hard to stop those practices."

"Oh" was all I could say. Helen had talked about some of that, but either I wasn't paying attention or I hadn't connected all of the dots.

"It wasn't just oracles and witches," Mrs. Wadsworth added. "It was a dark time for all of us."

Jordan nodded and explained, "The Council at the time helped to ensure the institutions were disbanded and laws were enacted by the Council Forum to protect everyone within the community should the humans try to bring back those practices."

Michael connected the dots first. "Which is why the director is hiding the money for that in a second set of books."

"Exactly," Helen answered.

"And you have evidence in the director's files of individuals who may be in that institution now?" Hazel asked.

"Yes."

Hazel sighed. "So, what do we do now?"

Helen gave her a sad but appreciative smile. "First, I want to make sure that this entire conclave agrees on what we are charging the director with."

Winthrop grunted, "I think we all do."

"Even so," Helen said, "I want us to be sure. There won't be any going back once we make a move."

The blanket of concern snuffed out the room again. Helen was right, everyone knew it, and everyone was worried.

Helen took a deep breath and then suggested, "Let's break for dinner and give everyone a chance to process what we've talked about this afternoon. We'll reconvene after dinner."

Mrs. Clark left the table quickly. Annie and I followed her to help. Dinner that night was a taco bar to accommodate everyone's dietary needs, except for the vampires. Winthrop had let me know that he and Ms. Wadsworth would enjoy their dinner later in the parlor to not upset anyone's appetite.

Setting out the buffet was quick and easy. We had just finished up as folks started to make their way downstairs. Everyone complimented Mrs. Clark, and I was glad to see that she stuck around to hear it. Plates were filled, and folks chose if they wanted to sit at the kitchen table, go eat in the living room, or head to one of the conference room tables.

Mostly, folks stuck with their partner representatives. Quiet conversations about the afternoon's reveal were happening all over the office. Soon I didn't have a task and could get my own dinner. But not having a task meant my brain had time to think. Suddenly I needed air. It was still cold outside, so no one else had gone to the patio table. I took my plate and headed that way.

"Do you want to be alone?" Annie asked softly with her dinner plate in hand.

"Not from you," I answered back.

She set her plate next to mine and sat down. "That was a lot."

"Yeah," I answered. "I don't think I realized what everything meant and the magnitude of it all."

"It did all come together fast," Annie said. "There wasn't a lot of time for you to process it with us because you had to be in San Francisco last week."

We took a few bites of our dinner and let each other sit in our feelings. I thought for a moment about telling Annie about the vision I had had just before the meeting, but Jordan popped her head out the door and told us that Helen wanted to talk with the team in her office really quick.

Annie and I exchanged puzzled looks and then headed inside. We dropped off our empty plates and went up to Helen's office. Soon the whole team—including our vampire consultant, Winthrop—stood around Helen's desk.

"Thank you all for eating quickly and coming up here," Helen said. "I just got some news and didn't want you to be surprised in the meeting. Winthrop, will you fill everyone in?"

We all turned to Winthrop with confused looks. He smiled back at us.

"I took the liberty of having the family in the area keep tabs on the director and her minions," he shared. "I just got word that Director Owens has boarded her plane and is heading to Seattle."

"She knows," I whispered. She must have learned something from watching me. I wanted to throw up.

Helen looked grim and said, "We think it's safe to assume that she is coming here and that she may know some of what is going on. But we don't know what she knows and we don't want anyone to panic."

"Maybe panic a little bit," Winthrop joked.

"No, we don't need to panic," Helen said, a bit annoyed. "But we do need to move fast to align the conclave and have a plan."

"Do we have a plan?" Jordan asked.

"I have one forming," Helen said. "But we'll need the conclave and their local members' help to pull it off."

"What do you need from us?" I asked, ready to help.

Helen smiled. "I'd like Jordan to stay with me and talk

through a few specifics. Cam, Steve, and Mrs. Clark, can you three check the security perimeter? The rest of you round up the conclave and get them back to the conference table in ten minutes without making them nervous."

A chorus of confirmations filled the room, and we all left to complete our jobs. We found everyone scattered about and gave them the ten-minute warning to finish up their dinners and head back to the table. No one complained. I wondered if they could sense that something was happening.

Right on time, we were all gathered back at the conference table in our assigned seats. Everyone sat quietly, waiting for Helen to restart the meeting.

"I was hoping we'd have some more time to work through things as a group," Helen started out. "But it appears that we are now on the clock. We received word that Director Owens is on her way to Seattle. We don't know what she knows. And she is likely to arrive in the next three hours."

As expected, the room broke out into overlapping conversations and exclamations of alarm.

"At this point in time, I think we need to take a quick vote of no confidence," Helen suggested.

Jordan stood and passed out three-by-five notecards to each representative at the table. She handed one to me with a whisper: "You'll vote as one of the rare community representatives. Doria asked me to help represent the demon vote."

"Just a reminder on protocol," Helen said. "This is anonymous, and the vote of no confidence only moves forward if it is unanimous. Please write *yes* if you agree or *no* if you do not agree. Jordan will collect the cards and then Linda will count the votes. We'll do three rounds if needed with discussion in between."

People were looking around the table. A few folks had already written on their cards and had them turned over in front of them. I scribbled a *yes* on my card and then waited for everyone to finish. Jordan collected all of the cards, shuffled them, and then handed the stack to me.

Helen leaned toward me and whispered, "Just sort them into yes or no piles and then tell us the total for each."

All eyes were on me as I picked up the stack of twelve cards that would determine the future. I looked at the first card; it said *yes*. So did the next six. The next card in the stack had a *no* crossed out and then *yes* written in. I added it to the stack of yeses. I was on the last card, relieved that everyone was a yes. But then, in bold letters, *No*.

That was the lone card in the no stack. Everyone was shocked. Before I could say anything, Mr. Gray stood and cleared his throat.

"I've seen too much violence in my time," he started quietly. "I will not be party to another cycle of bloodshed. It is often the ones on the edges who take the brunt of it."

I knew he was speaking up for those who usually didn't have a voice. His words sounded a lot like something my mom would have said.

"What would need to be true for you to vote yes?' I asked.

He looked over at me with kind eyes. "I need reassurance that death will not be the punishment for Director Owens or any of the offenders."

"She's killed witches," Hazel countered.

"Killing in response will just lead to more violence. It doesn't end," he said calmly.

"But then where is the justice?" Hazel asked.

"Justice can be in ensuring that no more people come to harm," I responded. "I think that's what my mom would want most."

"The young oracle is wise," Mr. Gray said.

Helen wiped away a tear. "I can agree to those terms, Mr. Gray," she said and looked around the table. "Can everyone else?"

Heads started to nod. Some took more time than others. But soon enough everyone agreed.

"Okay," Helen said. "Let's vote again."

We passed out new cards. I collected them, reading and sorting each one. All of the cards were yeses.

I looked up at the group with a smile, but everyone could see that there was only one stack of cards. I said it out loud anyway: "It's twelve yeses and zero noes."

Helen and most of the table let out a sigh of relief.

"Good," Helen said and composed herself. "Let's move forward and discuss what next steps we want to take."

"Well," Ms. Wadsworth started, "normally correction and confinement, if needed, would be left up to the group that the offender belongs to. But it's probably safe to assume that Linda, as an oracle, doesn't want this responsibility."

From the cases we had handled, I knew that was true,

but I agreed with Ms. Wadsworth. I didn't want that responsibility. My face gave that away to everyone at the table.

"Don't scare the child," Hazel admonished.

"Wouldn't the Council Forum handle her correction?" Mira asked.

"But they haven't done anything to stop her yet," I said, letting the anger that had been simmering come to the surface.

The room went silent at my small outburst, but I could tell that several people agreed with me.

"That is a good point," Helen agreed, and my anger lessened. "They haven't paid attention. Or, if they have, then they haven't taken action. I don't know if I trust them in this case."

"I agree," Michael offered.

Mr. Gray cleared his throat. "Oracles are considered part of the rare otherworldly community, correct?"

I leaned forward so that I could see him on our shared row of the table. He gave me a soft smile and a wink.

"Yes," Helen said. "They are. Are you offering to take responsibility for Director Owens?"

"I don't have the resources for that," he said. "But yes, I would take responsibility on behalf of the rare community. However, I would ask that the other groups help in the practical logistics."

Michael answered the request, "The werewolf community has often served as enforcement for the Council. We would take on the responsibility of confinement."

"Would that conflict with the werewolves within the Council?" Mr. Gray asked. "Can we trust all the packs?"

"The vampires can serve alongside, a system of checks and balances," Winthrop offered.

Mr. Gray nodded in agreement. Michael didn't look as happy, but he didn't protest the offer.

Hazel and Ivy exchanged glances, then Hazel said, "We could offer an everlasting tracking spell and any wards that would be needed. It would take some time and a full coven, but it would make it so that she couldn't escape or disappear."

"We know of an island that may be a good location for her confinement," Mira offered. "It belongs to the siren community, but we'd offer it up for this purpose as long as needed."

"Or I can just send her to another dimension," Doria offered. Everyone looked at her, a bit horrified. She laughed softly at the reactions. "Well, don't say I didn't offer."

Helen smiled at the group. "It sounds like we have a long-term plan. With the island, not the other dimension, to be clear. But we'll need a short-term plan for when she shows up."

Michael looked slightly guilty and admitted, "I have the local pack on standby. I trust them. They can be here within ten minutes to contain her and anyone she brings with her."

"Okay, thank you," Helen said. "We need to do it quietly. We can't have a showdown in a neighborhood full of humans."

"Understood," he responded. "I'll work on some options."

Ms. Wadsworth raised her hand for attention at the end of the table. "That's a good plan for the director, but what about the rest of the North American Council staff? Cora didn't do this on her own. They all need to be dealt with."

The table erupted again into side conversations.

"I think most of the Council people are just trying to do their job," I said loudly, getting everyone's attention. "There are probably some people who did bad things and need to be dealt with, but it's not everyone who works there."

"Also," Michael offered, "I do agree that we need a working Council, we can't just disband the whole thing."

"I agree," Hazel said. "We'll need a new director, and I think that as community representatives, we should appoint someone. At least as a temporary director until a permanent one can be put in place by the Council Forum."

Ms. Wadsworth added, "A new director can weed through the Council staff members to decide what to do with them. I'd be fine with that."

Mira asked softly, "Who could be the new director?"

The table again erupted into overlapping responses. Doria leaned forward and stared down Helen. I glanced between the two of them to try to make sense of the unspoken conversation that was happening.

"Okay," Helen said to settle everyone down. Then she turned on her *let's get down to business* voice. "We do need to appoint a new director, but that can wait until the morning. I don't think we need to make any rash decisions on that tonight."

She looked at her phone. "We have maybe an hour or two until Ms. Owens gets here, and if we are going to take her and her agents into custody, we need to start preparing. Those who need to be or want to be involved with that, please take five minutes for a break and then come back here. Everyone else can move to the living room downstairs. The safest place for you will be in your rooms; please be there by the top of the hour."

Everyone looked stunned for a moment and then quickly moved to clean up their things and head for the bathrooms or downstairs. I wasn't sure which group I should be in. I was likely to help the guests who wouldn't be involved with the containment mission, but I wanted to be on that mission.

"Linda and Annie, hold on for just one second." Helen got our attention to stay there and then turned to say something quietly to Jordan. Jordan nodded and turned to leave.

"Annie," Helen said and turned back to us, "would you look after the group that won't be involved with the containment mission? Mrs. Clark can help. Just make sure everyone gets settled into their rooms on time."

"I can do that," Annie confirmed.

"Linda," Helen said and looked at me, "can you help with the containment mission?"

"Yes, what do you need me to do?" I asked, eager to help.

"I don't know yet," she said truthfully. "But I have a feeling I'll need you close."

A SMALLER GROUP was back at the conference table after the five-minute break. Mrs. Clark and Annie were the only two missing from our team; they were downstairs with the other people who weren't going to be involved.

Michael, Sarah, Hazel, Winthrop, Doria, and Mr. Gray rounded out the group that would be involved in the confinement mission.

"I want to make it clear that phoenixes are pacifists," Mr. Gray said. "I'm here because I'm taking responsibility for Ms. Owens, and I will be ensuring that we hold to our agreement and no lasting harm comes to her from this encounter."

"Well noted," Helen said, "and I appreciate the extra oversight to ensure we act appropriately."

Everyone nodded their understanding of the situation that Helen had confirmed. This was not a revenge mission.

"Michael," Helen said, motioning to him, "would you please take point on this mission?"

"Yes," he said quickly. "As mentioned, we will supply the people to execute this mission. I do not expect any of you to be directly physically involved. But we do need to think through the approach."

Not everyone looked pleased with that expectation.

He didn't acknowledge the looks and continued, "We'll need a four-point plan. First, we'll want to isolate Ms.

Owens. This will best ensure her physical safety and increase our chances of securing her."

I noticed that people had started referring to her as Ms. Owens instead of the director or Director Owens. I also realized that I had made that switch in my head.

"Next," Michael continued, "we will need to apprehend any agents who accompany her or who are already near the office. We'll also want to hold them for questioning and to determine how best to release them so they won't cause harm."

"Does the local pack have enough resources and locations for that?" Steve asked.

"Yes," Michael confirmed. "But we may not have enough for the third aim. We need to apprehend any local Council personnel, not just the ones who come with Ms. Owens. I'm not sure we have enough for that."

"Do we even know who they are?" I asked.

"We do have that list," Helen confirmed. "It was in some of the records you obtained for us."

Winthrop raised his hand. "We can have the local family help, and we have locations we can use to hold them for questioning."

"Great, I'll put you in touch with the local pack alpha to coordinate," Michael agreed. "The fourth aim will be to lock down the Council offices and the institution in California. We need to keep staff out of the offices until we put a temporary director and plan in place."

"The local coven in San Francisco can spell the buildings to keep people out," Hazel offered. "It'll hold for several days until a firmer plan is in place."

"Thank you," Michael said. "Can you coordinate with the coven on that?"

"Yes."

"So the covens will restrict entry to the office buildings. The pack and the family can contain the agents," Helen summarized. "And I have an idea of how we can isolate Cora. Michael, you, me, and Linda should talk. Let's go to my office."

Everyone looked at me, but I didn't give away anything. The three of us went into Helen's office. She sat behind the desk and I took my normal chair, leaving the other for Michael.

"Linda, I apologize for putting you on the spot," she said gently, "but I think we need to tell Michael about what we learned recently. I think it can help us."

Michael shifted his attention to me. I gulped and then explained how Cora and I had connected in a vision.

"So you could use that to lure her somewhere. But you need her to be trying to view you with her oracle gift?" he asked.

"Yes," I answered.

"She can't do that here with the wards," he said and turned to Helen. "Does Cora know about the wards?"

"I think we should assume that she does now," Helen answered. "So we'd need another location."

"Taking Linda out of the house so that she can connect with Cora could be dangerous," he said, still looking at me with concern.

"But if it works, I can feed her information," I countered. "Like that we are gathering somewhere unprotected.

Or unprotected as far as she knows. I can get her to come where we need her to be."

"We would want to control what Cora sees," he said. "Only give her a limited view."

"We can't use wards for that," Helen said. "We can't get them up or down that fast, and she's likely to notice."

We all sat quiet for a moment thinking about our options.

"I got it," I blurted out. "Doria can shield me with physical contact. Cora can't see her or anyone she is touching. I'll keep in contact with Doria until we are ready to connect with Cora."

"That's right," Helen said, smiling proudly.

I rambled through a plan: "We can use the portal, go back to Doria's house, I can try to connect with Cora, feed her the information that we are at Doria's. Get her to come there, then we can spring a trap."

"It could work," Michael said. "Do you know how to connect with her?"

"Well, kind of," I admitted. "It only happened once. But it's worth a shot."

Michael was looking doubtful. "I'm not sure we should risk taking you out of this office."

I stayed firm. "We can't hide forever from Cora. If we don't make a move now, it's likely that we won't be able to surprise her again. This may be our only shot."

We rejoined the bigger group and updated them on the plan to get Cora to Doria's house so that we wouldn't have a showdown on the streets of the agency's neighborhood.

"Doria, I'm not sure who Cora will bring with her,"

Helen cautioned, "or what they may do to your home. Are you truly okay with us luring them there?"

Doria grinned. "Will the new Council pay for any damages?"

"If they don't, I will," Helen answered.

"Great, I've been wanting to remodel anyway."

The location chosen, the team then worked out the details. Well, all the details except one.

Jordan asked, "Linda, what are you going to tell her to get her to come and not suspect an ambush?"

"I'm not sure yet," I admitted. "Something to make her think I'm abandoning Helen and all of you to join her."

"Let me know if you need help on staging that play or any acting advice," Steve offered.

"That would be great." I'd take all the help I could get.

28

I followed Doria through the portal. She had told me that I'd just see a black nothingness and maybe get cold. It should only last a moment, like a long blink.

It wasn't black, like nothing. It was a mix of dark colors: purples, blues, and streaks of silver. They swirled around and formed images. Faces appeared in the swirls. Some I recognized. Others were new. The cold was there, but it was like a soothing cold of running water over a burn. And the moment, the long blink, that Doria had described felt like forever until the moment I emerged on the other side, then it condensed into a blink of an eye.

Doria looked at me, a mischievous smile breaking through. "How was the trip?" she asked me.

"Good," I shrugged.

"See anyone you know?"

I blinked to clear the images away. "Yes, I think so."

"Good. I thought you would." I started to ask her a

question, but she turned on her heels and loudly proclaimed, "Let's get this done with."

Doria led us out of the basement where the portal was. She held my hand firmly, keeping physical contact the whole time.

We set up in the living room. Doria and I sat across from each other with tea and cookies on the coffee table, our arms reaching across and holding hands to stay connected.

"Let me know when you are ready," Doria said.

I took a few more deep breaths, reviewed what Steve and I had practiced, and then said, "Ready."

Doria released my hand. Nothing happened. We waited.

"Tea," Doria offered.

I took it and sipped it slowly, waiting to feel like someone was just on the edge of my vision. The tea in my cup began to grow cold. I was on the verge of giving up when I felt it.

I nodded to Doria and blinked twice, the signal that Cora was watching. Then, I closed my eyes and let the pull in my gut take me.

We were moving. I was sitting up on a seat, something tight against my lap and chest. We were in a car. I looked to my right. Cora was sitting there, eyes closed, hands folded in her lap. Two werewolf agents in black suits sat in the front seats, one driving, the other on the phone. I couldn't tell what he was saying.

A movement to my right drew my attention back to

Cora. She opened her eyes, looked shocked for a moment, and then smiled.

"We found each other again," she said.

I looked ahead to see if either of the agents noticed anything. They hadn't moved.

"Cora?" I asked, making my voice sound like I was scared and pleading.

Cora looked surprised but quickly regained her confident exterior. "Good, you figured out how to talk this time."

I glanced nervously toward the two agents.

Cora chuckled. "They can't see us here. We can talk privately."

I said the words I had practiced with Steve: "I think I made a mistake."

"What mistake is that?" Cora asked, using her fake sweet tone that I'd come to identify. That was the tone I wanted from her; it meant she thought she was playing me.

"Trusting Helen," I answered. "I think she might be dangerous and I don't know what to do."

Cora smiled. "Well, it's a good thing you met me then, right?"

"You'll help me?" I said, trying to sound small and needy.

"Of course." Cora reached over and patted my hand. It took all my strength not to yank it away. "In fact, I'm actually in Seattle. Tell me where you are and I can come help you."

"I'm at a friend's house," I answered and gave her the

address. We had counted on her not knowing Doria or anything about her, including where she lived.

Cora typed the address into her phone. "I'll be there in about ten minutes."

"Thank you, I really need help."

"Yes, you do," she said. "Now open your eyes."

I opened my eyes and snapped back to Doria's couch. Doria reached out quickly for my hand.

"How did it go?" she asked as soon as we held hands.

"I think it went well," I answered. "She's coming here. I might have given it away at the end, though."

"What do you mean?"

"She told me to open my eyes," I said. The phrasing still puzzled me. "How did she know that would break the connection? I couldn't control my reaction, she may have noticed I looked angry."

"I bet she didn't notice," Doria reassured me. "How much time do we have?"

"Ten minutes."

"Great, let's call Helen."

Doria insisted we refill the tea—not an easy thing to do while holding hands. She wanted it to look like we were friends just chatting when Cora showed up. I thought she also wanted to keep me busy and calm. I jumped when the doorbell rang.

Doria released my hand. "Showtime."

I answered the door. Doria stayed on the couch.

"Linda, dear," Cora said and leaned in to give me a stiff hug. The two agents from the car stood at the bottom of the steps. "I'm so glad I found you. Everything will be okay now."

"Thank you for coming," I said and then leaned in to whisper. "My friend doesn't know about all of this." I made a sweeping gesture at the agents, who looked anything but friendly.

"I see," Cora said. She turned back to the agents. "You can wait in the car."

"Are you sure, Director?" the one on the left said.

"Did I stutter?" Cora said, the sweetness leaving her voice.

"No, ma'am," he answered. Both agents went to the car without another word.

Cora shifted her tone back. "Let's have a nice chat, and then we can decide what to do."

"Great," I said. "If we go sit in the basement lounge, then my friend won't be able to hear us."

"Lead the way."

We walked past the stairs, continuing on to the door to the basement. Doria had removed the bar and the lock that would normally secure it. The door was propped open to the carpeted stairs.

Cora huffed softly at the darkness below, but I continued forward without a word, hoping that Cora would follow and that Doria was ready for her part.

At the bottom of the steps I made a show of searching the wall. "Sorry, the switch is here somewhere," I said.

I walked farther down the dark hallway. Cora followed.

"A light would be nice," she said, her annoyance leaking through.

We were almost close enough. A few more steps.

"Maybe we can talk upstairs," Cora said, still annoyed.

"I can find it," I said, then gave the code word. "Oh, I remember, it's back here."

Two things happened very quickly. First, I flung open the heavy door to the portal. Then, Doria appeared at the top of the stairs and ran at Cora, wrapping her arms around her and continuing through the open door into the portal. Cora gasped but wasn't able to scream.

I followed quickly behind, closing the door before I stepped through the portal, gripping onto the back of Doria's shirt.

The other side of the portal was chaos. Cora was screaming for help. Michael was trying to place handcuffs on her while she was still being bear-hugged from behind by Doria. Helen was telling Jordan to give her the sedative injection.

Steve reached for me as I stood frozen at the portal and pulled me to the side, out of the chaos. "You okay?" he asked.

"Yes, I think so," I said, a little breathless as my adrenaline started to crash.

"Well, you got her here, so your acting must have been good."

"I had a good coach," I said and reached out to give Steve a hug. He held on, doing his box breathing so I could copy him and calm down.

The activity in the lab also calmed down. Cora was slumped over in a chair, out cold, her hands cuffed behind her. Jordan, always the doctor, was hooking her up to a heart monitor.

Helen turned to the room. "The coven should be radioing soon confirming the office lockdown. Linda, can you listen to that on the radio? If you don't hear anything in ten minutes, come find me. I need to talk with Michael and Steve."

"Sure," I answered and took the offered radio.

Helen, Steve, and Michael all left the lab, leaving Jordan, Doria, and me behind along with an unconscious Cora.

"Any way we can see what's going on outside?" Doria asked.

"Can we pull the camera feeds up on these computers?" I asked Jordan.

"Yep." She typed in a few things into one of the workstations, and the monitor filled with boxes showing different parts of the house. I took over from there, searching for the right cameras until I found the one that showed the back garden. "They surrendered quickly when they found out that Owens was in custody," Jordan explained as the video came up.

The outside team was already loading agents in black suits into vans, as planned for any agents hanging around the office. The local werewolf pack would question the agents to determine whether they were currently a threat or could be released. Similarly the sweep team, led by the vampire family, would be doing the same. The new director would have a lot to work through to decide who was a long-term threat or not.

The radio crackled, and a voice I didn't recognize reported, "Lockdown confirmed." That meant that the coven had successfully secured the office building and institution.

"Copy that," I replied and relaxed in the chair. Doria and I watched through the monitors.

"Do you think the agents at my house got picked up?" she asked.

"I bet they did," I said.

Doria grinned. "I hope they trashed the place first. New furniture would be nice."

I was about to offer to radio someone to ask when the sound of someone coming into the room startled us all.

"Cam," I said when I saw who it was. "Everything okay on your end?"

"Yes, the network at the Council office is shut down. And we've confirmed that the servers weren't tampered with, so all the data is secure."

"Good," I said.

"Linda," Cam said and then paused.

"What?" I asked.

"Do you think I should suggest using that new thing on Cora?"

She meant the suppression collar. I recoiled slightly, and Cam looked guilty.

"No," I said firmly. "If everyone does their part, then even if Cora can see what we are doing, she won't be able to do anything to harm anyone."

"But what if someone doesn't do their part?"

I sighed. I had struggled with that one as well. The

vision I had with Cora in the office hadn't helped me feel better about the situation.

"I think everyone has spent a long time not trusting each other," I offered. "We need to give trust a chance and see what happens when everyone works together instead."

Cam sank heavily into another chair in front of the monitors. "You're right."

"So are you going to destroy it?" I asked but tried not to push.

Cam smiled sadly. "Yes, and I'm going to find and destroy all the ones that the Council created too."

We sat silently for several minutes, both of us processing everything that had happened that day. Helen and Michael came back. They talked quietly to Jordan, then they gave Cora another shot. She woke up slightly, enough to stand. They unhooked the monitor and took her away.

The rest of us made our way upstairs to hang out somewhere more comfortable while we waited for instructions on what we should do next. A while after we got settled in the downstairs living room, Helen walked in, and we all looked up at her. "Linda, would you be willing to come talk to Cora?"

"Why?" I asked.

"She said that she would only talk to you," Helen answered. "We are trying to get a confession. It might not be necessary, but it will make things easier with the Forum."

"Okay," I said, handing the radio back to her as we walked to the back parlor.

Sarah was outside the door. "We'll be right out here if you need anything."

I nodded, my mouth too dry to say anything. Sarah knocked on the door, and Michael opened it. He looked at me, a sadness in his eyes, gave me a firm nod, and then gestured for me to go in.

The room was dark. Someone had closed the drapes. Cora sat in the chair facing the door. She still seemed groggy but looked straight at me as I walked in, her mouth pressed straight. Her hands were still bound, but they had been switched to be in front of her.

I sat in the chair opposite her and closest to the door. I jumped slightly when the door closed behind me.

Cora tilted her head and narrowed her eyes. "They'll do this to you someday, you know."

"Do what?" I asked, genuinely confused.

"Figure out a reason to lock you up."

I thought about why I was there. I couldn't take her bait. "And what's the reason that they are locking you up?"

Cora scoffed. "I know more than them, and I wasn't afraid to do something about it."

"What did you know?"

"I know who is dangerous to our world and way of life."

"How?"

"I could see it," she said and let out a maniacal laugh.

I steadied myself so I wouldn't recoil. "What did you see?"

"The plotting. The secrets. The lying. Everyone wanted something. I kept the balance."

"How did you keep the balance?"

She glared at me. We sat in silence for a few moments. I thought I had pushed too far and she wouldn't talk to me anymore, but then she smiled. "You look a lot like your mom."

I pressed my eyes closed and took a deep breath before I repeated, "How did you keep the balance?"

"I did what I had to."

"What?"

"What Helen would never have been willing to do."

"What is Helen not willing to do?"

"Be decisive. Be the bad guy, if it meant people stayed safe."

"You were keeping people safe?" I asked. That wasn't a confession, but it felt like she was opening up.

"Yes," she said.

"How?"

"I got rid of anything or anyone that was dangerous, that would upset the balance."

"Like what?"

Cora scoffed. "Like that nosy witch who was hiding people from me."

"Enid?" I asked before I could think better of it.

"Yes," she whispered.

"And my mom?" I pressed, wanting to hear her say it.

She closed her eyes and shook her head like she was sad or disappointed. "Your mom," she said as if remembering her. "Malinda had so much promise. We could have been great together."

I breathed and used Helen's silence strategy.

Cora looked up at me. Her eyes went wide when she

realized what she had revealed. "It's Helen's fault. Helen poisoned them all against me. Malinda. Frank. Mrs. Clark. All of them."

I stayed silent.

"Ask Helen," she said.

I didn't reply.

"Ask Helen," she demanded.

I recoiled.

"Ask Helen," she yelled and started banging her head against the back of the chair.

The door opened when the yelling started, and Michael rushed in to stop her from hurting herself. Helen came in next and ushered me out of the room.

I started to hyperventilate. The adrenaline was crashing my body. Helen gathered me up into a hug.

I heard Helen call out to someone, "Can you grab some juice and a banana?"

She held me to her side and slowly walked us both into the kitchen, which was surprisingly empty. She sat me down in a chair at the table. Annie came and put a Capri Sun up to my mouth and a banana in front of me. I drank the juice and began to feel better.

I looked up and saw Helen and Annie staring at me with concern.

"I'm alright," I said, not convincingly. "It was just scary. But I'm alright."

"Eat the banana," Annie said. I did as I was told.

The banana gone, I looked up at Helen. She looked back at me knowingly.

"I heard what she said at the end," Helen said.

"Why does she blame you?"

"I need to tell you a story, something I should have told you a long time ago," she said sadly. "Once there were three best friends who had a dream of how we could help people who needed it the most. Cora, me, and Frank. We started an agency with the goal of offering support to the hidden communities that couldn't seek out the normal avenues when they got into trouble.

"Soon we had more work than we could manage. So we expanded. We added Mrs. Clark to the team and bought a fancy house for our office. But then one day we got a case for a friend who was a woman we all loved, Malinda, and the baby still inside her. We needed to hide her from a very bad man."

Annie gasped and looked at me. We both knew she was talking about me. I was that baby.

"This mission was so important that Frank, Cora, and I all went across the country to bring Malinda back. Cora saw a vision that helped us decide when the right time to rescue her would be. But that vision was wrong, and Frank was killed during the fight."

All three of us had tears silently streaming down our faces.

"We were able to get Malinda away to safety. Cora and I fought. We each blamed the other for what had happened. Malinda isolated herself away from the community to protect her child. I remained at the agency that we had all built together. Cora left to find a place where she thought she could make a difference. We didn't talk for years." Helen gulped down tears and took a deep breath. "Cora has always blamed me for Frank's death, and she was resentful of Malinda. But I still don't know why she had Malinda killed."

"I do," I said. "My mom was helping hide people from Cora. People Cora thought were dangerous or would upset the balance of the communities. Maybe she had been looking for an excuse all along, or maybe it just turned out that way. But that doesn't matter now." I pulled out my cell phone and clicked to show the recording. "I recorded my conversation with her. She admitted to having people killed and specifically to having Enid killed."

Helen and Annie both looked at me in surprise. And then Helen smiled sadly. "Good work, Linda."

29

S urprisingly, I slept well in the bunk room of the basement bomb shelter with Ilka curled up at my feet. Everyone had decided to stay the night even though the threat had been contained.

The kitchen was buzzing that morning. Every seat was filled with people happily eating eggs, bacon, and hash browns. Mrs. Clark walked around with a fruit platter, insisting that everyone had at least one serving to balance their breakfast.

I loaded up my plate and gladly took a serving of fruit from Mrs. Clark. The table was full, so I went to join the group in the living room.

"Good morning," Jordan called out from the couch.

I went and sat in an empty chair opposite her. "Good morning."

"Did you sleep okay?"

"Yes, it was actually nice down there."

"It was," Jordan agreed.

"How is Steve doing?" I hadn't seen him yet that morning. He had taken a blow to the head in the struggle to bring in the agents. He insisted he was fine. Jordan told us he would be soon.

"Good," she answered. "I think he is still asleep. The pain meds I made him take are helping with that."

I laughed, remembering the grumbling fight that they had tried to hide from all of us in the bunk room the night before. Jordan had won, and Steve took the pills that she insisted on.

"I'll go get him," she added. "He'll never let me give him meds again if they make him miss this meeting."

I laughed again. A good night's sleep had done wonders for my mood. I knew there was still a lot to discuss, but the hard part seemed over. We talked about smaller things, like the friendship that Ilka and Juniper had established, until it was time to head up to the meeting.

"Don't let them start without us," Jordan said as she headed to the basement.

Not only had the team stayed overnight, but the whole conclave had also chosen to stay. There were a few jokes about it just being because they wanted Mrs. Clark's breakfast. But I thought people wanted to be together and feel safe after the ordeal, and there was still one big decision to make.

Everyone was gathered around the large conference table on the second floor. Even without the placards, people sat in their assigned seats from the day before. We were a few minutes late, and Helen was already there. She waited for Steve and Jordan to come upstairs and get seated before starting.

"I don't know how to thank everyone for their help in the successful mission yesterday," Helen said. "So I'm hoping that the big lunch that Mrs. Clark has planned for later will help show our appreciation."

We all looked at Mrs. Clark and gave her an anticipatory round of applause.

Helen's voice shifted to serious. "I've asked Michael to give a quick debrief of yesterday's events and an update. Michael?"

"All the teams successfully completed their tasks," Michael said. "Ms. Owens is still being held at an undisclosed location with the local pack. She does not have access to phones or a computer."

Several sighs of relief around the table made it clear that that was a concern.

"The agents who were apprehended yesterday were held overnight. Representatives of at least two groups will be working today to interview and clear the agents. If cleared, they will be released and asked to remain in the area until they are contacted by the new Council director's team. The Council offices are locked down. The staff has been informed that the director will be replaced and that they will be contacted about a return-to-office plan within a week." Michael looked around the table. "Any questions?"

Hazel raised her hand. "How are we going to determine the new director?"

Helen answered, "I spoke with the Council Forum members last night. They weren't happy with the situation, but they have all agreed that this conclave can appoint a temporary director."

Everyone was surprised. We hadn't talked about how and when to tell the Council Forum.

"What else did you share with them?" Ms. Wadsworth asked.

"I shared the general charges we have against the director," Helen replied. 'And that we had evidence. Also, that Cora was contained and that we'd be working with them to stabilize the North American region."

Ms. Wadsworth gave a sharp nod. "Good."

I searched the table for any negative reactions to Helen's plan. Everyone seemed okay with it.

Doria didn't waste a moment. "So when do we all vote for Helen to be the appointed director?"

Helen kept calm. "I think we need to see who all the candidates are first."

Everyone looked at her, and Michael announced, "We may have had a secret small group meeting last night without any of the agency, sorry. We've already decided that there is only one candidate."

Doria picked at the croissant in front of her, took a bite, and casually said, "And Helen has enough siren in her to appease the stupid rules of the Council Forum if she wants to be the director permanently."

My mouth dropped open, and the table erupted into shocked exclamations and surprised faces.

"Oh, sorry," Doria said. "Was that not common knowledge?"

It took Helen a few tries to calm down the table.

Mira and Ara looked the happiest with the news. "Is it true?" Mira asked.

Helen sighed. "Yes. I do have siren heritage, but I don't know much about it, and it's a very small percentage."

Mira and Ara looked at each other, then back at Helen, and then sang in harmony, "Welcome, sister."

I watched a tear fall from Helen's eye before she sniffled and regained control.

"Yes, yes, very nice," Doria said. "We should move this along. Are there any other candidates anyone wants to put forth?"

Everyone smiled and shook their heads.

"Great, can we vote?"

Jordan jumped up, took a stack of three-by-five cards from the side cabinet, and passed them around to the representatives. It didn't take long for everyone to fill them out and hand them back to Jordan. She handed me the stack with a smile.

I flipped through the cards, looking for any card that said *no*. I looked at Helen and smiled. "All twelve cards say *yes*."

WE ALL WAITED around the conference table for Helen to come out of her closed-door video call with the Council Forum. Every spot was filled except her seat. Forced casual conversations between small groups helped to pass the time. Even Mrs. Clark and Winthrop chatted amicably at the end of the table.

Every head perked up and the conversations stopped when the double doors that led to Helen's office opened. She walked out with a neutral face and joined us at the table in her normal spot. We all waited for her to give us the update.

"The call went as well as could be expected," Helen started off, calm and measured. "They agree with the conclave's vote and my temporary appointment as the North American Council director."

Sighs of relief and congratulations filled the space. No one had wanted to discuss what would happen if they disagreed with our vote.

"You have a lot of work to do," Michael said as he leaned toward Helen.

Helen smiled back at him. "I'll have a lot of help."

"Yes, you will."

Everyone dispersed into smaller groups to discuss in detail the agents who needed to be questioned and the long-term plans for Cora. Helen asked Jordan to talk with her in her office.

They came out about ten minutes later. Jordan looked shocked but happy. Helen then took Angela and Winthrop back to her office. After several minutes, the three of them walked out with neutral faces.

"Sorry to interrupt," Helen called out to everyone still gathered at the table. "Can I have my team meet in the large conference room downstairs in five minutes?"

Everyone acknowledged her request and we all headed in that direction.

WE SQUEEZED around the smaller table, each taking the position we would have at our normal meeting table. I held my breath. I knew what was coming. Change. I normally hated change, but this change felt right.

Helen waited for everyone to settle and then ripped the bandage off. "I have asked Jordan to take over the agency, and she has agreed."

I smiled over at Jordan. I hadn't known what would be the outcome of Helen leaving, but it made sense. Quick glances around the table made it clear that everyone was okay with the decision.

"Also," Helen continued, and heads snapped back to her from smiling at Jordan, "I have asked Angela to come with me to work at the Council."

Angela smiled, and Winthrop nodded.

Helen explained, "It's clear that there is a big financial mess to untangle with what Cora was doing, and Angela is well positioned to help me with that."

I noticed that Helen had slipped back into calling Director Owens by her first name. It reminded me of their history and that they had once been good friends. I could still see the pain behind Helen's eyes for her once friend and all the problems that had occurred over the last few decades. We wouldn't learn until later just how much Helen blamed herself.

THINGS MOVED FAST at the agency, as they always did. Helen moved into the apartment in San Francisco on Thursday. She said she wanted the Council office opened back up within a week. I was only slightly jealous of Willow that she'd have Helen as a boss. I needed to remember to call her after everything got settled.

I waited all day on Thursday for something to go wrong. That was the day that my mom had warned us about. Other than Helen leaving, nothing so bad happened. Maybe we prevented it or maybe I misunderstood what she meant. Either way, there wasn't anything more to do about it.

Jordan, at Helen's insistence, had moved into her office on Friday. Annie and I had helped her move all of her plants. They were going to love the big window in that space.

Monday morning, I sat in my familiar wingback chair in front of the big walnut desk. My laptop sat open next to me. I gave Jordan time to shuffle papers around and get settled. It was our first one-on-one with her in the new role. She looked more nervous than I had felt on my first day. I smiled to reassure her. Even bosses as badass as Jordan needed encouragement sometimes.

ALSO BY JANELLE SEEGMILLER

THE OTHERWORLDLY ADMIN

Otherworldly Onboarding

Magic, Meetings, and Murder

Demons, Databases, and Danger

MALINDA'S ADVENTURES (Novellas)

Fixed Fate

Fled Fate

Feel Fate

Fail Fate

Find Fate

ACKNOWLEDGMENTS

It's bittersweet to end a series. I've thought about Linda and her story so much over the past several years. It's hard to let go, but I'm excited to give her a conclusion. In my mind, she gets to continue on with a fulfilling job, supportive friends, and a wonderful life. It's unlikely I'll be able to give up these characters fully. Watch out for future work where they make some guest appearances.

I've gone through cycles of writing where it feels very independent and then where it feels like a community. The community feeling is what I'm leaning into. Special thanks to my community of friends, especially my beta readers: Olivia Harold, Tim Johnstone, Erin Spannan, and Jett Jones.

Thank you to my editors who continue to teach me more about writing and put up with my writing habits: Oren Ashkenazi, Ariel Anderson, and Erin Spannan.

As always, thank you to my family, Alyssa and Nick, for your encouragement and support.

To my readers, every page read or review left is a signal for me to keep going. It makes me unreasonably happy to know that even one person found joy in something I put out into the world. Thank you!

ABOUT THE AUTHOR

JANELLE SEEGMILLER spent thirteen years in corporate jobs until she decided to take a break and chase a dream. Now, she has fallen in love with the journey of writing fiction. She lives in Washington with her family. When she isn't writing, she can most likely be found reading, napping, or drinking tea.

www.ingramcontent.com/pod-product-compliance
Lightning Source LLC
Chambersburg PA
CBHW021128260626
47169CB00005B/1506